EXPLORERS OF SPACE

The Masks of Time
The Time Hoppers
Hawksbill Station
To Live Again
Recalled to Life
Starman's Quest
Tower of Glass
Earthmen and Strangers *(editor)*
Voyagers in Time *(editor)*
Men and Machines *(editor)*
Tomorrow's Worlds *(editor)*
Revolt on Alpha C
Lost Race of Mars
Time of the Great Freeze
Conquerors from the Darkness
Planet of Death
The Gate of Worlds
The Calibrated Alligator
Needle in a Timestack
To Open the Sky
Thorns
Worlds of Maybe *(editor)*
Mind to Mind *(editor)*
The Science Fiction Bestiary *(editor)*
The Day the Sun Stood Still *(compiler)*
Beyond Control *(editor)*
Chaims of the Sea (compiler)
Deep Space *(editor)*
Sundance and Other Science Fiction Stories
Mutants: Eleven Stories of Science Fiction *(editor)*
Threads of Time *(compiler)*
Sunrise on Mercury and Other Science Fiction Stories
Explorers of Space: Eight Stories of Science Fiction *(editor)*

EXPLORERS OF SPACE

Eight Stories of Science Fiction

edited and with an Introduction by
ROBERT SILVERBERG

THOMAS NELSON INC., PUBLISHERS

Nashville   New York

No character in these stories is intended to represent any actual person; all the incidents of the story are entirely fictional in nature.

First edition

Library of Congress Cataloging in Publication Data

Silverberg, Robert, comp.
  Explorers of space.

  CONTENTS: Leinster, M. Exploration team.—Simak, C.
D. Beachhead.—Anderson, P. Kyrie. [etc.]
  1. Science fiction. [1. Science fiction.
2. Short stories] I. Title.

PZ5.S596Ex [Fic] 74-30399
ISBN 0-8407-6439-1

ACKNOWLEDGMENTS

Exploration Team, by Murray Leinster, copyright © 1956 by Street & Smith Publications, Inc. Reprinted by permission of the author and Scott Meredith Literary Agency, Inc.

Beachhead, by Clifford D. Simak, copyright © 1951 by Ziff-Davis Publications, Inc. Reprinted by permission of the author and his agent, Robert P. Mills, Ltd.

Kyrie, by Poul Anderson, copyright © 1968 by Joseph Elder. Reprinted by permission of the author and his agents,

TABLE OF CONTENTS

EXPLORERS OF SPACE

INTRODUCTION

For centuries readers have found pleasure in wondrous tales of expeditions to far-off places. In the fourteenth and fifteenth centuries, before the era of printed books, such narratives as those of Marco Polo and Sir John Mandeville circulated widely in Europe in manuscript form. It mattered very little that Marco Polo's story of adventures in the Orient was authentic while Mandeville's far more flamboyant account turned out to be a clever literary hoax; both books, and others like them, were eagerly sought. In the sixteenth century came the huge printed anthology of Giambattista Ramusio, a compilation of dozens of explorers' narratives, and then the immense collection edited by Richard Hakluyt, which published the exploits of Columbus, the Cabots, Drake, Raleigh, and hundreds of others. These books were succeeded by even larger gatherings of first-hand tales of exploration in the seventeenth and eighteenth centuries—the many-volumed collections of Samuel Purchas, John Churchill, Alexander Dalrymple, and others.

Many motives drew the authors of those narratives of discovery into the world's most distant regions. Some, like Marco Polo, were merchants; some, such as Columbus, were explorers seeking new trade routes; Drake was a pirate; Raleigh hoped to found colonies. A few traveled out of sheer curiosity and the love of adventure; but none were engaged in what we would regard as pure scientific research. That came later.

One of the first true scientific expeditions was that of the British astronomer Edmund Halley, who commanded the sloop *Paramour Pink* from 1698 to 1700 on a voyage to study the Earth's magnetic field. In the decades that followed, such

11

French explorers as La Condamine, Bougainville, and La Pérouse brought back invaluable anthropological and geographical data from South America and the South Pacific, the great British explorer James Cook made three mighty voyages of scientific discovery that spanned the globe, Danish-born Vitus Bering penetrated the Arctic, and the eccentric Scot James Bruce went off to Ethiopia in search of the sources of the Nile.

The nineteenth century saw the indefatigable German scientist Alexander von Humboldt exploring South America, Charles Darwin circling the world aboard H.M.S. *Beagle,* Austen Henry Layard looking for the ruins of Nineveh in Iraq, Richard Burton prowling dark corners of Arabia and Africa, Heinrich Schliemann finding the ancient city of Troy in Asia Minor. In our own century we have seen Peary, Amundsen, and Byrd venturing into the polar wastelands, Beebe plumbing the ocean depths in his bathysphere, and a dozen American astronauts strolling across the face of the Moon. The narratives of these modern journeys of exploration have been as popular with readers as those of Marco Polo and Mandeville were five hundred years ago, and for the same reasons: they open new frontiers, they offer views of lands beyond the horizon.

Now space is our last frontier; and, though mankind has not yet gone beyond the orbit of the Moon, the imaginations of science-fiction writers have propelled explorers still unborn to the farthest reaches of the galaxy. Just as people turned to the accounts of Captain Cook's travels in the eighteenth century and Burton's in the nineteenth, contemporary readers have begun to look toward science fiction for a glimpse of the realms of strangeness that lie outside the world of everyday reality. Stories of interplanetary and interstellar expeditions are innumerable in the literature of science fiction; out of that vast body of stories I have chosen eight that illustrate some of the challenges we think human explorers will face as they embark on the scientific expeditions of the day after tomorrow. What these stories tell us is something that explorers have been telling us since the time of Marco Polo: that the universe about us is a perilous and challenging place, full of marvels and dangers, and that the human drive to learn what lies beyond the next valley will lead us onward and onward regardless of the risks, ever onward in an unending quest.

ROBERT SILVERBERG

EXPLORATION TEAM

Murray Leinster

*The first time a story labeled "by Murray Leinster" appeared
in print, Woodrow Wilson was in the White House and
Kaiser Wilhelm ruled Germany. Since then, kaisers and
presidents and kings and tsars have come and gone, but Murray
Leinster seems eternal. Actually, of course, there is no Murray
Leinster—the name is a pseudonym for Will F. Jenkins, a
courtly Southern type who, without fuss or effort, has
flourished for six decades as a successful writer in five or six
different branches of literature while carrying on a spectacular
second career as an inventor and gadgeteer. It is his science
fiction, perhaps, that has won him his most enduring literary
acclaim—particularly this powerful story of an oddly assorted
outfit of planetary explorers, for which he won the Hugo
Award of the 1956 World Science Fiction Convention.*

The nearer moon went by overhead. It was jagged and
irregular in shape, and was probably a captured asteroid.
Huyghens had seen it often enough, so he did not go out of
his quarters to watch it hurtle across the sky with seemingly
the speed of an atmosphere-flier, occulting the stars as it
went. Instead, he sweated over paper work, which should
have been odd because he was technically a felon and all his
labors on Loren Two felonious. It was odd, too, for a man
to do paper work in a room with steel shutters and a huge
bald eagle—untethered—dozing on a three-inch perch set

in the wall. But paper work was not Huyghens' real task. His only assistant had tangled with a night-walker and the furtive Kodius Company ships had taken him away to where Kodius Company ships came from. Huyghens had to do two men's work in loneliness. To his knowledge, he was the only man in this solar system.

Below him, there were snufflings. Sitka Pete got up heavily and padded to his water pan. He lapped the refrigerated water and sneezed violently. Sourdough Charley waked and complained in a rumbling growl. There were divers other rumblings and mutterings below. Huyghens called reassuringly, "Easy there!" and went on with his work. He finished a climate report, and fed figures to a computer, and while it hummed over them he entered the inventory totals in the station log, showing what supplies remained. Then he began to write up the log proper.

"Sitka Pete," he wrote, "has apparently solved the problem of killing individual sphexes. He has learned that it doesn't do to bug them and that his claws can't penetrate their hide—not the top hide, anyhow. Today Semper notified us that a pack of sphexes had found the scent-trail to the station. Sitka hid downwind until they arrived. Then he charged from the rear and brought his paws together on both sides of a sphex's head in a terrific pair of slaps. It must have been like two twelve-inch shells arriving from opposite directions at the same time. It must have scrambled the sphex's brains as if they were eggs. It dropped dead. He killed two more with such mighty pairs of wallops. Sourdough Charley watched, grunting, and when the sphexes turned on Sitka, he charged in his turn. I, of course, couldn't shoot too close to him, so he might have fared badly but that Faro Nell came pouring out of the bear quarters to help. The diversion enabled Sitka Pete to resume the use of his new technique, towering on his hind legs and swinging his paws in the new and grisly fashion. The fight ended promptly. Semper flew and screamed above the scrap, but as usual did not join in. Note: Nugget, the cub, tried to mix in but his mother cuffed him out of the way. Sourdough and Sitka ignored him as usual. Kodius Champion's genes are sound!"

The noises of the night went on outside. There were notes like organ tones—song lizards. There were the tittering giggling cries of night-walkers—not to be tittered back at. There were sounds like tack hammers, and doors closing, and from every direction came noises like hiccups in various keys. These were made by the improbable small creatures which on Loren Two took the place of insects.

Huyghens wrote out:

"Sitka seemed ruffled when the fight was over. He painstakingly used his trick on every dead or wounded sphex, except those he'd killed with it, lifting up their heads for his pile-driverlike blows from two directions at once, as if to show Sourdough how it was done. There was much grunting as they hauled the carcasses to the incinerator. It almost seemed—"

The arrival bell clanged, and Huyghens jerked up his head to stare at it. Semper, the eagle, opened icy eyes. He blinked.

Noises. There was a long, deep, contented snore from below. Something shrieked out in the jungle. Hiccups. Clatterings, and organ notes—

The bell clanged again. It was a notice that a ship aloft somewhere had picked up the beacon beam—which only Kodius Company ships should know about—and was communicating for a landing. But there shouldn't be any ships in this solar system just now! This was the only habitable planet of the sun, and it had been officially declared uninhabitable by reason of inimical animal life. Which meant sphexes. Therefore no colony was permitted, and the Kodius Company broke the law. And there were fewer graver crimes than unauthorized occupation of a new planet.

The bell clanged a third time. Huyghens swore. His hand went out to cut off the beacon—but that would be useless. Radar would have fixed it and tied it in with physical features like the nearby sea and the Sere Plateau. The ship could find the place, anyhow, and descend by daylight.

"The devil!" said Huyghens. But he waited yet again for the bell to ring. A Kodius Company ship would double ring to reassure him. But there shouldn't be a Kodius Company ship for months.

The bell clanged singly. The space phone dial flickered and a voice came out of it, tinny from stratospheric distortion:

"Calling ground! Calling ground! Crete Line ship Odysseus *calling ground on Loren Two. Landing one passenger by boat. Put on your field lights."*

Huyghens' mouth dropped open. A Kodius Company ship would be welcome. A Colonial Survey ship would be extremely unwelcome, because it would destroy the colony and Sitka and Sourdough and Faro Nell and Nugget—and Semper—and carry Huyghens off to be tried for unauthorized colonization and all that it implied.

But a commercial ship, landing one passenger by boat— There were simply no circumstances under which that would happen. Not to an unknown, illegal colony. Not to a furtive station!

Huyghens flicked on the landing-field lights. He saw the glare in the field outside. Then he stood up and prepared to take the measures required by discovery. He packed the paper work he'd been doing into the disposal safe. He gathered up all personal documents and tossed them in. Every record, every bit of evidence that the Kodius Company maintained this station went into the safe. He slammed the door. He touched his finger to the disposal button, which would destroy the contents and melt down even the ashes past their possible use for evidence in court.

Then he hesitated. If it was a Survey ship, the button had to be pressed and he must resign himself to a long term in prison. But a Crete Line ship—if the space phone told the truth—was not threatening. It was simply unbelievable.

He shook his head. He got into travel garb and armed himself. He went down into the bear quarters, turning on lights as he went. There were startled snufflings and Sitka Pete reared himself very absurdly to a sitting position to blink at him. Sourdough Charley lay on his back with his legs in the air. He'd found it cooler, sleeping that way. He rolled over with a thump. He made snorting sounds which somehow sounded cordial. Faro Nell padded to the door of her separate apartment—assigned her so that Nugget would not be underfoot to irritate the big males.

Huyghens, as the human population of Loren Two, faced the work force, fighting force, and—with Nugget—four-fifths of the terrestrial nonhuman population of the planet. They were mutated Kodiak bears, descendants of that Kodius Champion for whom the Kodius Company was named. Sitka Pete was a good twenty-two hundred pounds of lumbering, intelligent carnivore. Sourdough Charley would weigh within a hundred pounds of that figure. Faro Nell was eighteen hundred pounds of female charm—and ferocity. Then Nugget poked his muzzle around his mother's furry rump to see what was toward, and he was six hundred pounds of ursine infancy. The animals looked at Huyghens expectantly. If he'd had Semper riding on his shoulder, they'd have known what was expected of them.

"Let's go," said Huyghens. "It's dark outside, but somebody's coming. And it may be bad!"

He unfastened the outer door of the bear quarters. Sitka Pete went charging clumsily through it. A forthright charge was the best way to develop any situation—if one was an oversized male Kodiak bear. Sourdough went lumbering after him. There was nothing hostile immediately outside. Sitka stood up on his hind legs—he reared up a solid twelve feet—and sniffed the air. Sourdough methodically lumbered to one side and then the other, sniffing in his turn. Nell came out, nine-tenths of a ton of daintiness, and rumbled admonitorily at Nugget, who trailed her closely. Huyghens stood in the doorway, his night-sighted gun ready. He felt uncomfortable at sending the bears ahead into a Loren Two jungle at night. But they were qualified to scent danger, and he was not.

The illumination of the jungle in a wide path towards the landing field made for weirdness in the look of things. There were arching giant ferns and columnar trees which grew above them, and the extraordinary lanceolate underbrush of the jungle. The flood lamps, set level with the ground, lighted everything from below. The foliage, then, was brightly lit against the black night sky—brightly lit enough to dim out the stars. There were astonishing contrasts of light and shadow everywhere.

"On ahead!" commanded Huyghens, waving. "Hup!"

He swung the bear-quarters door shut. He moved towards the landing field through the lane of lighted forest. The two giant male Kodiaks lumbered ahead. Sitka Pete dropped to all fours and prowled. Sourdough Charley followed closely, swinging from side to side. Huyghens came alertly behind the two of them, and Faro Nell brought up the rear, with Nugget following her closely.

It was an excellent military formation for progress through dangerous jungle. Sourdough and Sitka were advance guard and point, respectively, while Faro Nell guarded the rear. With Nugget to look after she was espe-cially alert against attack from behind. Huyghens was, of course, the striking force. His gun fired explosive bullets which would discourage even sphexes, and his night-sight— a cone of light which went on when he took up the trigger-slack—told exactly where they would strike. It was not a sportsmanlike weapon, but the creatures of Loran Two were not sportsmanlike antagonists. The night-walkers, for example— But night-walkers feared light. They attacked only in a species of hysteria if it was too bright.

Huyghens moved towards the glare at the landing field. His mental state was savage. The Kodius Company station on Loren Two was completely illegal. It happened to be necessary, from one point of view, but it was still illegal. The tinny voice on the space phone was not convincing, in ignoring that illegality. But if a ship landed, Huyghens could get back to the station before men could follow, and he'd have the disposal safe turned on in time to protect those who'd sent him here.

But he heard the faraway and high harsh roar of a landing-boat rocket—not a ship's bellowing tubes—as he made his way through the unreal-seeming brush. The roar grew louder as he pushed on, the three big Kodiaks padding here and there, sniffing thoughtfully, making a perfect defensive-offensive formation for the particular conditions of this planet.

He reached the edge of the landing field, and it was blindingly bright, with the customary divergent beams slanting skyward so a ship could check its instrument land-ing by sight. Landing fields like this had been standard, once upon a time. Nowadays all developed planets had landing grids—monstrous structures which drew upon iono-spheres for power and lifted and drew down star ships with remarkable gentleness and unlimited force. This sort of landing field would be found where a survey team was at work, or where some strictly temporary investigation of ecology or bacteriology was under way, or where a newly authorized colony had not yet been able to build its landing grid. Of course it was unthinkable that anybody would attempt a settlement in defiance of the law!

Already, as Huyghens reached the edge of the scorched open space, the night-creatures had rushed to the light like moths on Earth. The air was misty with crazily gyrating, tiny flying things. They were innumerable and of every possible form and size, from the white midges of the night and multi-winged flying worms to those revoltingly naked-looking larger creatures which might have passed for plucked flying monkeys if they had not been carnivorous and worse. The flying things soared and whirred and danced and spun insanely in the glare. They made peculiarly plaintive humming noises. They almost formed a lamp-lit ceiling over the cleared space. They did hide the stars. Staring upwards, Huyghens could just barely make out the blue-white flame of the space boat's rocket through the fog of wings and bodies.

The rocket-flame grew steadily in size. Once, apparently it tilted to adjust the boat's descending course. It went back to normal. A speck of incandescence at first, it grew until it was like a great star, and then a more-than-brilliant moon, and then it was a pitiless glaring eye. Huyghens averted his gaze from it. Sitka Pete sat lumpily—more than a ton of him—and blinked wisely at the dark jungle away from the light. Sourdough ignored the deepening, increasing rocket roar. He sniffed the air delicately. Faro Nell held Nugget firmly under one huge paw and licked his head as if tidying him up to be seen by company. Nugget wriggled.

The roar became that of ten thousand thunders. A warm breeze blew outwards from the landing field. The rocket boat hurled downwards, and its flame touched the mist of flying things, and they shriveled and burned and were hot. Then there were churning clouds of dust everywhere, and the center of the field blazed terribly—and something slid down a shaft of fire, and squeezed it flat, and sat on it— and the flame went out. The rocket boat sat there, resting on its tail fins, pointing toward the stars from which it came.

There was a terrible silence after the tumult. Then, very faintly, the noises of the night came again. There were sounds like those of organ pipes, and very faint and apologetic noises like hiccups. All these sounds increased, and suddenly Huyghens could hear quite normally. Then a side-port opened with a quaint sort of clattering, and something unfolded from where it had been inset into the hull of the space boat, and there was a metal passageway across the flame-heated space on which the boat stood.

A man came out of the port. He reached back in and shook hands very formally. He climbed down the ladder rungs to the walkway. He marched above the steaming baked area, carrying a traveling bag. He reached the end of the walk and stepped gingerly to the ground. He moved hastily to the edge of the clearing. He waved to the space boat. There were ports. Perhaps someone returned the gesture. The walkway folded briskly back up to the hull and vanished in it. A flame exploded into being under the tail fins. There were fresh clouds of monstrous, choking dust and a brightness like that of a sun. There was noise past the possibility of endurance. Then the light rose swiftly through the dust cloud, and sprang higher and climbed more swiftly still. When Huyghens' ears again permitted him to hear anything, there was only a diminishing mutter in the heavens and a small bright speck of light ascending to the sky and swinging eastward as it rose to intercept the ship which had let it descend.

The night noises of the jungle went on. Life on Loren Two did not need to heed the doings of men. But there was a spot of incandescence in the day-bright clearing, and a short brisk man, with a traveling bag in his hand, looked puzzledly about him.

Huyghens advanced towards him as the incandescence dimmed. Sourdough and Sitka preceded him. Faro Nell trailed faithfully, keeping a maternal eye on her offspring. The man in the clearing stared at the parade they made. It would be upsetting, even after preparation, to land at night on a strange planet, and to have the ship's boat and all links with the rest of the cosmos depart, and then to find one's self approached—it might seem stalked—by two colossal male Kodiak bears, with a third bear and a cub behind them. A single human figure in such company might seem irrelevant.

The new arrival gazed blankly. He moved, startedly. Then Huyghens called:

"Hello, there! Don't worry about the bears! They're friends!"

Sitka reached the newcomer. He went warily downwind from him and sniffed. The smell was satisfactory. Man-smell. Sitka sat down with the solid impact of more than a ton of bear-meat landing on packed dirt. He regarded the man amiably. Sourdough said "Whoosh!" and went on to sample the air beyond the clearing. Huyghens approached. The newcomer wore the uniform of the Colonial Survey. That was bad. It bore the insignia of a senior officer. Worse.

"Hah!" said the just-landed man. "Where are the robots? What in all the nineteen hells are these creatures? Why did you shift your station? I'm Roane, here to make a progress report on your colony."

Huyghens said:

"What colony?"

"Loren Two Robot Installation—" Then Roane said indignantly, "Don't tell me that that idiot skipper dropped me at the wrong place! This is Loren Two, isn't it? And this is the landing field. But where are your robots? You should have the beginning of a grid up! What the devil's happened here and what are these beasts?"

Huyghens grimaced.

"This," he said politely, "is an illegal, unlicensed settlement. I'm a criminal. These beasts are my confederates. If you don't want to associate with criminals, you needn't, of course, but I doubt if you'll live till morning unless you accept my hospitality while I think over what to do about your landing. In reason, I ought to shoot you."

Faro Nell came to a halt behind Huyghens, which was her proper post in all outdoor movement. Nugget, however, saw a new human. Nugget was a cub, and, therefore, friendly. He ambled forward ingratiatingly. He was four feet high at the shoulders, on all fours. He wriggled bashfully as he approached Roane. He sneezed, because he was embarrassed.

His mother overtook him swiftly and cuffed him to one side. He wailed. The wail of a six-hundred-pound Kodiak bear cub is a remarkable sound. Roane gave ground a pace.

"I think," he said carefully, "that we'd better talk things over. But if this is an illegal colony, of course you're under arrest and anything you say will be used against you."

Huyghens grimaced again.

"Right," he said. "But now if you'll walk close to me, we'll head back to the station. I'd have Sourdough carry your bag—he likes to carry things—but he may need his teeth. We've half a mile to travel." He turned to the animals. "Let's go!" he said commandingly. "Back to the station! Hup!"

Grunting, Sitka Pete arose and took up his duties as advanced point of a combat team. Sourdough trailed, swinging widely to one side and another. Huyghens and Roane moved together. Faro Nell and Nugget brought up the rear. Which, of course, was the only relatively safe way for anybody to travel on Loren Two, in the jungle, a good half mile from one's fortress-like residence.

But there was only one incident on the way back. It was a night-walker, made hysterical by the lane of light. It poured through the underbrush, uttering cries like maniacal laughter.

Sourdough brought it down, a good ten yards from Huyghens. When it was all over, Nugget bristled up to the dead creature, uttering cub-growls. He feigned to attack it.

His mother whacked him soundly.

2

There were comfortable, settling-down noises below. The bears grunted and rumbled, but ultimately were still. The glare from the landing field was gone. The lighted lane through the jungle was dark again. Huyghens ushered the man from the space boat up into his living quarters. There was a rustling stir, and Semper took his head from under his wing. He stared coldly at the two humans. He spread monstrous, seven-foot wings and fluttered them. He opened his beak and closed it with a snap.

"That's Semper," said Huyghens. "Semper Tyrannis. He's the rest of the terrestrial population here. Not being a fly-by-night sort of creature, he didn't come out to welcome you."

Roane blinked at the huge bird, perched on a three-inch-thick perch set in the wall.

"An eagle?" he demanded. "Kodiak bears—mutated ones, you say, but still bears—and now an eagle? You've a very nice fighting unit in the bears."

"They're pack animals too," said Huyghens. "They can carry some hundreds of pounds without losing too much combat efficiency. And there's no problem of supply. They live off the jungle. Not sphexes, though. Nothing will eat a sphex, even if it can kill one."

He brought out glasses and a bottle. He indicated a chair. Roane put down his traveling bag. He took a glass.

"I'm curious," he observed. "Why Semper Tyrannis? I can understand Sitka Pete and Sourdough Charley as names. The home of their ancestors makes them fitting. But why Semper?"

"He was bred for hawking," said Huyghens. "You sic a dog on something. You sic Semper Tyrannis. He's too big to ride on a hawking glove, so the shoulders of my coats are padded to let him ride there. He's a flying scout. I've trained him to notify us of sphexes, and in flight he carries a tiny television camera. He's useful, but he hasn't the brains of the bears."

Roane sat down and sipped at his glass.

"Interesting . . . very interesting! But this is an illegal settlement. I'm a Colonial Survey officer. My job is reporting on progress according to plan, but nevertheless I have to arrest you. Didn't you say something about shooting me?"

Huyghens said doggedly:

"I'm trying to think of a way out. Add up all the penalties for illegal colonization and I'd be in a very bad fix if you got away and reported this set-up. Shooting you would be logical."

"I see that," said Roane reasonably. "But since the point has come up—I have a blaster trained on you from my pocket."

Huyghens shrugged.

"It's rather likely that my human confederates will be back here before your friends. You'd be in a very tight fix if my friends came back and found you more or less sitting on my corpse."

Roane nodded.

"That's true, too. Also it's probable that your fellow terrestrials wouldn't co-operate with me as they have with you. You seem to have the whip hand, even with my blaster trained on you. On the other hand, you could have killed me quite easily after the boat left, when I'd first landed. I'd have been quite unsuspicious. So you may not really intend to murder me."

Huyghens shrugged again.

"So," said Roane, "since the secret of getting along with people is that of postponing quarrels—suppose we postpone the question of who kills whom? Frankly, I'm going to send you to prison if I can. Unlawful colonization is very bad business. But I suppose you feel that you have to do something permanent about me. In your place I probably should, too. Shall we declare a truce?"

Huyghens indicated indifference. Roane said vexedly:

"Then I do! I have to! So—"

He pulled his hand out of his pocket and put a pocket blaster on the table. He leaned back, defiantly.

"Keep it," said Huyghens. "Loren Two isn't a place where you live long unarmed." He turned to a cupboard. "Hungry?"

"I could eat," admitted Roane.

Huyghens pulled out two meal-packs from the cupboard and inserted them in the readier below. He set out plates.

"Now—what happened to the official, licensed, authorized colony here?" asked Roane briskly. "License issued eighteen months ago. There was a landing of colonists with a drone fleet of equipment and supplies. There've been four ship-contacts since. There should be several thousand robots being industrious under adequate human supervision. There should be a hundred-mile-square clearing, planted with food plants for later human arrivals. There should be a landing grid at least half-finished. Obviously there should be a space beacon to guide ships to a landing. There isn't. There's no clearing visible from space. That Crete Line ship has been in orbit for three days, trying to find a place to drop me. Her skipper was fuming. Your beacon is the only one on the planet, and we found it by accident. What happened?"

Huyghens served the food. He said drily:

"There could be a hundred colonies on this planet without any one knowing of any other. I can only guess about your robots, but I suspect they ran into sphexes."

Roane paused, with his fork in his hand.

"I read up on this planet, since I was to report on its colony. A sphex is part of the inimical animal life here. Cold-blooded belligerent carnivore, not a lizard but a genus all its own. Hunts in packs. Seven to eight hundred pounds, when adult. Lethally dangerous and simply too numerous to fight. They're why no license was ever granted to human colonists. Only robots could work here, because they're machines. What animal attacks machines?"

Huyghens said:

"What machine attacks animals? The sphexes wouldn't bother robots, of course, but would robots bother the sphexes?"

Roane chewed and swallowed.

"Hold it! I'll agree that you can't make a hunting-robot. electric fence which no sphex could touch without frying."

A machine can discriminate, but it can't decide. That's why there's no danger of a robot revolt. They can't decide to do something for which they have no instructions. But this colony was planned with full knowledge of what robots can and can't do. As ground was cleared, it was enclosed in an

Huyghens thoughtfully cut his food. After a moment:

"The landing was in the winter-time," he observed. "It must have been, because the colony survived a while. And at a guess, the last ship-landing was before thaw. The years are eighteen months long here, you know."

Roane admitted:

"It was in winter that the landing was made. And the last ship-landing was before spring. The idea was to get mines in operation for material, and to have ground cleared and enclosed in sphex-proof fence before the sphexes came back from the tropics. They winter there, I understand."

"Did you ever see a sphex?" Huyghens asked. Then added, "No, of course not. But if you took a spitting cobra and crossed with it a wildcat, painted it tan-and-blue and then gave it hydrophobia and homicidal mania at once— why, you might have one sphex. But not the race of sphexes. They can climb trees, by the way. A fence wouldn't stop them."

"An electrified fence," said Roane. "Nothing could climb that!"

"No one animal," Huyghens told him. "But sphexes are a race. The smell of one dead sphex brings others running with blood in their eyes. Leave a dead sphex alone for six hours and you've got them around by the dozen. Two days and there are hundreds. Longer, and you've got thousands of them! They gather to caterwaul over their dead pal and hunt for whoever or whatever killed him."

He returned to his meal. A moment later he said:

"No need to wonder what happened to your colony. During the winter the robots burned out a clearing and put up an electrified fence according to the book. Come spring, the sphexes came back. They're curious, among their other madnesses. A sphex would try to climb the fence just to see what was behind it. He'd be electrocuted. His carcass would bring others, raging because a sphex was dead. Some of them would try to climb the fence—and die. And their corpses would bring others. Presently the fence would break down from the bodies hanging on it, or a bridge of dead beasts' carcasses would be built across it—and from as far downwind as the scent carried there'd be loping, raging, scent-crazed sphexes racing to the spot. They'd pour into the clearing through or over the fence, squalling and screeching for something to kill. I think they'd find it."

Roane ceased to eat. He looked sick.

"There were . . . pictures of sphexes in the data I read. I suppose that would account for . . . everything."

He tried to lift his fork. He put it down again.

"I can't eat," he said abruptly.

Huyghens made no comment. He finished his own meal, scowling. He rose and put the plates into the top of the cleaner. There was a whirring. He took them out of the bottom and put them away.

"Let me see those reports, eh?" he asked dourly. "I'd like to see what sort of a set-up they had—those robots."

Roane hesitated and then opened his traveling bag. There was a microviewer and reels of films. One entire reel was labeled "Specifications for Construction, Colonial Survey," which would contain detailed plans and all requirements of material and workmanship for everything from desks, office, administrative personnel, for use of, to landing grids, heavy-gravity planets, lift-capacity one hundred thousand Earth-tons. But Huyghens found another. He inserted it and spun the control swiftly here and there, pausing only briefly at index frames until he came to the section he wanted. He began to study the information with growing impatience.

"Robots, robots, robots!" he snapped. "Why don't they leave them where they belong—in cities to do the dirty work, and on airless planets where nothing unexpected ever happens! Robots don't belong in new colonies! Your colonists depended on them for defense! Dammit, let a man work with robots long enough and he thinks all nature is as limited as they are! This is a plan to set up a controlled environment! On Loren Two! Controlled environment—" He swore, luridly. "Complacent, idiotic, desk-bound half-wits!"

"Robots are all right," said Roane. "We couldn't run civilization without them."

"But you can't tame a wilderness with 'em!" snapped Huyghens. "You had a dozen men landed, with fifty assembled robots to start with. There were parts for fifteen hundred more—and I'll bet anything I've got that the ship-contacts landed more still."

"They did," admitted Roane.

"I despise 'em," growled Huyghens, "I feel about 'em the way the old Greeks and Romans felt about slaves. They're for menial work—the sort of work a man will perform for himself, but that he won't do for another man for pay. Degrading work!"

"Quite aristocratic!" said Roane with a touch of irony. "I take it that robots clean out the bear quarters downstairs."

"No!" snapped Huyghens, "I do! They're my friends! They fight for me! They can't understand the necessity and no robot would do the job right!"

He growled, again. The noises of the night went on outside. Organ tones and hiccupings and the sound of tack-hammers and slamming doors. Somewhere there was a singularly exact replica of the discordant squeaking of a rusty pump.

"I'm looking," said Huyghens at the microviewer, "for the record of their mining operations. An open-pit operation wouldn't mean a thing. But if they had driven a tunnel, and somebody was there supervising the robots when the colony was wiped out, there's an off-chance he survived a while."

Roane regarded him with suddenly intent eyes.

"And—"

"Dammit," snapped Huyghens, "if so I'll go see! He'd . . . they'd have no chance at all, otherwise. Not that the chance is good in any case!"

Roane raised his eyebrows.

"I'm a Colonial Survey officer," he said. "I've told you I'll send you to prison if I can. You've risked the lives of millions of people, maintaining non-quarantine communication with an unlicensed planet. If you did rescue somebody from the ruins of the robot colony, does it occur to you that they'd be witnesses to your unauthorized presence here?"

Huyghens spun the viewer again. He stopped. He switched back and forth and found what he wanted. He muttered in satisfaction: "They did run a tunnel!" Aloud he said, "I'll worry about witnesses when I have to."

He pushed aside another cupboard door. Inside it were odds and ends a man makes use of to repair the things about his house that he never notices until they go wrong. There was an assortment of wires, transistors, bolts, and similar stray items that a man living alone will need. When to his knowledge he's the only inhabitant of a solar system, he especially needs such things.

"What now?" asked Roane mildly.

"I'm going to try to find out if there's anybody left alive over there. I'd have checked before if I'd known the colony existed. I can't prove they're all dead, but I may prove that somebody's still alive. It's barely two weeks' journey away from here! Odd that two colonies picked spots so near!"

He absorbedly picked over the oddments he'd selected. Roane said vexedly:

"Confound it! How can you check whether somebody's alive some hundreds of miles away—when you didn't know he existed half an hour ago?"

Huyghens threw a switch and took down a wall panel, exposing electronic apparatus and circuits behind. He busied himself with it.

"Ever think about hunting for a castaway?" he asked over his shoulder. "There's a planet with some tens of millions of square miles on it. You know there's a ship down. You've no idea where. You assume the survivors have power—no civilized man will be without power very long, so long as he can smelt metals!—but making a space beacon calls for high-precision measurements and workmanship. It's not to be improvised. So what will your shipwrecked civilized man do, to guide a rescue ship to the one or two square miles he occupies among some tens of millions on the planet?"

Roane fretted visibly.

"What?"

"He's had to go primitive, to begin with," Huyghens explained. "He cooks his meat over a fire, and so on. He has to make a strictly primitive signal. It's all he can do without gauges and micrometers and very special tools. But he can fill all the planet's atmosphere with a signal that searchers for him can't miss. You see?"

Roane thought irritably. He shook his head.

"He'll make," said Huyghens, "a spark transmitter. He'll fix its output at the shortest frequency he can contrive—it'll be somewhere in the five-to-fifty-meter wave-band, but it will tune very broad—and it will be a plainly human signal. He'll start it broadcasting. Some of those frequencies will go all around the planet under the ionosphere. Any ship that comes in under the radio roof will pick up his signal, get a fix on it, move and get another fix, and then go straight to where the castaway is waiting placidly in a hand-braided hammock, sipping whatever sort of drink he's improvised out of the local vegetation."

Roane said grudgingly:

"Now that you mention it, of course—"

"My space phone picks up micro-waves," said Huyghens, "I'm shifting a few elements to make it listen for longer stuff. It won't be efficient, but it will pick up a distress signal if one's in the air. I don't expect it, though."

He worked. Roane sat still a long time, watching him. Down below a rhythmic sort of sound arose. It was Sourdough Charley, snoring. Sitka Pete grunted in his sleep. He was dreaming. In the general room of the station Semper the eagle blinked his eyes rapidly and then tucked his head under a gigantic wing and went to sleep. The noises of the Loren Two jungle came through the steel-shuttered windows. The nearer moon—which had passed overhead not long before the ringing of the arrival bell—again came soaring over the eastern horizon. It sped across the sky at the apparent speed of an atmosphere-flier. Overhead, it could be seen to be a jagged irregular mass of rock or metal, plunging blindly about the great planet forever.

Inside the station, Roane said angrily:

"See here, Huyghens! You've reason to kill me. Apparently you don't intend to. You've excellent reason to leave that robot colony strictly alone. But you're preparing to help, if there's anybody alive to need it. And yet you're a criminal—and I mean a criminal! There've been some ghastly bacteria exported from planets like Loren Two! There've been plenty of lives lost in consequence, and you're risking more! Why do you do it? Why do you do something that could produce monstrous results to other beings?"

Huyghens grunted.

"You're only assuming there are no sanitary and quarantine precautions taken in my communications. As a matter of fact, there are. They're taken, all right! As for the rest, you wouldn't understand."

"I don't understand," snapped Roane, "but that's no proof I can't! Why are you a criminal?"

Huyghens painstakingly used a screwdriver inside the wall panel. He delicately lifted out a small electronic assembly. He carefully began to fit in a spaghettied new assembly with larger units.

"I'm cutting my amplification here to hell-and-gone," he observed, "but I think it'll do. I'm doing what I'm doing," he added calmly, "I'm being a criminal because it seems to me befitting what I think I am. Everybody acts according to his own real notion of himself. You're a conscientious citizen, and a loyal official, and a well-adjusted personality. You consider yourself an intelligent rational animal. But you don't act that way! You're reminding me of my need to shoot you or something similar, which a merely rational animal would try to make me forget. You happen, Roane, to be a man. So am I. But I'm aware of it. Therefore, I deliberately do things a merely rational animal wouldn't, because they're my notion of what a man who's more than a rational animal should do."

He very carefully tightened one small screw after another. Roane said annoyedly:

"Oh. Religion."

"Self-respect," corrected Huyghens. "I don't like robots. They're too much like rational animals. A robot will do whatever it can that its supervisor requires it to do. A merely rational animal will do whatever it can that circumstances require it to do. I wouldn't like a robot unless it had some idea of what was befitting it and would spit in my eye if I tried to make it do something else. The bears downstairs, now—they're no robots! They are loyal and honorable beasts, but they'd turn and tear me to bits if I tried to make them do something against their nature. Faro Nell would fight me, and all creation together if I tried to harm Nugget. It would be unintelligent and unreasonable and irrational. She'd lose out and get killed. But I like her that way! And I'll fight you and all creation when you make me try to do something against my nature. I'll be stupid and unreasonable and irrational about it." Then he grinned over his shoulder. "So will you. Only you don't realize it."

He turned back to his task. After a moment he fitted a manual-control knob over a shaft in his haywire assembly.

"What did somebody try to make you do?" asked Roane shrewdly. "What was demanded of you that turned you into a criminal? What are you in revolt against?"

Huyghens threw a switch. He began to turn the knob that controlled the knob of his makeshift-modified receiver.

"Why," he said amusedly, "when I was young the people around me tried to make me into a conscientious citizen and a loyal employee and a well-adjusted personality. They tried to make me into a highly intelligent rational animal and nothing more. The difference between us, Roane, is that I found it out. Naturally, I rev—"

He stopped short. Faint, crackling, crisp frying sounds came from the speaker of the space phone now modified to receive what once were called short waves.

Huyghens listened. He cocked his head intently. He turned the knob very, very slowly. Then Roane made an arrested gesture, to call attention to something in the sibilant sound. Huyghens nodded. He turned the knob again, with infinitesimal increments.

Out of the background noise came a patterned mutter. As Huyghens shifted the tuning, it grew louder. It reached a volume where it was unmistakable. It was a sequence of sounds like discordant buzzing. There were three half-second buzzings with half-second pauses between. A two-second pause. Three full-second buzzings with half-second pauses between. Another two-second pause and three half-second buzzings, again. Then silence for five seconds. Then the pattern repeated.

"The devil!" said Huyghens. "That's a human signal! Mechanically made, too In fact, it used to be a standard distress call. It was termed an SOS, though I've no idea what that meant. Anyhow, somebody must have read old-fashioned novels, some time, to know about it. And so someone is still alive over at your licensed, but now smashed-up, robot colony. And they're asking for help. I'd say they're likely to need it."

He looked at Roane.

"The intelligent thing to do is sit back and wait for a ship—either of my friends or yours. A ship can help survivors or castaways much better than we can. A ship can even find them more easily. But maybe time is important to the poor devils! So I'm going to take the bears and see if I can reach them. You can wait here, if you like. What say? Travel on Loren Two isn't a picnic! I'll be fighting nearly every foot of the way. There's plenty of 'inimical animal life' here!"

Roane snapped angrily:

"Don't be a fool! Of course I'm coming! What do you take me for? And two of us should have four times the chance of one!"

Huyghens grinned.

"Not quite. You forget Sitka Pete and Sourdough Charley and Faro Nell. There'll be five of us if you come, instead of four. And, of course, Nugget has to come—and he'll be no help—but Semper may make up for him. You won't quadruple our chances, Roane, but I'll be glad to have you if you want to be stupid and unreasonable and not at all rational and come along."

3

There was a jagged spur of stone looming precipitously

over a river valley. A thousand feet below, a broad stream ran westward to the sea. Twenty miles to the east, a wall of mountains rose sheer against the sky. Its peaks seemed to blend to a remarkable evenness of height. There was rolling, tumbled ground between for as far as the eye could see.

A speck in the sky came swiftly downwards. Great pinions spread, and flapped, and icy eyes surveyed the rocky space. With more great flappings, Semper the eagle came to ground. He folded his huge wings and turned his head jerkily, his eyes unblinking. A tiny harness held a miniature camera against his chest. He strutted over the bare stone to the highest point. He stood there, a lonely and arrogant figure in the vastness.

There came crashings and rustlings, and then snuffling sounds. Sitka Pete came lumbering out into the clear space. He wore a harness too, and a pack. The harness was complex, because it had not only to hold a pack in normal travel, but, when he stood on his hind legs, it must not hamper the use of his forepaws in combat.

He went cagily all over the open area. He peered over the edge of the spur's farthest tip. He prowled to the other side and looked down. He scouted carefully. Once he moved close to Semper and the eagle opened his great curved beak and uttered an indignant noise. Sitka paid no attention.

He relaxed, satisfied. He sat down untidily, his hind legs sprawling. He wore an air approaching benevolence as he surveyed the landscape about and below him.

More snufflings and crashings. Sourdough Charley came into view, with Huyghens and Roane behind him. Sourdough carried a pack, too. Then there was a squealing and Nugget scurried up from the rear, impelled by a whack from his mother. Faro Nell appeared, with the carcass of a staglike animal lashed to her harness.

"I picked this place from a space photo," said Huyghens, "to make a directional fix from. I'll get set up."

He swung his pack from his shoulders to the ground. He extracted an obviously self-constructed device which he set on the ground. It had a whip aerial, which he extended. Then he plugged in a considerable length of flexible wire and unfolded a tiny, improvised directional aerial with an even tinier booster at its base. Roane slipped his pack from his shoulders and watched. Huyghens slipped headphones over his ears. He looked up and said sharply:

"Watch the bears, Roane. The wind's blowing up the way we came. Anything that trails us—sphexes, for example—will send its scent on before. The bears will tell us."

He busied himself with the instruments he'd brought. He heard the hissing, frying background noise that could be anything at all except a human signal. He reached out and swung the small aerial around. Rasping, buzzing tones came in, faintly and then loudly. This receiver, though, had been made for this particular wave band. It was much more efficient than the modified space phone had been. It picked up three short buzzes, three long ones, and three short ones again. Three dots, three dashes, and three dots. Over and over again. SOS. SOS. SOS.

Huyghens took a reading and moved the directional aerial a carefully measured distance. He took another reading. He shifted it yet again and again, carefully marking and measuring each spot and taking notes of the instrument readings. When he finished, he had checked the direction of the signal not only by loudness but by phase—he had as accurate a fix as could possibly be had with portable apparatus.

Sourdough growled softly. Sitka Pete whiffed the air and arose from his sitting position. Faro Nell whacked Nugget, sending him whimpering to the farthest corner of the flea place. She stood bristling, facing downhill the way they'd come.

"Damn!" said Huyghens.

He got up and waved his arm at Semper, who had turned his head at the stirrings. Semper squawked in a most un-eaglelike fashion and dived off the spur and was immediately fighting the downdraft beyond it. As Huyghens reached for his weapon, the eagle came back overhead. He went magnificently past, a hundred feet high, careening and flapping in the tricky currents. He screamed, abruptly, and circled and screamed again. Huyghens swung a tiny vision plate from its strap to where he could look into it. He saw, of course, what the little camera on Semper's chest could see—reeling, swaying terrain as Semper saw it, though without his breadth of field. There were moving objects to be seen through the shifting trees. Their coloring was unmistakable.

"Sphexes," said Huyghens dourly. "Eight of them. Don't look for them to follow our track, Roane. They run parallel to a trail on either side. That way they attack on breadth and all at once when they catch up. And listen! The bears can handle anything they tangle with! It's our job to pick off the loose ones! And aim for the body! The bullets explode."

He threw off the safety of his weapon. Faro Nell, uttering thunderous growls, went padding to a place between Sitka Pete and Sourdough. Sitka glanced at her and made a whuffing noise, as if derisive of her blood-curdling sounds. Sourdough grunted in a somehow solid fashion. He and Sitka moved farther away from Nell to either side. They would cover a wider front.

There was no other sign of life than the shrillings of the incredibly tiny creatures which on this planet were birds, and Faro Nell's deep-bass, raging growls, and then the click of Roane's safety going off as he got ready to use the weapon Huyghens had given him.

Semper screamed again, flapping low above the treetops, following parti-colored, monstrous shapes beneath.

Eight blue-and-tan fiends came racing out of the under-brush. They had spiny fringes, and horns, and glaring eyes, and they looked as if they had come straight out of hell. On the instant of their appearance they leaped, emitting squall-ing, spitting squeals that were like the cries of fighting tomcats ten thousand times magnified. Huyghens' rifle cracked, and its sound was wiped out in the louder detona-tion of its bullet in sphexian flesh. A tan-and-blue monster tumbled over, shrieking. Faro Nell charged, the very im-personation of white-hot fury. Roane fired, and his bullet exploded against a tree. Sitka Pete brought his massive forepaws in a clapping, monstrous ear-boxing motion. A sphex died.

Then Roane fired again. Sourdough Charley whuffed. He fell forward upon a spitting bi-colored fiend, rolled him over, and raked with his hind claws. The belly-side of the sphex was tenderer than the rest. The creature rolled away, snapping at its own wounds. Another sphex found itself shaken loose from the tumult about Sitka Pete. It whirled to leap on him from behind—and Huyghens fired very coldly—and two plunged upon Faro Nell and Roane blasted one and Faro Nell disposed of the other in truly awesome fury. Then Sitka Pete heaved himself erect—seeming to drip sphexes—and Sourdough waddled over and pulled one off and killed it and went back for another. And both rifles cracked together and there was suddenly nothing left to fight.

The bears prowled from one to another of the corpses. Sitka Pete rumbled and lifted up a limp head. Crash! Then another. He went over the lot, whether or not they showed signs of life. When he had finished, they were wholly still.

Semper came flapping down out of the sky. He had screamed and fluttered overhead as the fight went on. Now he landed with a rush. Huyghens went soothingly from one bear to another, calming them with his voice. It took longest

to calm Faro Nell, licking Nugget with impassioned solici-
tude and growling horribly as she licked.

"Come along now," said Huyghens, when Sitka showed
signs of intending to sit down again. "Heave these carcasses
over a cliff. Come along! Sitka! Sourdough! Hup!"

He guided them as the two big males somewhat fastid-
iously lifted up the nightmarish creatures they and the guns
together had killed, and carried them to the edge of the
spur of stone. They let the dead beasts go bouncing and
sliding down into the valley.

"That," said Huyghens, "is so their little pals will gather
round them and caterwaul their woe where there's no trail
of ours to give them ideas. If we'd been near a river, I'd
have dumped them in to float downriver and gather
mourners wherever they stranded. Around the station I
incinerate them. If I had to leave them, I'd make tracks
away. About fifty miles upwind would be a good idea."

He opened the pack Sourdough carried and extracted
giant-sized swabs and some gallons of antiseptic. He tended
the three Kodiaks in turn, swabbing not only the cuts and
scratches they'd received, but deeply soaking their fur
where there could be suspicion of spilled sphex blood.

"This antiseptic deodorizes, too," he told Roane. "Or
we'd be trailed by any sphex who passed to leeward of us.
When we start off, I'll swab the bears' paws for the same
reason."

Roane was very quiet. He'd missed his first shot with a
bullet-firing weapon—a beam hasn't the stopping-power of
an explosive bullet—but he'd seemed to grow savagely
angry with himself. The last few seconds of the fight, he'd
fired very deliberately and every bullet hit. Now he said
bitterly:

"If you're instructing me so I can carry on should you be
killed, I doubt that it's worth while!"

Huyghens felt in his pack and unfolded the enlargements

he'd made of the space photos of this part of the planet. He carefully oriented the map with distant landmarks. He drew a painstakingly accurate line across the photo.

"The SOS signal comes from somewhere close to the robot colony," he reported. "I think a little to the south of it. Probably from a mine they'd opened up, on the far side—of course—of the Sere Plateau. See how I've marked this map? Two fixes, one from the station and one from here. I came away off-course to get a fix here so we'd have two position-lines to the transmitter. The signal could have come from the other side of the planet. But it doesn't."

"The odds would be astronomical against other castaways," protested Roane.

"No-o-o-o," said Huyghens. "Ships have been coming here. To the robot colony. One could have crashed. And I have friends, too."

He repacked his apparatus and gestured to the bears. He led them beyond the scene of combat and very carefully swabbed off their paws, so they could not possibly leave a trail of sphex-blood scent behind them. He waved Semper the eagle aloft.

"Let's go," he told the Kodiaks. "Yonder! Hup!"

The party headed downhill and into the jungle again. Now it was Sourdough's turn to take the lead, and Sitka Pete prowled more widely behind him. Faro Nell trailed the men, with Nugget. She kept an extremely sharp eye upon the cub. He was a baby, still. He only weighed six hundred pounds. And of course she watched against danger from the rear.

Overhead, Semper fluttered and flew in giant circles and spirals, never going very far away. Huyghens referred constantly to the screen which showed what the air-borne camera saw. The image tilted and circled and blanked and swayed. It was by no means the best air-reconnaissance that could be imagined. But it was the best that would work. Presently Huyghens said:

"We swing to the right, here. The going's bad straight ahead, and it looks like a pack of sphexes has killed and is feeding."

Roane was upset. He was dissatisfied with himself. So he said:

"It's against reason for carnivores to be as thick as you say! There has to be a certain amount of other animal life for every meat-eating beast! Too many of them would eat all the game and starve!"

"They're gone all winter," explained Huyghens, "which around here isn't as severe as you might think. And a good many animals seem to breed just after the sphexes go south. Also, the sphexes aren't around all the warm weather. There's a sort of peak, and then for a matter of weeks you won't see a one of them, and suddenly the jungle swarms with them again. Then, presently, they head south. Apparently they're migratory in some fashion, but nobody knows." He said drily: "There haven't been many naturalists around on this planet. The animal life is inimical."

Roane fretted. He was a senior officer in the Colonial Survey, and he was accustomed to arrival at a partly or completely finished colonial setup, and to pass upon the completion or non-completion of the planned installation as designed. Now he was in an intolerably hostile environment, depending upon an illegal colonist for his life, engaged upon a demoralizingly indefinite enterprise—because the mechanical spark-signal could be working long after its constructors were dead—and his ideas about a number of matters were shaken. He was alive, for example, because of three giant Kodiak bears and a bald eagle. He and Huyghens could have been surrounded by ten thousand robots, and they'd have been killed. Sphexes and robots would have ignored each other, and sphexes would have made straight for the men, who'd have had less than four seconds in which to discover for themselves that they were attacked, prepare to defend themselves, and kill eight sphexes.

Roane's convictions as a civilized man were shaken. Robots were marvelous contrivances for doing the expected: accomplishing the planned; coping with the predicted. But they also had defects. Robots could only follow instructions—if this thing happens, do this, if that thing happens, do that. But before something else, neither this nor that, robots were helpless. So a robot civilization worked only in an environment where nothing unanticipated ever turned up, and human supervisors never demanded anything unexpected. Roane was appalled. He'd never encountered the truly unpredictable before in all his life and career.

He found Nugget, the cub, ambling uneasily in his wake. The cub flattened his ears miserably when Roane glanced at him. It occurred to the man that Nugget was receiving a lot of disciplinary thumpings from Faro Nell. He was knocked about physically, pretty much as Roane was being knocked about psychologically. His lack of information and unfitness for independent survival in this environment was being hammered into him.

"Hi, Nugget," said Roane ruefully. "I feel just about the way you do!"

Nugget brightened visibly. He frisked. He tended to gambol. He looked very hopefully up into Roane's face— and he stood four feet high at the shoulder and would overtop Roane if he stood erect.

Roane reached out and patted Nugget's head. It was the first time in all his life he'd ever patted an animal.

He heard a snuffling sound behind him. Skin crawled at the back of his neck. He whirled.

Faro Nell regarded him—eighteen hundred pounds of she-bear only ten feet away and looking into his eyes. For one panicky instant Roane went cold all over. Then he realized that Faro Nell's eyes were not burning. She was not snarling. She did not emit those blood-curdling sounds which the bare prospect of danger to Nugget had produced upon the rocky spur. She looked at him blandly. In fact, after a moment she swung off in some independent investigation of a matter that had aroused her curiosity.

The traveling party went on, Nugget frisking beside Roane and tending to bump into him out of pure cub-clumsiness. Now and again he looked adoringly at Roane, in the instant and overwhelming affection of the very young.

Roane trudged on. Presently he glanced behind again. Faro Nell was now ranging more widely. She was well satisfied to have Nugget in the immediate care of a man. From time to time he got on her nerves.

A little while later, Roane called ahead.

"Huyghens! Look here! I've been appointed nursemaid to Nugget!"

Huyghens looked back.

"Oh, slap him a few times and he'll go back to his mother."

"The devil I will!" said Roane querulously. "I like it!"

The traveling party went on.

When night fell, they camped. There could be no fire, of course, because all the minute night-things about would come eagerly to dance in the glow. But there could not be darkness, equally, because night-walkers hunted in the dark. So Huyghen set out the barrier lamps, which made a wall of twilight about their halting place, and the staglike creature Faro Nell had carried became their evening meal. Then they slept—at least the men did—and the bears dozed and snorted and waked and dozed again. But Semper sat immobile with his head under his wing on a tree limb. And presently there was a glorious cool hush and all the world glowed in morning light diffused through the jungle by a newly risen sun. And they arose, and traveled again.

This day they stopped stock-still for two hours while sphexes puzzled over the trail the bears had left. Huyghens discoursed calmly on the need for an anti-scent, to be used on the boots of men and the paws of bears, which would make the following of their trails unpopular with sphexes. And Roane seized upon the idea and absorbedly suggested that a sphex-repellent odor might be worked out, which would make a human revolting to a sphex. If that were done—why—humans could go freely about unmolested.

"Like stink-bugs," said Huyghens, sardonically. "A very intelligent idea! Very rational! You can feel proud!"

And suddenly Roane, very obscurely, was not proud of the idea at all.

They camped again. On the third night they were at the base of that remarkable formation, the Sere Plateau, which from a distance looked like a mountain-range but was actually a desert tableland. And it was not reasonable for a desert to be raised high, while lowlands had rain, but on the fourth morning they found out why. They saw, far, far away, a truly monstrous mountain-mass at the end of the long-way expanse of the plateau. It was like the prow of a ship. It lay, so Huyghens observed, directly in line with the prevailing winds, and divided them as a ship's prow divides the waters. The moisture-bearing air currents flowed beside the plateau, not over it, and its interior was pure sere desert in the unscreened sunshine of high altitudes.

It took them a full day to get halfway up the slope. And here, twice as they climbed, Semper flew screaming over aggregations of sphexes to one side of them or the other. These were much larger groups than Huyghens had ever seen before—fifty to a hundred monstrosities together, where a dozen was a large hunting pack elsewhere. He looked in the screen which showed him what Semper saw, four or five miles away. The sphexes padded uphill towards the Sere Plateau in a long line. Fifty—sixty—seventy tan-and-azure beasts out of hell.

"I'd hate to have that bunch jump us," he said candidly to Roane. "I don't think we'd stand a chance."

"Here's where a robot tank would be useful," Roane observed.

"Anything armored," conceded Huyghens. "One man in an armored station like mine would be safe. But if he killed a sphex he'd be besieged. He'd have to stay holed up, breathing the smell of dead sphex, until the odor had gone away. And he mustn't kill any others or he'd be besieged until winter came."

Roane did not suggest the advantages of robots in other directions. At that moment, for example, they were working their way up a slope that averaged fifty degrees. The bears climbed without effort despite their burdens. For the men it was infinite toil. Semper the eagle manifested impatience with bears and men alike, who crawled so slowly up an incline over which he soared.

He went ahead up the mountainside and teetered in the air currents at the plateau's edge. Huyghens looked in the vision-plate by which he reported.

"How the devil," panted Roane—they had stopped for a breather, and the bears waited patiently for them—"do you train bears like these? I can understand Semper."

"I don't train them," said Huyghens, staring into the plate. "They're mutations. In heredity the sex-linkage of physical characteristics is standard stuff. But there's been some sound work done on the gene-linkage of psychological factors. There was need, on my home planet, for an animal who could fight like a fiend, live off the land, carry a pack, and get along with men at least as well as dogs do. In the old days they'd have tried to breed the desired physical properties into an animal who already had the personality they wanted. Something like a giant dog, say. But back home they went at it the other way about. They picked the wanted physical characteristics and bred for the personality—the psychology. The job got done over a century ago—a Kodiak bear named Kodius Champion was the first real success. He had everything that was wanted. These bears are his descendants."

"They look normal," commented Roane.

"They are!" said Huyghens warmly. "Just as normal as an honest dog! They're not trained, like Semper. They train themselves!" He looked back into the plate in his hands, which showed the ground five and six and seven thousand feet higher. "Semper, now, is a trained bird without too much brains. He's educated—a glorified hawk. But the bears want to get along with men. They're emotionally dependent on us! Like dogs. Semper's a servant, but they're companions and friends. He's trained, but they're loyal. He's conditioned. They love us. He'd abandon me if he ever realized he could—he thinks he can only eat what men feed him. But the bears wouldn't want to. They like us. I admit that I like them. Maybe because they like me."

Roane said deliberately:

"Aren't you a trifle loose-tongued, Huyghens? I'm a Colonial Survey officer. I have to arrest you sooner or later. You've told me something that will locate and convict the people who set you up here. It shouldn't be hard to find where bears were bred for psychological mutations, and where a bear named Kodius Champion left descendants! I can find out where you came from now, Huyghens!"

Huyghens looked up from the plate with its tiny swaying

television image, relayed from where Semper floated impatiently in mid-air.

"No harm done," he said amiably. "I'm a criminal there, too. It's officially on record that I kidnaped these bears and escaped with them. Which, on my home planet, is about as heinous a crime as a man can commit. It's worse than horsetheft back on Earth in the old days. The kin and cousins of my bears are highly thought of. I'm quite a criminal, back home."

Roane stared.

"Did you steal them?" he demanded.

"Confidentially," said Huyghens, "no. But prove it!" Then he said: "Take a look in this plate. See what Semper can see at the plateau's edge."

Roane squinted aloft, where the eagle flew in great sweeps and dashes. Somehow, by the experience of the past few days, Roane knew that Semper was screaming fiercely as he flew. He made a dart towards the plateau's border.

Roane looked at the transmitted picture. It was only four inches by six, but it was perfectly without grain and in accurate color. It moved and turned as the camera-bearing eagle swooped and circled. For an instant the screen showed the steeply sloping mountainside, and off at one edge the party of men and bears could be seen as dots. Then it swept away and showed the top of the plateau.

There were sphexes. A pack of two hundred trotted towards the desert interior. They moved at leisure, in the open. The viewing camera reeled, and there were more. As Roane watched and as the bird flew higher, he could see still other sphexes moving up over the edge of the plateau from a small erosion-defile here and another one there. The Sere Plateau was alive with the hellish creatures. It was inconceivable that there should be game enough for them to live on. They were visable as herds of cattle would be visible on grazing plants.

It was simply impossible.

"Migrating," observed Huyghens. "I said they did. They're headed somewhere. Do you know, I doubt that it would be healthy for us to try to cross the plateau through such a swarm of sphexes."

Roane swore, in abrupt change of mood.

"But the signal's still coming through! Somebody's alive over at the robot colony! Must we wait till the the migration's over?"

"We don't know," Huyghens pointed out, "that they'll stay alive. They may need help badly. We have to get to them. But at the same time—"

He glanced at Sourdough Charley and Sitka Pete, clinging patiently to the mountainside while the men rested and talked. Sitka had managed to find a place to sit down, though one massive paw anchored him in his place.

Huyghens waved his arm, pointing in a new direction.

"Let's go!" he called briskly. "Let's go! Yonder! Hup!"

4

They followed the slopes of the Sere Plateau, neither ascending to its level top, where sphexes congregated, nor descending into the foothills, where sphexes assembled. They moved along hillsides and mountain-flanks which sloped anywhere from thirty to sixty degrees, and they did not cover much distance. They practically forgot what it was to walk on level ground. Semper, the eagle, hovered overhead during the daytime, not far away. He descended at nightfall for his food from the pack of one of the bears.

"The bears aren't doing too well for food," said Huyghens drily. "A ton of bear needs a lot to eat. But they're loyal to us. Semper hasn't any loyalty. He's too stupid. But he's been conditioned to think that he can only eat what men feed him. The bears know better, but they stick to us regardless. I rather like these bears."

It was the most self-evident of understatements. This was at an encampment on the top of a massive boulder which projected from a mountainous stony wall. This was six days from the start of their journey. There was barely room on the boulder for all the party. And Faro Nell fussily insisted that Nugget should be in the safest part, which meant near the mountain-flank. She would have crowded the men outwards, but Nugget whimpered for Roane. Wherefore, when Roane moved to comfort him, Faro Nell contentedly drew back and snorted at Sitka and Sourdough and they made room for her near the edge.

It was a hungry camp. They had come upon tiny rills upon occasion, flowing down the mountainside. Here the bears had drunk deeply and the men had filled canteens. But this was the third night, and there had been no game at all. Huyghens made no move to bring out food for Roane or himself. Roane made no comment. He was beginning to participate in the relationship between bears and men, which was not the slavery of the bears but something more. It was two-way. He felt it.

"It would seem," he said fretfully, "that since the sphexes don't seem to hunt on their way uphill, that there should be some game. They ignore everything as they file uphill."

This was true enough. The normal fighting formation of sphexes was line abreast, which automatically surrounded anything that offered to flee and outflanked anything that offered fight. But here they ascended the mountain in long lines, one after the other, following apparently long-established trails. The wind blew along the slopes and carried scent only sideways. But the sphexes were not diverted from their chosen paths. The long processions of hideous blue-and-tawny creatures—it was hard to think of them as natural beasts, male and female and laying eggs like reptiles on other planets—simply climbed.

"There've been other thousands of beasts before them," said Huyghens. "They must have been crowding this way for days or even weeks. We've seen tens of thousands in Semper's camera. They must be uncountable, altogether. The first-comers ate all the game there was, and the last-comers have something else on whatever they use for minds."

Roane protested:

"But so many carnivores in one place is impossible! I know they are here, but they can't be!"

"They're cold-blooded," Huyghens pointed out. "They don't burn food to sustain body temperature. After all, lots of creatures go for long periods without eating. Even bears hibernate. But this isn't hibernation—or estivation, either."

He was setting up the radiation-wave receiver in the darkness. There was no point in attempting a fix here. The transmitter was on the other side of the Sere Plateau, which inexplicably swarmed with the most ferocious and deadly of all the creatures of Loren Two. The men and bears would commit suicide by crossing here.

But Huyghens turned on the receiver. There came the whispering, scratchy sound of background noise. Then the signal. Three dots, three dashes, three dots. Three dots, three dashes, three dots. It went on and on and on. Huyghens turned it off. Roane said:

"Shouldn't we have answered that signal before we left the station? To encourage them?"

"I doubt they have a receiver," said Huyghens. "They won't expect an answer for months, anyhow. They'd hardly listen all the time, and if they're living in a mine-tunnel and trying to sneak out for food to stretch their supplies—why, they'll be too busy to try to make complicated recorders or relays."

Roane was silent for a moment or two.

"We've got to get food for the bears," he said presently. "Nugget's weaned, and he's hungry."

"We will," Huyghens promised. "I may be wrong, but it seems to me that the number of sphexes climbing the mountain is less than yesterday and the day before. We may have just about crossed the path of their migration. They're thinning out. When we're past their trail, we'll have to look out for night-walkers and the like again. But I think they wiped out all animal life on their migration route."

He was not quite right. He was waked in darkness by the sound of slappings and the grunting of bears. Feather-light puffs of breeze beat upon his face. He struck his belt-lamp sharply and the world was hidden by a whitish film that snatched itself away. Something flapped. Then he saw the stars and the emptiness on the edge of which they camped. Then big white things flapped towards him.

Sitka Pete whuffed mightly and swatted. Faro Nell grunted and swung. She caught something in her claws. She crunched. The light went off as Huyghens realized. Then he said:

"Don't shoot, Roane!" He listened, and heard the sounds of feeding in the dark. It ended. "Watch this!" said Huyghens.

The belt-light came on again. Something strangely shaped and pallid like human skin reeled and flapped crazily towards him. Something else. Four. Five—ten—twenty— more . . .

A huge hairy paw reached up into the light-beam and snatched a flying thing out of it. Another great paw. Huyghens shifted the light and the three great Kodiaks were on their hind legs, swatting at creatures which flittered insanely, unable to resist the fascination of the glaring lamp. Because of their wild gyrations it was impossible to see them in detail, but they were those unpleasant night-creatures which looked like plucked flying monkeys but were actually something quite different.

The bears did not snarl or snap. They swatted, with a remarkable air of businesslike competence and purpose. Small mounds of broken things built up about their feet.

Suddenly there were no more. Huyghens snapped off the light. The bears crunched and fed busily in the darkness.

"Those things are carnivores *and* blood-suckers, Roane," said Huyghens calmly. "They drain their victims of blood like vampire bats—they've some trick of not waking them— and when they're dead the whole tribe eats. But bears have thick furs, and they wake when they're touched. And they're omnivorous—they'll eat anything but sphexes, and like it. You might say that those night-creatures came to lunch. But they stayed. They are it—for the bears, who are living off the country as usual."

Roane uttered a sudden exclamation. He made a tiny light, and blood flowed down his hand. Huyghens passed over his pocket kit of antiseptic and bandages. Roane stanched the bleeding and bound up his hand. Then he realized that Nugget chewed on something. When he turned the light, Nugget swallowed convulsively. It appeared that he had caught and devoured the creature which had drawn blood from Roane. But Roane had lost none to speak of, at that.

In the morning they started along the sloping scarp of the plateau once more. During the morning, Roane said painfully:

"Robots wouldn't have handled those vampire-things, Huyghens."

"Oh, they could be built to watch for them," said Huyghens, tolerantly. "But you'd have to swat for yourself. I prefer the bears."

He led the way on. Here their jungle-formation could not apply. On a steep slope the bears ambled comfortably, the tough pads of their feet holding fast on the slanting rock, but the men struggled painfully. Twice Huyghens halted to examine the ground about the mountain's base through binoculars. He looked encouraged as they went on. The monstrous peak, which was like the bow of a ship at the end of the Sere Plateau, was visibly nearer. Towards midday, indeed, it looked high above the horizon, no more than fifteen miles away. And at midday Huyghens called a final halt.

"No more congregations of sphexes down below," he said cheerfully, "and we haven't seen a climbing line of them in miles." The crossing of a sphex-trail meant simply waiting until one party had passed, and then crossing before another came in view. "I've a hunch we've crossed their migration-route. Let's see what Semper tells us!"

He waved the eagle aloft. And Semper, like all creatures other than men, normally functioned only for the satisfaction of his appetite, and then tended to loaf or sleep. He had ridden the last few miles perched on Sitka Pete's pack. Now he soared upwards and Huyghens watched in the small vision-plate.

Semper went soaring—and the image on the plate swayed and turned and turned—and in minutes was above the plateau's edge. And here there was some vegetation and the ground rolled somewhat, and there were even patches of brush. But as Semper towered higher still, the inner desert appeared. But nearby it was clear of beasts. Only once, when the eagle banked sharply and the camera looked along the long dimension of the plateau, did Huyghens see any sign of the blue-and-tan beasts. There he saw what looked like masses amounting to herds. But, of course, carnivores do not gather in herds.

"We go straight up," said Huyghens in satisfaction. "We cross the plateau here—and we can edge downwind a bit, even. I think we'll find something interesting on our way to your robot colony."

He waved to the bears to go ahead uphill.

They reached the top hours later—barely before sunset. And they saw game. Not much, but game at the grassy, brushy border of the desert. Huyghens brought down a shaggy ruminant which surely would not live on a desert. When night fell there was an abrupt chill in the air. It was much colder than night temperatures on the slopes. The air was thin. Roane thought confusedly and presently guessed at the cause. In the lee of the prow-mountain the air was calm. There were no clouds. The ground radiated its heat to empty space. It could be bitterly cold in the nighttime, here.

"And hot by day," Huyghens agreed when he mentioned it. "The sunshine's terrifically hot where the air is thin, but on most mountains there's wind. By day, here, the ground will tend to heat up like the surface of a planet without atmosphere. It may be a hundred and forty or fifty degrees on the sand at midday. But it should be cold at night."

It was. Before midnight Huyghens built a fire. There could be no danger of night-walkers where the temperature dropped to freezing.

In the morning the men were stiff with cold, but the bears snorted and moved about briskly. They seemed to revel in the morning chill. Sitka and Sourdough Charley, in fact, became festive and engaged in a mock fight, whacking each other with blows that were only feigned, but would have crushed in the skull of any man. Nugget sneezed with excitement as he watched them. Faro Nell regarded them with female disapproval.

They went on. Semper seemed sluggish. After a single brief flight he descended and rode on Sitka's pack, as on the previous day. He perched there, surveying the landscape as it changed from semi-arid to pure desert in their progress. His air was arrogant. But he would not fly. Soaring birds do not like to fly when there are no winds to make currents of which to take advantage. On the way, Huyghens pains-takingly pointed out to Roane exactly where they were on the enlarged photograph taken from space, and the exact spot from which the distress signal seemed to come.

"You're doing it in case something happens to you," said Roane. "I admit it's sense, but—what could I do to help those survivors even if I got to them, without you?"

"What you've learned about sphexes would help," said Huyghens. "The bears would help. And we left a note back at my station. Whoever grounds at the landing field back there—and the beacon's working again—will find instructions to come to the place we're trying to reach."

Roane plodded alongside him. The narrow non-desert border of the Sere Plateau was behind them, now. They marched across powdery desert sand.

"See here," said Roane, "I want to know something! You tell me you're listed as a bear-thief on your home planet. You tell me it's a lie—to protect your friends from prosecution by the Colonial Survey. You're on your own, risking your life every minute of every day. You took a risk in not shooting me. Now you're risking more in going to help men who'd have to be witnesses that you were a criminal. What are you doing it for?"

Huyghens grinned.

"Because I don't like robots. I don't like the fact that they're subduing men—making men subordinate to them."

"Go on," insisted Roane. "I don't see why disliking robots should make you a criminal. Nor men subordinating themselves to robots, either!"

"But they are," said Huyghens mildly. "I'm a crank, of course. But—I live like a man on this planet. I go where I please and do what I please. My helpers, the bears, are my friends. If the robot colony had been a success, would the humans in it have lived like men? Hardly! They'd have to live the way the robots let them! They'd have to stay inside a fence the robots built. They'd have to eat foods that robots could raise, and no others. Why—a man couldn't move his bed near a window, because if he did the house-tending robots couldn't work! Robots would serve them—the way the robots determined—but all they'd get out of it would be jobs servicing the robots!"

Roane shook his head.

"As long as men want robot service, they have to take the service that robots can give. If you don't want those services—"

"I want to decide what I want," said Huyghens, again mildly, "instead of being limited to choose among what I'm offered. On my home planet we halfway tamed it with dogs and guns. Then we developed the bears, and we finished the job with them. Now there's population-pressure and the room for bears and dogs—and men—is dwindling. More and more people are being deprived of the power of decision, and being allowed only the power of choice among the things robots allow. The more we depend on robots, the more limited those choices become. We don't want our children to limit themselves to wanting what robots can provide! We don't want them shriveling to where they abandon everything robots can't give—or won't! We want them to be men—and women. Not damned automatons who live *by* pushing robot-controls so they can live *to* push robot-controls. If that's not subordination to robots—"

"It's an emotional argument," protested Roane. "Not everybody feels that way."

"But I feel that way," said Huyghens. "And so do a lot of others. This is a big galaxy and it's apt to contain some surprises. The one sure thing about a robot and a man who depends on them is that they can't handle the unexpected. There's going to come a time when we need men who can. So on my home planet, some of us asked for Loren Two, to colonize. It was refused—too dangerous. But men can colonize anywhere if they're men. So I came here to study the planet. Especially the sphexes. Eventually, we expected to ask for a license again, with proof that we could handle even those beasts. I'm already doing it in a mild way. But the Survey licensed a robot colony—and where is it?"

Roane made a sour face.

"You picked the wrong way to go about it, Huyghens. It was illegal. It is. It was the pioneer spirit, which is admirable enough, but wrongly directed. After all, it was pioneers who left Earth for the stars. But—"

Sourdough raised up on his hind legs and sniffed the air. Huyghens swung his rifle around to be handy. Roane slipped off the safety-catch of his own. Nothing happened.

"In a way," said Roane vexedly, "you're talking about liberty and freedom, which most people think is politics. You say it can be more. In principle, I'll concede it. But the way you put it, it sounds like a freak religion."

"It's self-respect," corrected Huyghens.

"You may be—"

Faro Nell growled. She bumped Nugget with her nose, to drive him closer to Roane. She snorted at him. She trotted swiftly to where Sitka and Sourdough faced towards the broader, sphex-filled expanse of the Sere Plateau. She took up her position between them.

Huyghens gazed sharply beyond them and then all about.

"This could be bad!" he said softly. "But luckily there's no wind. Here's a sort of hill. Come along, Roane!"

He ran ahead, Roane following and Nugget plumping heavily with him. They reached the raised place—actually a mere hillock no more than five or six feet above the surrounding sand, with a distorted cactuslike growth protruding from the ground. Huyghens stared again. He used his binoculars.

"One sphex," he said curtly. "Just one. And it's out of all

reason for a sphex to be alone! But it's not rational for them to gather in hundreds of thousands, either!" He wetted his finger and held it up. "No wind at all."

He used the binoculars again.

"It doesn't know we're here," he added. "It's moving away. Not another one in sight—" He hesitated, biting his lips. "Look here, Roane! I'd like to kill that one lone sphex and find out something. There's fifty percent chance I could find out something really important. But—I might have to run. If I'm right—" Then he said grimly. "It'll have to be done quickly. I'm going to ride Faro Nell—for speed. I doubt Sitka or Sourdough would stay behind. But Nugget can't run fast enough. Will you stay here with him?"

Roane drew in his breath. Then he said calmly:

"You know what you're doing. Of course."

"Keep your eyes open. If you see anything, even at a distance, shoot and we'll be back—fast! Don't wait until something's close enough to hit. Shoot the instant you see anything—if you do!"

Roane nodded. He found it peculiarly difficult to speak again. Huyghens went over to the embattled bears. He climbed up on Faro Nell's back, holding fast by her shaggy fur.

"Let's go!" he snapped. "That way! Hup!"

The three Kodiaks plunged away at a dead run, Huyghens lurching and swaying on Faro Nell's back. The sudden rush dislodged Semper from his perch. He flapped wildly and got aloft. Then he followed effortfully, flying low.

It happened very quickly. A Kodiak bear can travel as fast as a racehorse on occasion. These three plunged arrow-straight for a spot perhaps half a mile distant, where a blue-and-tawny shape whirled to face them. There was the crash of Huyghens' weapon from where he rode on Faro Nell's back—the explosion of the weapon and the bullet were one sound. The somehow unnatural spiky monster leaped and died.

Huyghens jumped down from Faro Nell. He became feverishly busy at something on the ground—where the parti-colored sphex had fallen. Semper banked and whirled and came down to the ground. He watched, with his head on one side.

Roane stared, from a distance. Huyghens was doing something to the dead sphex. The two male bears prowled about. Faro Nell regarded Huyghens with intense curiosity. Back at the hillock, Nugget whimpered a little. Roane patted him roughly. Nugget whimpered more loudly. In the distance, Huyghens straightened up and took three steps toward Faro Nell. He mounted. Sitka turned his head back toward Roane. He seemed to see or sniff something dubious. He reared upwards. He made a noise, apparently, because Sourdough ambled to his side. The two great beasts began to trot back. Semper flapped wildly and—lacking wind—lurched crazily in the air. He landed on Huyghens' shoulder and his talons clung there.

Then Nugget howled hysterically and tried to swarm up Roane, as a cub tries to swarm up the nearest tree in time of danger. Roane collapsed, and the cub upon him—and there was a flash of stinking scaly hide, while the air was filled with the snarling, spitting squeals of a sphex in full leap. The beast had over-jumped, aiming at Roane and the cub while both were upright and arriving when they had fallen. It went tumbling.

Roane heard nothing but the fiendish squalling, but in the distance Sitka and Sourdough were coming at rocketship speed. Faro Nell let out a roar and fairly split the air. And then there was a furry cub streaking towards her, bawling, while Roane rolled to his feet and snatched up his gun. He raged through pure instinct. The sphex crouched to pursue

the cub and Roane swung his weapon as a club. He was lit-
erally too close to shoot—and perhaps the sphex had seen
the fleeing bear cub. But he swung furiously.

And the sphex whirled. Roane was toppled from his feet.
An eight-hundred-pound monstrosity straight out of hell—
half wildcat and half spitting cobra with hydrophobia and
homicidal mania added—such a monstrosity is not to be
withstood when in whirling its body strikes one in the chest.

That was when Sitka arrived, bellowing. He stood on his
hind legs, emitting roars like thunder, challenging the sphex
to battle. He waddled forward. Huyghens arrived, but he
could not shoot with Roane in the sphere of an explosive
bullet's destructiveness. Faro Nell raged and snarled, torn
between the urge to be sure that Nugget was unharmed and
the frenzied fury of a mother whose offspring has been
endangered.

Mounted on Faro Nell, with Semper clinging idiotically to
his shoulder, Huyghens watched helplessly as the sphex spat
and squalled at Sitka, having only to reach out one claw to
let out Roane's life.

5

They got away from there, though Sitka seemed to want
to lift the limp carcass of his victim in his teeth and dash it
repeatedly to the ground. He seemed doubly raging because
a man—with whom all Kodius Champion's descendants had
an emotional relationship—had been mishandled. But
Roane was not grievously hurt. He bounced and swore as
the bears raced for the horizon. Huyghens had flung him up
on Sourdough's back and snapped for him to hold on. He
bumped and chattered furiously:

"Dammit, Huyghens! This isn't right! Sitka got some deep
scratches! That horror's claws may be poisonous!"

But Huyghens snapped "Hup! Hup!" to the bears, and
they continued their race against time. They went on for a

good two miles, when Nugget wailed despairingly of his exhaustion and Fargo Nell halted firmly to nuzzle him.

"This may be good enough," said Huyghens. "Considering that there's no wind and the big mass of beasts is down the plateau and there were only those two around here. Maybe they're too busy to hold a wake, even! Anyhow——"

He slid to the ground and extracted the antiseptic and swabs.

"Sitka first," snapped Roane. "I'm all right!"

Huyghens swabbed the big bear's wounds. They were trivial, because Sitka Pete was an experienced sphex-fighter. Then Roane grudgingly let the curiously smelling stuff—it reeked of ozone—be applied to the slashes on his chest. He held his breath as it stung. Then he said dourly:

"It was my fault, Huyghens. I watched you instead of the landscape. I couldn't imagine what you were doing."

"I was doing a quick dissection," Huyghens told him. "By luck, that first sphex was a female, as I hoped. And she was just about to lay her eggs. Ugh! And now I know why the sphexes migrate, and where, and how it is that they don't need game up here."

He slapped a quick bandage on Roane. He led the way eastwards, still putting distance between the dead sphexes and his party. It was a crisp walk, only, but Semper flapped indignantly overhead, angry that he was not permitted to ride again.

"I'd dissected them before," said Huyghens. "Not enough's been known about them. Some things needed to be found out if men were ever to be able to live here."

"With bears?" asked Roane ironically.

"Oh, yes," said Huyghens. "But the point is that sphexes come to the desert here to breed—to mate and lay their eggs for the sun to hatch. It's a particular place. Seals return to a special place to mate—and the males, at least, don't eat for weeks on end. Salmon return to their native streams to

spawn. They don't eat, and they die afterwards. And eels—
I'm using Earth examples, Roane—travel some thousands
of miles to the Sargasso to mate and die. Unfortunately,
sphexes don't appear to die, but it's clear that they have an
ancestral breeding place and that they come here to the Sere
Plateau to deposit their eggs!"

Roane plodded onward. He was angry: angry with himself because he hadn't taken elementary precautions; because
he'd felt too safe, as a man in a robot-served civilization
forms the habit of doing; because he hadn't used his brain
when Nugget whimpered, in even a bear cub's awareness
that danger was near.

"And now," Huyghens added, "I need some equipment
that the robot colony had. With it, I think we can make a
start towards making this a planet that men can live like men
on!"

Roane blinked.

"What's that?"

"Equipment," said Huyghens impatiently. "It'll be at the
robot colony. Robots were useless because they wouldn't pay
attention to sphexes. They'd still be. But take out the robot
controls and the machines will do! They shouldn't be ruined
by a few months' exposure to weather!"

Roane marched on and on. Presently he said:

"I never thought you'd want anything that came from that
colony, Huyghens!"

"Why not?" demanded Huyghens impatiently. "When
men make machines do what they want, that's all right. Even
robots—when they're where they belong. But men will have
to handle flame-casters in the job I want them for. There
have to be some, because there was a hundred-mile clearing
to be burned off. And Earth-sterilizers—intended to kill the
seeds of any plants that robots couldn't handle. We'll come
back up here, Roane, and at least we'll destroy the spawn of
these infernal beasts! If we can't do more than that—just

doing that every year will wipe out the race in time. There are probably other hordes than this, with other breeding places. But we'll find them, too. We'll make this planet into a place where men from my world can come—and still be men!"

Roane said sardonically:

"It was sphexes that beat the robots. Are you sure you aren't planning to make this world safe for robots?"

Huyghens laughed shortly.

"You've only seen one night-walker," he said. "And how about those things on the mountain-slope—which would have drained you of blood and then feasted? Would you care to wander about this planet with only a robot bodyguard, Roane? Hardly! Men can't live on this planet with only robots to help them—and stop them from being fully men! You'll see!"

They found the colony after only ten days more of travel and after many sphexes and more than a few staglike creatures and shaggy ruminants had fallen to their weapons and the bears. But first they found the survivors of the colony.

There were three of them, hard-bitten and bearded and deeply embittered. When the electrified fence went down, two of them were away at a mine-tunnel, installing a new control panel for the robots who worked in it. The third was in charge of the mining operation. They were alarmed by the stopping of communication with the colony and went back in a tank-truck to find out what had happened, and only the fact that they were unarmed saved them. They found sphexes prowling and caterwauling about the fallen colony, in numbers they still did not wholly believe. And the sphexes smelled men inside the armored vehicle, but couldn't break in. In turn, the men couldn't kill them, or they'd have been trailed to the mine and besieged there for as long as they could kill an occasional monster.

The survivors stopped all mining—of course—and tried

to use remote-controlled robots for revenge and to get supplies for them. Their mining-robots were not designed for either task. And they had no weapons. They improvised miniature throwers of burning rocket fuel, and they sent occasional prowling sphexes away screaming with scorched hides. But this was useful only because it did not kill the beasts. And it cost fuel. In the end they barricaded themselves and used the fuel only to keep a spark-signal going against the day when another ship came to seek the colony. They stayed in the mine as in a prison, on short rations, waiting without real hope. For diversion they could only contemplate the mining-robots they could not spare fuel to run and which could not do anything but mine.

When Huyghens and Roane reached them, they wept. They hated robots and all things robotic only a little less than they hated sphexes. But Huyghens explained, and armed them with weapons from the packs of the bears, and they marched to the dead colony with the male Kodiaks as point and advance guard, and with Faro Nell bringing up the rear. They killed sixteen sphexes on the way. In the now overgrown clearing there were four more. In the shelters of the colony they found only foulness and the fragments of what had been men. But there was some food—not much, because the sphexes clawed at anything that smelled of men, and had ruined the plastic packets of radiation-sterilized food. But there were some supplies in metal containers which were not destroyed.

And there was fuel, which men could dispense when they got to the control panels of the equipment. There were robots everywhere, bright and shining and ready for operation, but immobile, with plants growing up, around, and over them.

They ignored those robots. But lustfully they fueled tracked flame-casters—adapting them to human rather than robot operation—and the giant soil-sterilizer, which had been built to destroy vegetation that robots could not be made to weed out or cultivate. And they headed back for the Sere Plateau, burning-eyed and filled with hate.

But Nugget became a badly spoiled bear cub, because the freed men approved passionately of anything that would even grow up to kill sphexes. They petted him to excess, when they camped.

And they reached the plateau by a sphex-trail to the top. And Semper scouted for sphexes, and the giant Kodiaks disturbed them and the sphexes came squalling and spitting to destroy them—and while Roane and Huyghens fired steadily, the great machines swept up with their special weapons. The Earth-sterilizer, it was found, was deadly against animal life as well as seeds, when its diathermic beam was raised and aimed. But it had to be handled by a man. No robot could decide just when it was to be used, and against what target.

Presently the bears were not needed, because the scorched corpses of sphexes drew live ones from all parts of the plateau even in the absence of noticeable breezes. The official business of the sphexes was presumably finished, but they came to caterwaul and seek vengeance—which they did not find. Presently the survivors of the robot colony drove machines—as men needed to do, here—in great circles around the huge heap of slaughtered finds, destroying new arrivals as they came. It was such a killing as men had never before made on any planet, but there would not be many left of the sphex-horde which had bred in this particular patch of desert. There might be other hordes elsewhere, and other breeding places, but the normal territory of this mass of monsters would see few of them this year.

Or next year, either. Because the soil-sterilizer would go over the dug-up sand where the sphex-spawn lay hidden for the sun to hatch. And the sun would never hatch them.

But Huyghens and Roane, by that time, were camped on

the edge of the plateau with the Kodiaks. They were technically upwind from the scene of slaughter—and somehow it seemed more befitting for the men of the robot colony to conduct it. After all, it was those men whose companions had been killed.

There came an evening when Huyghens amiably cuffed Nugget away from where he sniffed too urgently at a stagsteak cooking on the camp-fire. Nugget ambled dolefully behind the protecting form of Roane and sniveled.

"Huyghens," said Roane painfully, "we've got to come to a settlement of our affairs. I'm a Colonial Survey officer. You're an illegal colonist. It's my duty to arrest you."

Huyghens regarded him with interest.

"Will you offer me lenience if I tell on my confederates," he asked mildly, "or may I plead that I can't be forced to testify against myself?"

Roane said vexedly:

"It's irritating! I've been an honest man all my life, but—I don't believe in robots as I did, except in their place. And their place isn't here. Not as the robot colony was planned, anyhow. The sphexes are nearly wiped out, but they won't be extinct and robots can't handle them. Bears and men will have to live here or—the people who do will have to spend their lives behind sphex-proof fences, accepting only what robots can give them. And there's much too much on this planet for people to miss it! To live in a robot-managed controlled environment on a planet like Loren Two wouldn't . . . it wouldn't be self-respecting!"

"You wouldn't be getting religious, would you?" asked Huyghens drily. "That was your term for self-respect."

Sempér the eagle squawked indignantly as Sitka Pete almost stepped on him, approaching the fire. Sitka Pete sniffed and Huyghens spoke to him sharply, and he sat down with a thump. He remained sitting in an untidy lump, looking at the steak and drooling.

"You don't let me finish!" protested Roane querulously. "I'm a Colonial Survey officer, and it's my job to pass on the work that's done on a planet before any but the first-landed colonists may come there to live. And of course to see that specifications are followed. Now—the robot colony I was sent to survey was practically destroyed. As designed, it wouldn't work. It couldn't survive."

Huyghens grunted. Night was falling. He turned the meat over the fire.

"Now, in emergencies," said Roane carefully, "colonists have the right to call on any passing ship for aid. Naturally! So—I've always been an honest man before, Huyghens—my report will be that the colony as designed was impractical, and that it was overwhelmed and destroyed except for three survivors who holed up and signaled for help. They did, you know!"

"Go on," grunted Huyghens.

"So, said Roane querulously, "it just happened—just happened, mind you—that a ship with you and Sitka and Sourdough and Faro Nell on board—and Nugget and Semper, too, of course—picked up the distress call. So you landed to help the colonists. And you did. That's the story. Therefore it isn't illegal for you to be here. It was only illegal for you to be here when you were needed. But we'll pretend you weren't."

Huyghens glanced over his shoulder in the deepening night. He said calmly:

"I wouldn't believe that if I told it myself. Do you think the Survey will?"

"They're not fools," said Roane tartly. "Of course they won't! But when my report says that because of this unlikely series of events it is practical to colonize the planet, whereas before it wasn't—and when my report proves that a robot colony alone is stark nonsense, but that with bears and men from your world added, so many thousand colonists can be received per year—And when that much is true, anyhow—"

Huyghens seemed to shake a little as a dark silhouette against the flames. A little way off, Sourdough sniffed the air hopefully. With a bright light like the fire, presently naked-looking flying things might appear to be slapped down out of the air. They were succulent—to a bear.

"My reports carry weight," insisted Roane. "The deal will be offered, anyhow! The robot colony organizers will have to agree or they'll have to fold up. It's true! And your people can hold them up for nearly what terms they choose."

Huyghens' shaking became understandable. It was laughter.

"You're a lousy liar, Roane," he said, chuckling. "Isn't it unintelligent and unreasonable and irrational to throw away a lifetime of honesty just to get me out of a jam? You're not acting like a rational animal, Roane. But I thought you wouldn't, when it came to the point."

Roane squirmed.

"That's the only solution I can think of. But it'll work."

"I accept it," said Huyghens, grinning. "With thanks. If only because it means another few generations of men living like men on a planet that is going to take a lot of taming. And—if you want to know—because it keeps Sourdough and Sitka and Nell and Nugget from being killed because I brought them here illegally."

Something pressed hard against Roane. Nugget, the cub, pushed urgently against him in his desire to get closer to the fragrantly cooking meat. He edged forward. Roane toppled from where he squatted on the ground. He sprawled. Nugget sniffed luxuriously.

"Slap him," said Huyghens. "He'll move back."

"I won't!" said Roane indignantly from where he lay. "I won't do it! He's my friend!"

BEACHHEAD

Clifford D. Simak

*Cliff Simak's stories tend to be quiet, warmhearted, intelligent,
and thoughtful—and anyone looking for ways to describe
Simak himself would probably use much the same terms. This
gentle Minnesotan has enjoyed two careers side by side: in
daily life an editor for the Minneapolis* Tribune, *and after
hours a writer of science fiction, one of the great figures of the
genre. His novels include such classics as* City, Time and Again,
and Ring Around the Sun; *he has written one Hugo-winning
shorter story, "The Big Front Yard"; in 1971 he was guest of
honor at the World Science Fiction Convention in Boston. The
theme of interplanetary exploration is a frequent one in Simak's
works; the story chosen here, not nearly as well known as
it should be, is one of his most moving examinations of the
collision between Earthmen and the natives of a distant world.*

There was nothing, absolutely nothing, that could stop a
human planetary survey party. It was a specialized unit
created for and charged with one purpose only—to establish
a bridgehead on an alien planet, to blast out the perimeters
of that bridgehead and establish a base where there would be
some elbow room. Then hold that elbow room against all
comers until it was time to go.

After the base was once established, the brains of the
party got to work. They turned the place inside out. They
put it on tape and captured it within the chains of symbols
they scribbled in their field books. They pictured it and

wrote it and plotted it and reduced it to a neat assembly of keyed and symbolic facts to be inserted in the galactic files.

If there was life, and sometimes there was, they prodded it to get reaction. Sometimes the reaction was extremely violent, and other times it was much more dangerously subtle. But there were ways in which to handle both the violent and the subtle, for the legionnaires and their robots were trained to a razor's edge and knew nearly all the answers.

There was nothing in the galaxy so far known that could stop a human survey party.

Tom Decker sat at ease in the empty lounge and swirled the ice in the highball glass, well contented, watching the first of the robots emerge from the bowels of the cargo space. They dragged a conveyor belt behind them as they emerged, and Decker, sitting idly, watched them drive supports into the ground and rig up the belt.

A door clicked open back of Decker and he turned his head.

"May I come in, sir?" Doug Jackson asked.

"Certainly," said Decker.

Jackson walked to the great curving window and looked out. "What does it look like, sir?" he asked.

Decker shrugged. "Another job," he said. "Six weeks. Six months. Depends on what we find."

Jackson sat down beside him. "This one looks tough," he said. "Jungle worlds always are a bit meaner than any of the others."

Decker grunted at him. "A job. That's all. Another job to do. Another report to file. Then they'll either send out an exploitation gang or a pitiful bunch of bleating colonists."

"Or," said Jackson, "they'll file the report and let it gather dust for a thousand years or so."

"They can do anything they want," Decker told him. "We turn it in. What someone else does with it after that is their affair, not ours."

They sat quietly watching the six robots roll out the first of the packing cases, rip off its cover and unpack the seventh robot, laying out his various parts neatly in a row in the tramped-down, waist-high grass. Then, working as a team, with not a single fumble, they put No. 7 together, screwed his brain case into his metal skull, flipped up his energizing switch, and slapped the breastplate home.

No. 7 stood groggily for a moment. He swung his arms uncertainly, shook his head from side to side. Then, having oriented himself, he stepped briskly forward and helped the other six heave the packing box containing No. 8 off the conveyor belt.

"Takes a little time this way," said Decker, "but it saves a lot of space. Have to cut our robot crew in half if we didn't pack them at the end of every job. They stow away better."

He sipped at his highball speculatively. Jackson lit a cigarette.

"Someday," said Jackson, "we're going to run up against something that we can't handle."

Decker snorted.

"Maybe here," insisted Jackson, gesturing at the nightmare jungle world outside the great curved sweep of the vision plate.

"You're a romanticist," Decker told him shortly. "In love with the unexpected. Besides that, you're new. Get a dozen trips under your belt and you won't feel this way."

"It could happen," insisted Jackson.

Decker nodded, almost sleepily, "Maybe," he said, "Maybe it could, at that. It never has, but I suppose it could. And when it does, we take it on the lam. It's not part of our job to fight a last-ditch battle. When we bump up against something that's too big to handle, we don't stick around. We don't take any risks."

He took another sip. "Not even calculated risks," he added.

The ship rested on the top of a low hill, in a small clearing masked by tall grass, sprinkled here and there with patches of exotic flowers. Below the hill a river flowed sluggishly, a broad expanse of chocolate-colored water moving in a sleepy tide through the immense vine-entangled forest.

As far as the eye could see, the jungle stretched away, a brooding darkness that even from behind the curving quartz of the vision plate seemed to exude a heady, musty scent of danger that swept up over the grass-covered hilltop. There was no sign of life, but one knew, almost instinctively, that sentiency lurked in the buried pathways and tunnels of the great tree-land.

Robot No. 8 had been energized, and now the eight, split into two groups, ran out two packing cases at a time instead of one. Soon there were twelve robots, and then they formed themselves into three working groups.

"Like that," said Decker, picking up the conversation where they had left it lying. He gestured with his glass, now empty. "No calculated risks. We send the robots first. They unpack and set up their fellows. Then the whole gang turns to and uncrates the machinery and sets it up and gets it operating. A man doesn't even put his foot on the ground until he has a steel ring around the ship to give him protection."

Jackson sighed. "I guess you're right," he said. "Nothing can happen. We don't take any chances. Not a single one."

"Why should we?" Decker asked. He heaved himself out of the chair, stood up and stretched. "Got a thing or two to do," he said. "Last-minute checks and so on."

"I'll sit here for a while," said Jackson. "I like to watch. It's all new to me."

"You'll get over it," Decker told him. "In another twenty years."

In his office, Decker lifted a sheaf of preliminary reports off his desk and ran through them slowly, checking each one carefully, filing away in his mind the basic facts of the world outside.

He worked stolidly, wetting a big, blunt thumb against his outthrust tongue to flip the report pages off the top of the next stack and deposit them, in not so neat a pile, to his right, face downward.

Atmosphere—pressure slightly more than Earth. High in oxygen. Gravity—a bit more than Earth. Temperature—hot. Jungle worlds always were. There was a breeze outside now, he thought. Maybe there'd be a breeze most of the time. That would be a help. Rotation—thirty-six-hour day.

Radiation—none of local origin, but some hard stuff getting through from the sun. He made a mental note: Watch that.

Bacterial and virus count—as usual. Lots of it. Apparently not too dangerous. Not with every single soul hypoed and immunized and hormoned to his eyebrows. But you never can be sure, he thought. Not entirely sure. No calculated risks, he had told Jackson. But here was a calculated risk, and one you couldn't do a single thing about. If there was a bug that picked you for a host and you weren't loaded for bear to fight him, you took him on and did the best you could. Life factor—lot of emanation. Probably the vegetation, maybe even the soil, was crawling with all sorts of loathsome life. Vicious stuff, more than likely. But that was something you took care of as a matter of routine. No use taking any chances. You went over the ground even if there was no life—just to be sure there wasn't.

A tap came on the door and Decker called out for the man to enter.

It was Captain Carr, commander of the Legion unit.

Carr saluted snappily. Decker did not rise. He made his answering salute a sloppy one on purpose. No use, he told himself, letting the fellow establish any semblance of equality, for there was no such equality in fact. A captain of the Legion simply did not rank with the commandant of a galactic survey party.

"Reporting, sir," said Carr. "We are ready for a landing."

"Fine, Captain. Fine." What was the matter with the fool? The Legion always was ready, always would be ready—that was no more than tradition. Why, then, carry out such an empty, stiff formality?

But it was the nature of a man like Carr, he supposed. The Legion, with its rigid discipline, with its ancient pride of service and tradition, attracted men like Carr, was a perfect finishing school for accomplished martinets.

Tin soldiers, Decker thought, but accomplished ones. As hardbitten a gang of fighting men as the galaxy had ever known. They were drilled and disciplined, serum- and hormone-injected against all known diseases of an alien world, trained and educated in alien psychology and strictly indoctrinated with high survival characteristics which stood up under even the most adverse circumstances.

"We shall not be ready for some time, Captain," Decker said. "The robots have just started their uncrating."

"Very well," said Carr. "We await your orders, sir."

"Thank you, Captain," Decker told him, making it quite clear that he wished he would get out. But when Carr turned to go, Decker called him back.

"What is it, sir?" asked Carr.

"I've been wondering," said Decker. "Just wondering, you understand. Can you imagine any circumstances which might arise that the Legion could not handle?"

Carr's expression was a pure delight to see. "I'm afraid, sir, that I don't understand your question."

Decker sighed. "I didn't think you would," he said.

Before nightfall, the full working force of robots had been uncrated and had set up some of the machines, enough to establish a small circle of alarm posts around the ship.

A flame thrower burned a barren circle on the hilltop, stretching five hundred feet around the ship. A hard-radiations generator took up its painstaking task, pouring pure death into the soil. The toll must have been terrific. In some spots the ground virtually boiled as the dying life forms fought momentarily and fruitlessly to escape the death that cut them down.

The robots rigged up huge batteries of lamps that set the hilltop ablaze with a light as bright as day, and the work went on.

As yet, no human had set foot outside the ship.

Inside the ship, the robot stewards set up a table in the lounge so that the human diners might see what was going on outside the ship.

The entire company, except for the legionnaires, who stayed in quarters, had gathered for the meal when Decker came into the room.

"Good evening, gentlemen," he said.

He strode to the table's head and the others ranged themselves along the side. He sat down and there was a scraping of drawn chairs as the others took their places.

He clasped his hands in front of him and bowed his head and parted his lips to say the customary words. He halted even as he was about to speak, and when the words did come they were different from the ones he had said by rote a thousand times before.

"Dear Father, we are Thy servants in an unknown land and there is a deadly pride upon us. Teach us humility and lead us to the knowledge, before it is too late, that men, despite their far traveling and their mighty works, still are as children in Thy sight. Bless the bread we are about to break, we beg Thee, and keep us forever in Thy compassion. Amen."

He lifted his head and looked down the table. Some of them, he saw, were startled. The others were amused.

They wonder if I'm cracking, he thought. They think the Old Man is breaking up. And that may be true, for all I know. Although I was all right until this afternoon. All right until young Doug Jackson . . .

"Those were fine words, lad," said Old MacDonald, the chief engineer. "I thank you for them, sir, and there is them among us who would do well to take some heed upon them."

Platters and plates were being passed up and down the table's length and there was the commonplace, homely clatter of silverware and china.

"This looks an interesting world," said Waldron, the anthropologist. "Dickson and I were up in observation just before the sun set. We thought we saw something down by the river. Some sort of life."

Decker grunted, scooping fried potatoes out of a bowl onto his plate. "Funny if we don't run across a lot of life here. The radiation wagon stirred up a lot of it when it went over the field today."

"What Waldron and I saw," said Dickson, "looked humanoid."

Decker squinted at the biologist. "Sure of that?" he asked.

Dickson shook his head. "The seeing was poor. Couldn't be absolutely sure. Seemed to me there were two or three of them. Matchstick men."

Waldron nodded. "Like a picture a kid would draw," he said. "One stroke for the body. Two strokes each for arms and legs. A circle for a head. Angular. Ungraceful. Skinny."

"Graceful enough in motion, though," said Dickson. "When they moved, they went like cats. Flowed, sort of."

"We'll know plenty soon enough," Decker told them mildly. "In a day or two we'll flush them."

Funny, he thought. On almost every job someone popped up to report he had spotted humanoids. Usually there weren't any. Usually it was just imagination. Probably wishful thinking, he told himself, the yen of men far away from their fellow men to find in an alien place a type of life that somehow seemed familiar.

Although the usual humanoid, once you met him in the flesh, turned out to be so repulsively alien that alongside him an octopus would seem positively human.

Franey, the senior geologist, said, "I've been thinking about those mountains to the west of us, the ones we caught sight of when we were coming in. Had a new look about them. New mountains are good to work in. They haven't worn down. Easier to get at whatever's in them."

"We'll lay out our first survey lines in that direction," Decker told him.

Outside the curving vision plate, the night was alive with the blaze of the batteries of lights. Gleaming robots toiled in shining gangs. Ponderous machines lumbered past. Smaller ones scurried like frightened beetles. To the south, great gouts of flame leaped out, and the sky was painted red with the bursts of a squad of flame throwers going into action.

"Chewing out a landing field," said Decker. "A tongue of jungle juts out there. Absolutely level ground. Like a floor. Won't take a great deal of work to turn it into a field."

The stewards brought coffee and brandy and a box of good cigars. Decker and his men settled back into their chairs, taking life easy, watching the work going on outside the ship.

"I hate this waiting," Franey said, settling down comfortably to his cigar.

"Part of the job," said Decker. He poured more brandy into his coffee.

By dawn the last machines were set up and had either been moved out to their assigned positions or were parked in the motor pool. The flamers had enlarged the burned-out area and three radiation wagons were busy on their rounds. To the south, the airfield had been finished and the jets were lined up and waiting in a plumb-straight row.

Some of the robots, their work done for the moment, formed themselves in solid ranks to form a solid square, neat and orderly and occupying a minimum of space. They stood there in the square, waiting against the time when they would be needed, a motor pool of robots, a reservoir of manpower.

Finally the gangplank came down and the legionnaires marched out in files of two, with clank and glitter and a remorseless precision that put machines to shame. There were no banners and there were no drums, for these are useless things and the Legion, despite its clank and glitter, was an organization of ruthless efficiency.

The column wheeled and became a line, and the line broke up and the platoons moved out toward the planet-head perimeter. There machines and legionnaires and robots manned the frontier that Earth had set up on an alien world.

Busy robots staked out and set up an open-air pavilion of gaudily striped canvas that rippled in the breeze, placed tables and chairs beneath its shade, moved in a refrigerator filled with beer and with extra ice compartments.

At last it was safe and comfortable for ordinary men to leave the shelter of the ship.

Organization, Decker told himself—organization and

efficiency and leaving not a thing to chance. Plug every loophole before it becomes a loophole. Crush possible resistance before it develops as resistance. Gain absolute control over a certain number of square feet of planet and operate from there.

Later, of course, there were certain chances taken; you just couldn't eliminate them all. There would be field trips, and even with all the precautions that robot and machine and legionnaire could offer, there would be certain risks. There would be aerial survey and mapping, and these, too, would have elements of chance, but with these elements reduced to the very minimum.

And always there would be the base, an absolutely safe and impregnable base to which a field party or a survey flight could retreat, from which reinforcements could be sent out or counteraction taken.

Foolproof, he told himself. As foolproof as it could be made.

He wondered briefly what had been the matter with him the night before. It had been that young fool, Jackson, of course—a capable biochemist, possibly, but certainly the wrong kind of man for a job like this. Something had slipped up: the screening board should have stopped a man like Jackson, should have spotted his emotional instability. Not that he could do any actual harm, of course, but he could be upsetting. An irritant, thought Decker, that is what he is. Just an irritant.

Decker laid an armload of paraphernalia on the long table underneath the gay pavilion. From it he selected a rolled-up sheet of map paper, unrolled it, spread it flat and thumbtacked it at four corners. On it a portion of the river and the mountains to the west had been roughly penciled in. The base was represented by an X'ed-through square— but the rest of it was blank.

But it would be filled in—as the days went by it would take shape and form.

From the field to the south a jet whooshed into the sky, made a lazy turn and straightened out to streak toward the west. Decker walked to the edge of the pavilion's shade and watched it as it dwindled out of sight. That would be Jarvis and Donnelly, assigned to the preliminary survey of the southwest sector between the base and the western mountains.

Another jet rose lazily, trailing its column of exhaust, gathered speed and sprang into the sky. Freeman and Johns, he thought.

Decker went back to the table, pulled out a chair and sat down. He picked up a pencil and tapped it idly on the almost blank map paper. Behind his back he heard another jet whoom upward from the field.

He let his eyes take in the base. Already it was losing its raw, burned-over look. Already it had something of the look of Earth about it, of the efficiency and common sense and get-the-job-done attitude of the men of Earth.

Small groups of men stood around talking. One of them, he saw, squatted on the ground, talking something over with three squatting robots. Others walked around, sizing up the situation.

Decker grunted with satisfaction. A capable gang of men, he thought. Most of them would have to wait around to really get down to work until the first surveys came in, but even while they waited they would not be idle.

They'd take soil samples and test them. The life that swarmed in the soil would be captured and brought in by grinning robots, and the squirming vicious things would be pinned down and investigated—photographed, X-rayed, dissected, analyzed, observed, put through reaction tests. Trees and plants and grasses would be catalogued and attempts made to classify them. Test pits would be dug for a look at soil strata. The river's waters would be analyzed. Seines would dredge up some of the life they held. Wells would be driven to establish water tables.

All of this here, at the moment, while they waited for the first preliminary flights to bring back data that would pinpoint other areas worthy of investigation.

Once those reports were in, the work would be started in dead earnest. Geologists and mineral men would probe into the planet's hide. Weather observation points would be set up. Botanists would take far-ranging check samples. Each man would do the work for which he had been trained. Field reports would pour back to the base, there to be correlated and fitted into the picture.

Work then, work in plenty. Work by day and night. And all the time the base would be a bit of Earth, a few square yards held inviolate against all another world might muster.

Decker sat easily in his chair and felt the breeze that came beneath the canvas, a gentle breeze that ruffled through his hair, rattled the papers on the table and twitched the tacked-down map. It was pleasant here, he thought. But it wouldn't stay pleasant long. It almost never did.

Someday, he thought, I'll find a pleasant planet, a paradise planet where the weather's always perfect and there is food for the picking of it and natives that are intelligent to talk with and companionable in other ways, and I will never leave it. I'll refuse to leave when the ship is ready to blast off. I'll live out my days in a fascinating corner of a lousy galaxy—a galaxy that is gaunt with hunger and mad with savagery and lonely beyond all that may be said of loneliness.

He looked up from his reverie and saw Jackson standing at the pavilion's edge, watching him.

"What's the matter, Jackson?" Decker asked with sudden bitterness. "Why aren't you—"

"They're bringing in a native, sir," said Jackson, breathlessly. "One of the things Waldron and Dickson saw."

The native was humanoid, but he was not human.

As Waldron and Dickson had said, he was a matchstick man, a flesh-and-blood extension of a drawing a four-year-old might make. He was black as the ace of spades, and he wore no clothing, but the eyes that looked out of the pumpkin-shaped head at Decker were bright with a light that might have been intelligence.

Decker tensed as he looked into those eyes. Then he looked away and saw the men standing silently around the pavilion's edge, silent and waiting, tense as he was.

Slowly Decker reached out his hand to one of the two headsets of the mentograph. His fingers closed over it and for a moment he felt a vague, but forceful, reluctance to put it on his head. It was disturbing to contact, or attempt to contact, an alien mind. It gave one a queasy feeling in the pit of the stomach. It was a thing, he thought, that Man never had been intended to do—an experience that was utterly foreign to any human background.

He lifted the headset slowly, fitted it over his skull, made a sign toward the second set.

For a long moment the alien eyes watched him, the creature standing erect and motionless.

Courage, thought Decker. Raw and naked courage, to stand there in this suddenly unfamiliar environment that had blossomed almost overnight on familiar ground, to stand there motionless and erect, surrounded by creatures that must look as if they had dropped from some horrible nightmare.

The humanoid took one step closer to the table, reached out a hand and took the headset. Fumbling with its unfamiliarity, he clamped it on his head. And never for a moment did the eyes waver from Decker's eyes, always alert and watchful.

Decker forced himself to relax, tried to force his mind into an attitude of peace and calm. That was a thing you had to be careful of. You couldn't scare these creatures— you had to lull them, quiet them down, make them feel your friendliness. They would be upset, and a sudden thought, even a suggestion of human brusqueness would wind them up tighter than a drum.

There was intelligence here, he told himself, being careful to keep his mind unruffled, a greater intelligence than one would think, looking at the creature. Intelligence enough to know that he should put on the headset, and guts enough to do it.

He caught the first faint mental whiff of the matchstick man, and the pit of his stomach contracted suddenly and there was an ache around his chest. There was nothing in the thing he caught, nothing that could be put into words, but there was an alienness, as a smell is alien. There was a nonhuman connotation that set one's teeth on edge. He fought back the gagging blackness of repulsive disgust that sought to break the smooth friendliness he held within his mind.

"We are friendly," Decker forced himself to think. "We are friendly. We are friendly. We are friendly. We are friendly. We are—"

"You should not have come," said the thought of the matchstick man.

"We will not harm you," Decker thought. "We are friendly. We will not harm you. We will not harm—"

"You will never leave," said the humanoid.

"Let us be friends," thought Decker. "Let us be friends. We have gifts. We will help you. We will—"

"You should not have come," said the matchstick thought. "But since you are here, you can never leave."

Humor him, thought Decker to himself. Humor him.

"All right, then," he thought. "We will stay. We will stay and we will be friendly. We will stay and teach you. We will give you the things we have brought for you and we will stay with you."

"You will not leave," said the matchstick man's thought, and there was something so cold and logical and matter-of-fact about the way the thought was delivered that Decker suddenly was cold.

The humanoid meant it—meant every word he said. He was not being dramatic, nor was he blustering—but neither was he bluffing. He actually thought that the humans would not leave, that they would not live to leave the planet. Decker smiled softly to himself.

"You will die here," said the humanoid thought.

"Die?" asked Decker. "What is die?"

The matchstick man's thought was pure disgust. Deliberately he reached up, took off the headset and laid it carefully back upon the table. Then he turned and walked away, and not a man made a move to stop him.

Decker took off his headset and slammed it on the table top.

"Jackson," he said, "pick up that phone and tell the Legion to let him through. Let him leave. Don't try to stop him."

He sat limply in his chair and looked at the ring of faces that were watching him.

Waldron asked, "What is it, Decker?"

"He sentenced us to death," said Decker. "He said that we would not leave the planet. He said that we would die here."

"Strong words," said Waldron.

"He meant them," Decker said.

He lifted a hand, flipped it wearily. "He doesn't know, of course," he said. "He really thinks that he can stop us from leaving. He thinks that we will die."

It was an amusing situation, really. That a naked humanoid should walk out of the jungle and threaten to do away with a human survey party, that he should really think that he could do it. That he should be so positive about it.

But there was not a single smile on any of the faces that looked at Decker.

"We can't let it get us," Decker said.

"Nevertheless," Waldron declared, "we should take precautions."

Decker nodded. "We'll go on emergency alert immediately," he said. "We'll stay that way until we're sure . . . until we're . . ." His voice trailed off. Sure of what? Sure that an alien savage who wore no clothing, who had not a sign of culture about him could wipe out a group of humans protected by a ring of steel, held within a guard of machines and robots and a group of fighting men who knew all there was to know concerning the refinements of dealing out swift and merciless extermination to anything that moved against them?

Ridiculous!

Of course it was ridiculous! And yet the eyes had held intelligence. The being had not only intelligence but courage. He had stood within a circle of—to him—alien beings, and he had not flinched. He had faced the unknown and said what there was to say, and then had walked away with a dignity any human would have been proud to wear. He must have guessed that the alien beings within the confines of the base were not of his own planet, for he had said that they should not have come, and his thought had implied that he was aware they were not of this world of his. He had understood that he was supposed to put on the headset, but whether that was an act more of courage than of intelligence one would never know—for you could not know if he had realized what the headset had been for. Not knowing, the naked courage of clamping it to his head was of an order that could not be measured.

"What do you think?" Decker asked Waldron.

"We'll have to be careful," Waldron told him evenly. "We'll have to watch our step. Take all precautions, now that we are warned. But there's nothing to be scared of, nothing we can't handle."

"He was bluffing," Dickson said. "Trying to scare us into leaving."

Decker shook his head. "I don't think he was," he said. "I tried to bluff him and it didn't work. He's just as sure as we are."

The work went on. There was no attack.

The jets roared out and thrummed away, mapping the land. Field parties went out cautiously. They were flanked by robots and by legionnaires and preceded by lumbering machines that knifed and tore and burned a roadway through even the most stubborn of the terrain they went up against. Radio weather stations were set up at distant points, and at the base the weather tabulators clicked off on tape the data that the stations sent back.

Other field parties were flown into the special areas pinpointed for more extensive exploration and investigation.

And nothing happened.

The days went past. The weeks went past. The machines and robots watched, and the legionnaires stood ready, and the men hurried with their work so they could get off the planet.

A bed of coal was found and mapped. An iron range was discovered. One area in the mountains to the west crawled with radioactive ores. The botanists found twenty-seven species of edible fruit. The base swarmed with animals that had been trapped as specimens and remained as pets.

And a village of the matchstick men was found. It wasn't much of a place. Its huts were primitive. Its sanitation was nonexistent. Its people were peaceful.

Decker left his chair under the striped pavilion to lead a party to the village.

The party entered cautiously, weapons ready, but being very careful not to move too fast, not to speak too quickly, not to make a motion that might be construed as hostile.

The natives sat in their doorways and watched them. They did not speak and they scarcely moved a muscle. They simply watched the humans as they marched to the center of the village.

There the robots set up a table and placed a mentograph upon it. Decker sat down in a chair and put one of the headsets on his skull. The rest of the party waited off to one side. Decker waited at the table.

They waited for an hour and not a native stirred. None came forward to put on the other headset.

Decker took off the headset wearily and placed it on the table.

"It's no use," he said. "It won't work. Go ahead and take your pictures. Do anything you wish. But don't disturb the natives. Don't touch a single thing."

He took a handkerchief out of his pocket and mopped his steaming face.

Waldron came and leaned on the table. "What do you make of it?" he asked.

Decker shook his head. "It haunts me," he said. "There's just one thing that I am thinking. It must be wrong. It can't be right. But the thought came to me, and I can't get rid of it."

"Sometimes that happens," Waldron said. "No matter how illogical a thing may be, it sticks with a man, like a burr inside his brain."

"The thought is this," said Decker. "That they have told us all that they have to tell us. That they have nothing more they wish to say to us."

"That's what you thought," said Waldron.

Decker nodded. "A funny thing to think," he said. "Out of a clear sky. And it can't be right."

"I don't know," said Waldron. "Nothing's right here. Notice that they haven't got a single iron tool. Not a scrap of metal in evidence at all. Their cooking utensils are stone, a sort of funny stuff like soapstone. What few tools they have are stone. And yet they have a culture. And they have it without metal."

"They're intelligent," said Decker. "Look at them watching us. Not afraid. Just waiting. Calm and sure of themselves. And that fellow who came into the base. He knew what to do with the headset."

Waldron sucked thoughtfully at a tooth. "We'd better be getting back to base," he said. "It's getting late." He held his wrist in front of him. "My watch has stopped. What time do you have, Decker?"

Decker lifted his arm and Waldron heard the sharp gasp of his indrawn breath. Slowly Decker raised his head and looked at the other man.

"My watch has stopped, too," he said, and his voice was scarcely louder than a whisper.

For a moment they were graven images, shocked into immobility by a thing that should have been no more than an inconvenience. Then Waldron sprang erect from the table, whirled to face the men and robots.

"Assemble!" he shouted. "Back to the base. Quick!"

The men came running. The robots fell into place. The column marched away. The natives sat quietly in their doorways and watched them as they left.

Decker sat in his camp chair and listened to the canvas of the pavilion snapping softly in the wind, alive in the wind, talking and laughing to itself. A lantern, hung on a ring above his head, swayed gently, casting fleeting shadows that seemed at times to be the shadows of living, moving things. A robot stood stiffly and quietly beside one of the pavilion poles.

Stolidly, Decker reached out a finger and stirred the little pile of wheels and springs that lay upon the table.

Sinister, he thought. Sinister and queer.

The guts of watches, lying on the table. Not of two watches alone, not only his and Waldron's watches, but many other watches from the wrists of other men. All of them silent, stilled in their task of marking time.

Night had fallen hours before, but the base still was astir with activity that was at once feverish and furtive. Men moved about in the shadows and crossed the glaring patches of brilliance shed by the batteries of lights set up by the robots many weeks before. Watching the men, one would have sensed that they moved with a haunting sense of doom, would have known as well that they knew, deep in their inmost hearts, that there was no doom to fear. No definite thing that one could put a finger on and say, this is the thing to fear. No direction that one might point toward and say, doom lies here, waiting to spring upon us.

Just one small thing.

Watches had stopped running. And that was a simple thing for which there must be some simple explanation.

Except, thought Decker, on an alien planet no occurrence,

no accident or incident, can be regarded as a simple thing for which a simple explanation must necessarily be anticipated. For the matrix of cause and effect, the mathematics of chance may not hold true on an alien planet as they hold true on Earth.

There was one rule, Decker thought grimly. One rule: Take no chances. That was the one safe rule to follow, the only rule to follow.

Following it, he had ordered all field parties back to base, had ordered the crew to prepare the ship for emergency takeoff, had alerted the robots to be ready at an instant to get the machines aboard. Even to be prepared to desert the machines and leave without them if circumstances should dictate that this was necessary.

Having done that, there was no more to do but wait. Wait until the field parties came back from their advance camps. Wait until some reason could be assigned to the failure of the watches.

It was not a thing, he told himself, that should be allowed to panic one. It was something to recognize, not to disregard. It was a circumstance that made necessary a certain number of precautions, but it was not a situation that should make one lose all sense of proportion.

You could not go back to Earth and say, "Well, you see, our watches stopped and so . . ."

A footstep sounded and he swung around in his chair. It was Jackson.

"What is it, Jackson?" Decker asked.

"The camps aren't answering, sir," said Jackson. "The operator has been trying to raise them and there is no answer. Not a single peep."

Decker grunted. "Take it easy," he said. "They will answer. Give them time."

He wished, even as he spoke, that he could feel some of the assurance that he tried to put into his voice. For a second, a rising terror mounted in his throat and he choked it back.

"Sit down," he said. "We'll sit here and have a beer and then we'll go down to the radio shack and see what's doing."

He rapped on the table. "Beer," he said. "Two beers."

The robot standing by the pavilion pole did not answer.

He made his voice louder. The robot did not stir.

Decker put his clenched fists upon the table and tried to rise, but his legs were suddenly cold and had turned unaccountably to water, and he could not raise himself.

"Jackson," he panted, "go and tap that robot on the shoulder. Tell him we want beer."

He saw the fear that whitened Jackson's face as he rose and moved slowly forward. Inside himself he felt the terror start and worry at his throat.

Jackson stood beside the robot and reached out a hesitant hand, tapped him gently on the shoulder, tapped him harder—and the robot fell flat upon its face!

Feet hammered across the hard-packed ground, heading for the pavilion.

Decker jerked himself around, sat foursquare and solid in his chair, waiting for the man who ran.

It was MacDonald, the chief engineer.

He halted in front of Decker and his hands, scarred and grimy with years of fighting balky engines, reached down and gripped the boards of the table's edge. His seamy face was twisted as if he were about to weep.

"The ship, sir. The ship . . ."

Decker nodded, almost idly. "I know, Mr. MacDonald. The ship won't run."

MacDonald gulped. "The big stuff's all right, sir. But the little gadgets . . . the injector mechanism . . . the—"

He stopped abruptly and stared at Decker. "You knew," he said. "How did you know?"

"I knew," said Decker, "that someday it would come. Not

like this, perhaps. But in any one of several ways. I knew that the day would come when our luck would run too thin. I talked big, like the rest of you, of course, but I knew that it would come. The day when we'd covered all the possibilities but the one that we could not suspect, and that, of course, would be the one that would ruin us."

He was thinking, the natives had no metal. No sign of any metal in their village at all. Their dishes were soapstone, and they wore no ornaments. Their implements were stone. And yet they were intelligent enough, civilized enough, cultured enough to have fabricated metal. For there was metal here, a great deposit of it in the western mountains. They had tried perhaps, many centuries ago, had fashioned metal tools and had them go to pieces underneath their fingers in a few short weeks.

A civilization without metal. A culture without metal. It was unthinkable. Take metal from a man and he went back to the caves. Take metal from a man and he was earth-bound, and his bare hands were all he had.

Waldron came into the pavilion, walking quietly in the silence. "The radio is dead," he said, "and the robots are dying like flies. The place is littered with them, just so much scrap metal."

Decker nodded. "The little stuff, the finely fabricated, will go first," he said. "Like watches and radio innards and robot brains and injector mechanisms. Next, the generators will go and we will have no lights or power. Then the machines will break down and the Legion's weapons will be no more than clubs. After that, the big stuff, probably."

"The native told us," Waldron said, "when you talked to him. 'You will never leave,' he said."

"We didn't understand," said Decker. "We thought he was threatening us and we knew that we were too big, too well guarded for any threat of his to harm us. He wasn't threatening us at all, of course. He was just telling us."

He made a hopeless gesture with his hands. "What is it?"

"No one knows," said Waldron quietly. "Not yet, at least. Later we may find out, but it won't help us any. A microbe, maybe. A virus. Something that eats iron after it has been subjected to heat or alloyed with other metals. It doesn't go for iron ore. If it did, that deposit we found would have been gone long ago."

"If that is true," said Decker, "we've brought it the first square meal it's had in a long, long time. A thousand years. Maybe a million years. There is no fabricated metal here. How would it survive? Without stuff to eat, how would it live?"

"I wouldn't know," said Waldron. "It might not be a metal-eating organism at all. It might be something else. Something in the atmosphere."

"We tested the atmosphere." But, even as the words left his mouth, Decker saw how foolish they were. They had tested the atmosphere, but how could they have detected something they had never run across before? Man's yardstick was limited—limited to the things he knew about, limited by the circle of his own experience. He guarded himself against the obvious and the imaginable. He could not guard himself against the unknowable or the unimaginable.

Decker rose and saw Jackson still standing by the pavilion pole, with the robot stretched at his feet.

"You have your answer," he told the biochemist. "Remember that first day here? You talked with me in the lounge."

Jackson nodded. "I remember, sir."

And suddenly, Decker realized, the entire base was quiet.

A gust of wind came out of the jungle and rattled the canvas.

Now, for the first time since they had landed, he caught in the wind the alien smell of an alien world.

KYRIE

Poul Anderson

A haunting and touching story of a strange form of life and a strange kind of love, by a writer whose crowded shelf of Hugo and Nebula awards testifies to the skill and the art with which he mixes science and fiction.

On a high peak in the Lunar Carpathians stands a convent of St. Martha of Bethany. The walls are native rock; they lift, dark and cragged as the mountainside itself, into a sky that is always black. As you approach from Northpole, flitting low to keep the force screen along Route Plato between you and the meteoroidal rain, you see the cross which surmounts the tower, stark athwart Earth's blue disk. No bells resound from there—not in airlessness.

You may hear them inside at the canonical hours, and throughout the crypts below where machines toil to maintain a semblance of terrestrial environment. If you linger a while you will also hear them calling to requiem mass. For it has become a tradition that prayers be offered at St. Martha's for those who have perished in space; and they are more with every passing year.

This is not the work of the sisters. They minister to the sick, the needy, the crippled, the insane, all whom space has broken and cast back. Luna is full of such, exiles because they can no longer endure Earth's pull or because it is feared they may be incubating a plague from some unknown planet or because men are so busy with their frontiers that they have no time to spare for the failures. The sisters wear spacesuits as often as habits, are as likely to hold a medikit as a rosary.

But they are granted some time for contemplation. At night, when for half a month the sun's glare has departed, the chapel is unshuttered and stars look down through the glaze-dome to the candles. They do not wink and their light is winter cold. One of the nuns in particular is there as often as may be, praying for her own dead. And the abbess sees to it that she can be present when the yearly mass, that she endowed before she took her vows, is sung.

> *Requiem aeternam dona eis, Domine, et lux*
> *perpetua luceat eis.*
> *Kyrie eleison, Christe eleison, Kyrie eleison.*

The Supernova Sagittarii expedition comprised fifty human beings and a flame. It went the long way around from Earth orbit, stopping at Epsilon Lyrae to pick up its last member. Thence it approached its destination by stages.

This is the paradox: time and space are aspects of each other. The explosion was more than a hundred years past when noted by men on Lasthope. They were part of a generations-long effort to fathom the civilization of creatures altogether unlike us; but one night they looked up and saw a light so brilliant it cast shadows.

That wave front would reach Earth several centuries hence. By then it would be so tenuous that nothing but another bright point would appear in the sky. Meanwhile, though, a ship overleaping the space through which light must creep could track the great star's death across time.

Suitably far off, instruments recorded what had been before the outburst: incandescence collapsing upon itself after the last nuclear fuel was burned out. A jump, and they saw what happened a century ago: convulsion, storm of quanta and neutrinos, a radiation equal to the massed hundred billion suns of this galaxy.

It faded, leaving an emptiness in heaven, and the *Raven* moved closer. Fifty light-years—fifty years—inward, she studied a shrinking fieriness in the midst of a fog which shone like lightning.

Twenty-five years later the central globe had dwindled more, the nebula had expanded and dimmed. But because the distance was now so much less, everything seemed larger and brighter. The naked eye saw a dazzle too fierce to look straight at, making the constellations pale by contrast. Telescopes showed a blue-white spark in the heart of an opalescent cloud delicately filamented at the edges.

The *Raven* made ready for her final jump, to the immediate neighborhood of the supernova.

Captain Teodor Szili went on a last-minute inspection tour. The ship murmured around him, running at one gravity of acceleration to reach the desired intrinsic velocity. Power droned, regulators whickered, ventilation systems rustled. He felt the energies quiver in his bones. But metal surrounded him, blank and comfortless. Viewports gave on a dragon's hoard of stars, the ghostly arch of the Milky Way: on vacuum, cosmic rays, cold not far above absolute zero, distance beyond imagination to the nearest human hearthfire. He was about to take his people where none had ever been before, into conditions none was sure about, and that was a heavy burden on him.

He found Eloise Waggoner at her post, a cubbyhole with intercom connections directly to the command bridge. Music drew him, a triumphant serenity he did not recognize. Stopping in the doorway, he saw her seated with a small tape machine on the desk.

"What's this?" he demanded.

"Oh!" The woman (he could not think of her as a girl though she was barely out of her teens) started. "I . . . I was waiting for the jump."

"You were to wait at the alert."

"What have I to do?" she answered less timidly than was her wont. "I mean, I'm not a crewman or a scientist."

"You are in the crew. Special communications technician."

"With Lucifer. And he likes the music. He says we come closer to oneness with it than in anything else he knows about us."

Szili arched his brows. "Oneness?"

A blush went up Eloise's thin cheeks. She stared at the deck and her hands twisted together. "Maybe that isn't the right word. Peace, harmony, unity . . . God? . . . I sense what he means, but we haven't any word that fits."

"Hm. Well, you are supposed to keep him happy." The skipper regarded her with a return of the distaste he had tried to suppress. She was a decent sort, he supposed, in her gauche and inhibited way; but her looks! Scrawny, big-footed, big-nosed, pop eyes, and stringy dust-colored hair—and, to be sure, telepaths always made him uncomfortable. She said she could only read Lucifer's mind, but was that true?

No. Don't think such things. Loneliness and otherness can come near breaking you out here, without adding suspicion of your fellows.

If Eloise Waggoner was really human. She must be some kind of mutant at the very least. Whoever could communicate thought to thought with a living vortex had to be.

"What are you playing, anyhow?" Szili asked.

"Bach. The Third Brandenburg Concerto. He, Lucifer, he doesn't care for the modern stuff. I don't either."

You wouldn't, Szili decided. Aloud: "Listen, we jump in half an hour. No telling what we'll emerge in. This is the first time anyone's been close to a recent supernova. We can only be certain of so much hard radiation that we'll be dead if the screenfields give way. Otherwise we've nothing to go on except theory. And a collapsing stellar core is so unlike anything anywhere else in the universe that I'm skeptical about how good the theory is. We can't sit daydreaming. We have to prepare."

"Yes, sir." Whispering, her voice lost its usual harshness.

He stared past her, past the ophidian eyes of meters and controls, as if he could penetrate the steel beyond and look straight into space. There, he knew, floated Lucifer.

The image grew in him: a fireball twenty meters across, shimmering white, red, gold, royal blue, flames dancing like Medusa locks, cometary tail burning for a hundred meters behind, a shiningness, a glory, a piece of hell. Not the least of what troubled him was the thought of that which paced his ship.

He hugged scientific explanations to his breast, though they were little better than guesses. In the multiple-star system of Epsilon Aurigae, in the gas and energy pervading the space around, things took place which no laboratory could imitate. Ball lightning on a planet was perhaps analogous, as the formation of simple organic compounds in a primordial ocean is analogous to the life which finally evolves. In Epsilon Aurigae, magnetohydrodynamics had done what chemistry did on Earth. Stable plasma vortices had appeared, had grown, had added complexity, until after millions of years they became something you must needs call an organism. It was a form of ions, nuclei and force-fields. It metabolized electrons, nucleons, X rays; it maintained its configuration for a long lifetime; it reproduced; it thought.

But what did it think? The few telepaths who could communicate with the Aurigeans, who had first made humankind aware that the Aurigeans existed, never explained clearly. They were a queer lot themselves.

Wherefore Captain Szili said, "I want you to pass this on to him."

"Yes, sir." Eloise turned down the volume on her taper. Her eyes unfocused. Through her ears went words, and her brain (how efficient a transducer was it?) passed the meanings on out to him who loped alongside *Raven* on his own reaction drive.

"Listen, Lucifer. You have heard this often before, I know, but I want to be positive you understand in full. Your psychology must be very foreign to ours. Why did you agree to come with us? I don't know. Technician Waggoner said you were curious and adventurous. Is that the whole truth?

"No matter. In half an hour we jump. We'll come within five hundred million kilometers of the supernova. That's where your work begins. You can go where we dare not, observe what we can't, tell us more than our instruments would ever hint at. But first we have to verify we can stay in orbit around the star. This concerns you too. Dead men can't transport you home again.

"So. In order to enclose you within the jumpfield, without disrupting your body, we have to switch off the shield screens. We'll emerge in a lethal radiation zone. You must promptly retreat from the ship, because we'll start the screen generator up sixty seconds after transit. Then you must investigate the vicinity. The hazards to look for—" Szili listed them. "Those are only what we can foresee. Perhaps we'll hit other garbage we haven't predicted. If anything seems like a menace, return at once, warn us, and prepare for a jump back to here. Do you have that? Repeat."

Words jerked from Eloise. They were a correct recital; but how much was she leaving out?

"Very good." Szili hesitated. "Proceed with your concert

if you like. But break it off at zero minus ten minutes and stand by."

"Yes, sir." She didn't look at him. She didn't appear to be looking anywhere in particular.

His footsteps clacked down the corridor and were lost.

—Why did he say the same things over? asked Lucifer.

"He is afraid," Eloise said.

—?—.

"I guess you don't know about fear," she said.

—Can you show me? . . . No, do not. I sense it is hurtful. You must not be hurt.

"I can't be afraid anyway, when your mind is holding mine."

(Warmth filled her. Merriment was there, playing like little flames over the surface of Father-leading-her-by-the-hand-when-she-was-just-a-child-and-they-went-out-one-summer's-day-to-pick-wildflowers; over strength and gentleness and Bach and God.) Lucifer swept around the hull in an exuberant curve. Sparks danced in his wake.

—Think flowers again. Please.

She tried.

—They are like (image, as nearly as a human brain could grasp, of fountains blossoming with gamma-ray colors in the middle of light, everywhere light). But so tiny. So brief a sweetness.

"I don't understand how you can understand," she whispered.

—You understand for me. I did not have that kind of thing to love, before you came.

"But you have so much else. I try to share it, but I'm not made to realize what a star is."

—Nor I for planets. Yet ourselves may touch.

Her cheeks burned anew. The thought rolled on, interweaving its counterpoint to the marching music. —That is why I came, do you know? For you. I am fire and air. I had not tasted the coolness of water, the patience of earth, until you showed me. You are moonlight on an ocean.

"No, don't," she said. "Please."

Puzzlement: —Why not? Does joy hurt? Are you not used to it?

"I, I guess that's right." She flung her head back. "No! Be damned if I'll feel sorry for myself!"

—Why should you? Have we not all reality to be in, and is it not full of suns and songs?

"Yes, To you. Teach me."

—If you in turn will teach me— The thought broke off. A contact remained, unspeaking, such as she imagined must often prevail among lovers.

She glowered at Motilal Mazundar's chocolate face, where the physicist stood in the doorway. "What do you want?"

He was surprised. "Only to see if everything is well with you, Miss Waggoner."

She bit her lip. He had tried harder than most aboard to be kind to her. "I'm sorry," she said. "I don't mean to bark at you. Nerves."

"We are everyone on edge." He smiled. "Exciting though this venture is, it will be good to come home, correct?"

Home, she thought: four walls of an apartment above a banging city street. Books and television. She might present a paper at the next scientific meeting, but no one would invite her to the parties afterward.

Am I that horrible? she wondered. *I know I'm not anything to look at, but I try to be nice and interesting. Maybe I try too hard.*

—You do not with me. Lucifer said.

"You're different," she told him.

Mazundar blinked. "Beg pardon?"

"Nothing," she said in haste.

"I have wondered about an item." Mazundar said in an effort at conversation. "Presumably Lucifer will go quite near the supernova. Can you still maintain contact with him? The time dilation effect, will that not change the frequency of his thoughts too much?"

"What time dilation?" she forced a chuckle. "I'm no physicist. Only a little librarian who turned out to have a wild talent."

"You were not told? Why, I assumed everybody was. An intense gravitational field affects time just as a high velocity does. Roughly speaking, processes take place more slowly than they do in clear space. That is why light from a massive star is somewhat reddened. And our supernova core retains almost three solar masses. Furthermore, it has acquired such a density that its attraction at the surface is, ah, incredibly high. Thus by our clocks it will take infinite time to shrink to the Schwarzschild radius; but an observer on the star itself would experience this whole shrinkage in a fairly short period."

"Schwarzschild radius? Be so good as to explain." Eloise realized that Lucifer had spoken through her.

"If I can without mathematics. You see, this mass we are to study is so great and so concentrated that no force exceeds the gravitational. Nothing can counterbalance. Therefore the process will continue until no energy can escape. The star will have vanished out of the universe. In fact, theoretically the contraction will proceed to zero volume. Of course, as I said, that will take forever as far as we are concerned. And the theory neglects quantum-mechanical considerations, which come into play toward the end. Those are still not very well understood. I hope, from this expedition, to acquire more knowledge." Mazundar shrugged. "At any rate, Miss Waggoner. I was wondering if the frequency shift involved would not prevent our friend from communicating with us when he is near the star."

"I doubt that." Still Lucifer spoke, she was his instrument and never had she known how good it was to be used by one who cared. "Telepathy is not a wave phenomenon. Since it transmits instantaneously, it cannot be. Nor does it appear limited by distance. Rather, it is a resonance. Being attuned, we two may well be able to continue thus across the entire breadth of the cosmos; and I am not aware of any material phenomenon which could interfere."

"I see." Mazundar gave her a long look. "Thank you," he said uncomfortably. "Ah . . . I must get to my own station. Good luck." He bustled off without stopping for an answer.

Eloise didn't notice. Her mind was become a torch and a song. "Lucifer!" she cried aloud. "Is that true?"

—I believe so. My entire people are telepaths, hence we have more knowledge of such matters than yours do. Our experience leads us to think there is no limit.

"You can always be with me? You always will?"

—If you so wish, I am gladdened.

The comet body curvetted and danced, the brain of fire laughed low. —Yes, Eloise, I would like very much to remain with you. No one else has ever— Joy. Joy. Joy.

They named you better than they knew, Lucifer, she wanted to say, and perhaps she did. *They thought it was a joke; they thought by calling you after the devil they could make you safely small like themselves. But Lucifer isn't the devil's real name. It means only Light Bearer. One Latin prayer even addresses Christ as Lucifer. Forgive me, God, I can't help remembering that. Do You mind? He isn't Christian, but I think he doesn't need to be, I think he must never have felt sin, Lucifer, Lucifer.*

She sent the music soaring for as long as she was permitted.

The ship jumped. In one shift of world line parameters she crossed twenty-five light-years to destruction.

Each knew it in his own way, save for Eloise, who also lived it with Lucifer.

She felt the shock and heard the outraged metal scream, she smelled the ozone and scorch and tumbled through the infinite falling that is weightlessness. Dazed, she fumbled at the intercom. Words crackled through: ". . . unit blown . . . back EMF surge . . . how should I know how to fix the blasted thing? . . . stand by, stand by . . ." Over all hooted the emergency siren.

Terror rose in her, until she gripped the crucifix around her neck and the mind of Lucifer. Then she laughed in the pride of this might.

He had whipped clear of the ship immediately on arrival. Now he floated in the same orbit. Everywhere around, the nebula filled space with unrestful rainbows. To him, *Raven* was not the metal cylinder which human eyes would have seen, but a lambency, the shield screen reflecting a whole spectrum. Ahead lay the supernova core, tiny at this remove but alight, alight.

—Have no fears (he caressed her). I comprehend. Turbulence is extensive, so soon after the detonation. We emerged in a region where the plasma is especially dense. Unprotected for the moment before the guardian field was reestablished, your main generator outside the hull was short-circuited. But you are safe. You can make repairs. And I, I am in an ocean of energy. Never was I so alive. Come, swim these tides with me.

Captain Szili's voice yanked her back. "Waggoner! Tell that Aurigean to get busy. We've spotted a radiation source on an intercept orbit, and it may be too much for our screen." He specified coordinates. "What *is* it?"

For the first time, Eloise felt alarm in Lucifer. He curved about and streaked from the ship.

Presently his thought came to her, no less vivid. She lacked words for the terrible splendor she viewed with him: a million-kilometer ball of ionized gas where luminance blazed and electric discharges leaped, booming through the haze around the star's exposed heart. The thing could not have made any sound, for space here was still almost a vacuum by Earth's parochial standards; but she heard it thunder, and felt the fury that spat from it.

She said for him: "A mass of expelled material. It must have lost radial velocity to friction and static gradients, been drawn into a cometary orbit, held together for a while by internal potentials. As if this sun were trying yet to bring planets to birth—"

"It'll strike us before we're in shape to accelerate," Szili said, "and overload our shield. If you know any prayers, use them."

"Lucifer!" she called; for she did not want to die, when he must remain.

—I think I can deflect it enough, he told her with a grimness she had not hitherto met in him.—My own fields, to mesh with its; and free energy to drink; and an unstable configuration; yet, perhaps I can help you. But help me, Eloise. Fight by my side.

His brightness moved toward the juggernaut shape.

She felt how its chaotic electromagnetism clawed at his. She felt him tossed and torn. The pain was hers. He battled to keep his own cohesion, and the combat was hers. They locked together, Aurigean and gas cloud. The forces that shaped him grappled as arms might; he poured power from his core, hauling that vast tenuous mass with him down the magnetic torrent which streamed from the sun; he gulped atoms and thrust them backward until the jet splashed across the heaven.

She sat in her cubicle, lending him what will to live and prevail she could, and beat her fists bloody on the desk.

The hours brawled past.

In the end, she could scarcely catch the message that flickered out of his exhaustion:—Victory.

"Yours," she wept.

—Ours.

Through instruments, men saw the luminous death pass them by. A cheer lifted.

"Come back," Eloise begged.

—I cannot. I am too spent. We are merged, the cloud and I, and are tumbling in toward the star. (Like a hurt hand reaching forth to comfort her:) Do not be afraid for me. As we get closer, I will draw fresh strength from its glow, fresh substance from the nebula. I will need a while to spiral out against that pull. But how can I fail to come back to you, Eloise? Wait for me. Rest. Sleep.

Her shipmates led her to sickbay. Lucifer sent her dreams of fire flowers and mirth and the suns that were his home.

But she woke at last, screaming. The medic had to put her under heavy sedation.

He had not really understood what it would mean to confront something so violent that space and time themselves were twisted thereby.

His speed increased appallingly. That was in his own measure; from *Raven* they saw him fall through several days. The properties of matter were changed. He could not push hard enough or fast enough to escape.

Radiation, stripped nuclei, particles born and destroyed and born again, sleeted and shouted through him. His substance was peeled away, layer by layer. The supernova core was a white delirium before him. It shrank as he approached, ever smaller, denser, so brilliant that brilliance ceased to have meaning. Finally the gravitational forces laid their full grip upon him.

—Eloise! he shrieked in the agony of his disintegration —Oh, Eloise, help me!

The star swallowed him up. He was stretched infinitely long, compressed infinitely thin, and vanished with it from existence.

The ship prowled the farther reaches. Much might yet be learned.

Captain Szili visited Eloise in sickbay. Physically she was recovering.

"I'd call him a man," he declared through the machine mumble, "except that's not praise enough. We weren't even his kin, and he died to save us."

She regarded him from eyes more dry than seemed natural. He could just make out her answer. "He is a man. Doesn't he have an immortal soul too?"

"Well, uh, yes, if you believe in souls, yes, I'd agree."

She shook here head. "But why can't he go to his rest?"

He glanced about for the medic and found they were alone in the narrow metal room. "What do you mean?" He made himself pat her hand. "I know, he was a good friend of yours. Still, his must have been a merciful death. Quick, clean; I wouldn't mind going out like that."

"For him . . . yes, I suppose so. It has to be. But—" She could not continue. Suddenly she covered her ears. "Stop! Please!"

Szili made soothing noises and left. In the corridor he encountered Mazundar. "How is she?" the physicist asked.

The captain scowled. "Not good. I hope she doesn't crack entirely before we can get her to a psychiatrist."

"Why, what is wrong?"

"She thinks she can hear him."

Mazundar smote fist into palm. "I hoped otherwise," he breathed.

Szili braced himself and waited.

"She does," Mazundar said. "Obviously she does."

"But that's impossible! He's dead!"

"Remember the time dilation," Mazundar replied. "He fell from the sky and perished swiftly, yes. But in supernova time. Not the same as ours. To us, the final stellar collapse takes an infinite number of years. And telepathy has no distance limits." The physicist started walking fast away from that cabin. "He will always be with her."

JUPITER FIVE

Arthur C. Clarke

One of the many virtues of the motion picture 2001 *was the quiet, unspectacular way that it showed us, through a myriad of tiny touches, what the texture of life a generation from now is likely to be. Everything had been thought through with care, from the technology of airlocks to the tone of advertisements. Arthur C. Clarke was co-author of that movie's screenplay, and most of those little touches were his; for that genius with small imaginative detail is a hallmark of this man whose name has become virtually synonymous with science fiction. It is displayed throughout his classic novel* Childhood's End *and in all his other work, up to his latest novel,* Rendezvous with Rama; *and it is apparent on every page of the ingenious story of Jovian exploration you are about to read.*

Professor Forster is such a small man that a special spacesuit had to be made for him. But what he lacked in physical size he more than made up—as is so often the case—in sheer drive and determination. When I met him, he'd spent twenty years pursuing a dream. What is more to the point, he had persuaded a whole succession of hard-headed businessmen, World Council delegates, and administrators of scientific trusts to underwrite his expenses and to fit out a ship for him. Despite everything that happened later, I still think that was his most remarkable achievement.

The *Arnold Toynbee* had a crew of six aboard when we left Earth. Besides the Professor and Charles Aston, his chief assistant, there was the usual pilot-navigator-engineer triumvirate and two graduate students—Bill Hawkins and myself. Neither of us had ever gone into space before, and we were still so excited over the whole thing that we didn't care in the least whether we got back to Earth before the next term started. We had a strong suspicion that our tutor had very similar views. The reference he had produced for us was a masterpiece of ambiguity, but as the number of people who could even begin to read Martian script could be counted, if I may coin a phrase, on the fingers of one hand, we'd got the job.

As we were going to Jupiter, and not to Mars, the purpose of this particular qualification seemed a little obscure, though, knowing something about the Professor's theories, we had some pretty shrewd suspicions. They were partly confirmed when we were ten days out from Earth.

The Professor looked at us very thoughtfully when we answered his summons. Even under zero g he always managed to preserve his dignity, while the best we could do was to cling to the nearest handhold and float around like drifting seaweed. I got the impression—though I may of course be wrong—that he was thinking: What have *I* done to deserve this? as he looked from Bill to me and back again. Then he gave a sort of "It's too late to do anything about it now" sigh and began to speak in that slow, patient way he always does when he has something to explain. At least, he always uses it when he's speaking to *us,* but it's just occurred to me—oh, never mind.

"Since we left Earth," he said, "I've not had much chance of telling you the purpose of this expedition. Perhaps you've guessed it already."

"I think I have," said Bill.

"Well, go on," replied the Professor, a peculiar gleam in his eye. I did my best to stop Bill, but have you ever tried to kick anyone when you're in free fall?

"You want to find some proof—I mean, some *more* proof—of your diffusion theory of extraterrestrial culture."

"And have you any idea why I'm going to Jupiter to look for it?"

"Well, not exactly. I suppose you hope to find something on one of the moons."

"Brilliant, Bill, brilliant. There are fifteen known satellites, and their total area is about half that of Earth. Where would you start looking if you had a couple of weeks to spare? I'd rather like to know."

Bill glanced doubtfully at the Professor, as if he almost suspected him of sarcasm.

"I don't know much about astronomy," he said. "But there are four big moons, aren't there? I'd start on those."

"For your information, Io, Europa, Ganymede, and Callisto are each about as big as Africa. Would you work through them in alphabetical order?"

"No," Bill replied promptly. "I'd start on the one nearest Jupiter and go outward."

"I don't think we'll waste any more time pursuing your logical processes," sighed the Professor. He was obviously impatient to begin his set speech. "Anyway, you're quite wrong. We're not going to the big moons at all. They're been photographically surveyed from space and large areas have been explored on the surface. They've got nothing of archaeological interest. *We're* going to a place that's never been visited before."

"Not to Jupiter!" I gasped.

"Heavens no, nothing as drastic as that! But we're going nearer to him than anyone else has ever been."

He paused thoughtfully.

"It's a curious thing, you know—or you probably don't— that it's nearly as difficult to travel between Jupiter's satellites as it is to go between the planets, although the distances are so much smaller. This is because Jupiter's got such a terrific gravitational field and his moons are traveling so quickly. The innermost moon's moving almost as fast as Earth, and the journey to it from Ganymede costs almost as much fuel as the trip from Earth to Venus, even though it takes only a day and a half.

"And it's *that* journey which we're going to make. No one's ever done it before because nobody could think of any good reason for the expense. Jupiter Five is only thirty kilometers in diameter, so it couldn't possibly be of much interest. Even some of the outer satellites, which are far easier to reach, haven't been visited because it hardly seemed worth while to waste the rocket fuel."

"Then why are *we* going to waste it?" I asked impatiently. The whole thing sounded like a complete wild-goose chase, though as long as it proved interesting, and involved no actual danger, I didn't greatly mind.

Perhaps I ought to confess—though I'm tempted to say nothing, as a good many others have done—that at this time I didn't believe a word of Professor Forster's theories. Of course I realize that he was a very brilliant man in his field, but I did draw the line at some of his more fantastic ideas. After all, the evidence was so slight and the conclusions so revolutionary that one could hardly help being skeptical.

Perhaps you can still remember the astonishment when the first Martian expedition found the remains not of one ancient civilization, but of two. Both had been highly advanced, but both had perished more than five million years ago. The reason was unknown (and still is). It did not seem to be warfare, as the two cultures appear to have lived amicably together. One of the races had been insectlike, the other vaguely reptilian. The insects seem to have been the genuine, original Martians. The reptile-people—usually referred to as "Culture X"—had arrived on the scene later.

So, at least, Professor Forster maintained. They had certainly possessed the secret of space travel, because the ruins of their peculiar cruciform cities had been found on —of all places—Mercury. Forster believed that they had tried to colonize all the smaller planets—Earth and Venus having been ruled out because of their excessive gravity. It was a source of some disappointment to the Professor that no traces of Culture X had ever been found on the Moon, though he was certain that such a discovery was only a matter of time.

The "conventional" theory of Culture X was that it had originally come from one of the smaller planets or satellites, had made peaceful contact with the Martians—the only other intelligent race in the known history of the System— and had died out at the same time as the Martian civilization. But Professor Forster had more ambitious ideas: he was convinced that Culture X had entered the Solar System from interstellar space. The fact that no one else believed this annoyed him, though not very much, for he is one of those people who are happy only when in a minority.

From where I was sitting, I could see Jupiter through the cabin porthole as Professor Forster unfolded his plan. It was a beautiful sight: I could just make out the equatorial cloud belts, and three of the satellites were visible as little stars close to the planet. I wondered which was Ganymede, our first port of call.

"If Jack will condescend to pay attention," the Professor continued, "I'll tell you why we're going such a long way from home. You know that last year I spent a good deal of time poking among the ruins in the twilight belt of Mercury. Perhaps you read the paper I gave on the subject at the London School of Economics. You may even have been there—I do remember a disturbance at the back of the hall.

"What I didn't tell anyone then was that while I was on Mercury I discovered an important clue to the origin of Culture X. I've kept quiet about it, although I've been sorely tempted when fools like Dr. Haughton have tried to be funny at my expense. But I wasn't going to risk letting someone else get here before I could organize this expedition.

"One of the things I found on Mercury was a rather well-preserved bas-relief of the Solar System. It's not the first that's been discovered—as you know, astronomical motifs are common in true Martian and Culture X art. But there were certain peculiar symbols against various planets, including Mars and Mercury. I think the pattern had some historic significance, and the most curious thing about it is that little Jupiter Five—one of the least important of all the satellites—seemed to have the most attention drawn to it. I'm convinced that there's something on Five which is the key to the whole problem of Culture X, and I'm going there to discover what it is."

As far as I can remember now, neither Bill nor I was particularly impressed by the Professor's story. Maybe the people of Culture X had left some artifacts on Five for obscure reasons of their own. It would be interesting to unearth them, but hardly likely that they would be as important as the Professor thought. I guess he was rather disappointed at our lack of enthusiasm. If so, it was his fault since, as we discovered later, he was still holding out on us.

We landed on Ganymede, the largest moon, about a week later. Ganymede is the only one of the satellites with a permanent base on it; there's an observatory and a geophysical station with a staff of about fifty scientists. They were rather glad to see visitors, but we didn't stay long as the Professor was anxious to refuel and set off again. The fact that we were heading for Five naturally aroused a good deal of interest, but the Professor wouldn't talk and we couldn't; he kept too close an eye on us.

Ganymede, by the way, is quite an interesting place and we managed to see rather more of it on the return journey. But as I've promised to write an article for a magazine about that, I'd better not say anything else here. (You might like to keep your eyes on the *National Astrographic* magazine next spring.)

The hop from Ganymede to Five took just over a day and a half, and it gave us an uncomfortable feeling to see Jupiter expanding hour by hour until it seemed as if he were going to fill the sky. I don't know much about astronomy, but I couldn't help thinking of the tremendous gravity field into which we were falling. All sorts of things could go wrong so easily. If we ran out of fuel we'd never be able to get back to Ganymede, and we might even drop into Jupiter himself.

I wish I could describe what it was like seeing that colossal globe, with its raging storm belts spinning in the sky ahead of us. As a matter of fact I *did* make the attempt, but some literary friends who have read this MS advised me to cut out the result. (They also gave me a lot of other advice which I don't think they could have meant seriously, because if I'd followed it there would have been no story at all.)

Luckily there have been so many color close-ups of Jupiter published by now that you're bound to have seen some of them. You may even have seen the one which, as I'll explain later, was the cause of all our trouble.

At last Jupiter stopped growing: we'd swung into the orbit of Five and would soon catch up with the tiny moon as it raced around the planet. We were all squeezed in the control room waiting for our first glimpse of our target.

At least, all of us who could get in were doing so. Bill and I were crowded out into the corridor and could only crane over other people's shoulders. Kingsley Searle, our pilot, was in the control seat looking as unruffled as ever: Eric Fulton, the engineer, was thoughtfully chewing his moustache and watching the fuel gauges, and Tony Groves was doing complicated things with his navigation tables.

And the Professor appeared to be rigidly attached to the eyepiece of the teleperiscope. Suddenly he gave a start and we heard a whistle of indrawn breath. After a minute, without a word, he beckoned to Searle, who took his place at the eyepiece. Exactly the same thing happened, and then Searle handed over to Fulton. It got a bit monotonous by the time Groves had reacted identically, so we wormed our way in and took over after a bit of opposition.

I don't know quite what I'd expected to see, so that's probably why I was disappointed. Hanging there in space was a tiny gibbous moon, its "night" sector lit up faintly by the reflected glory of Jupiter. And that seemed to be all.

Then I began to make out additional markings, in the way that you do if you look through a telescope for long enough. There were faint crisscrossing lines on the surface of the satellite, and suddenly my eye grasped their full pattern. For it *was* a pattern: those lines covered Five with the same geometrical accuracy as the lines of latitude and longitude divide up a globe of the Earth. I suppose I gave my whistle of amazement, for then Bill pushed me out of the way and had his turn to look.

The next thing I remember is Professor Forster looking very smug while we bombarded him with questions.

"Of course," he explained, "this isn't as much a surprise to me as it is to you. Besides the evidence I'd found on Mercury, there were other clues. I've a friend at the Ganymede Observatory whom I've sworn to secrecy and who's been under quite a strain this last few weeks. It's rather surprising to anyone who's not an astronomer that the Observatory has never bothered much about the satellites. The big instruments are all used on extra-galactic nebulae, and the little ones spend all their time looking at Jupiter.

"The only thing the Observatory had ever done to Five was to measure its diameter and take a few photographs. They weren't quite good enough to show the markings we've just observed, otherwise there would have been an investigation before. But my friend Lawton detected them through the hundred-centimeter reflector when I asked him to look, and he also noticed something else that should have been spotted before. Five is only thirty kilometers in diameter, but it's much brighter than it should be for its size. When you compare its reflecting power—its aldeb—its—"

"Its albedo."

"Thanks, Tony—its albedo with that of the other moons, you find that it's a much better reflection than it should be. In fact, it behaves more like polished metal than rock."

"So that explains it!" I said. "The people of Culture X must have covered Five with an outer shell—like the domes they built on Mercury, but on a bigger scale."

The Professor looked at me rather pityingly.

"So you still haven't guessed!" he said.

I don't think this was quite fair. Frankly, would you have done any better in the same circumstances?

We landed three hours later on an enormous metal plain. As I looked through the portholes, I felt completely dwarfed by my surroundings. An ant crawling on the top of an oil-storage tank might have had much the same feelings—and the looming bulk of Jupiter up there in the sky didn't help. Even the Professor's usual cockiness now seemed to be overlaid by a kind of reverent awe.

The plain wasn't quite devoid of features. Running across it in various directions were broad bands where the stupendous metal plates had been joined together. These bands, or the crisscross pattern they formed, were what we had seen from space.

About a quarter of a kilometer away was a low hill—at least, what would have been a hill on a natural world. We had spotted it on our way in after making a careful survey of the little satellite from space. It was one of six such projections, four arranged equidistantly around the equator and the other two at the Poles. The assumption was pretty obvious that they would be entrances to the world below the metal shell.

I know that some people think it must be very entertaining to walk around on an airless, low-gravity planet in spacesuits. Well, it isn't. There are so many points to think about, so many checks to make and precautions to observe that the mental strain outweighs the glamour—at least as far as I'm concerned. But I must admit that this time, as we climbed out of the airlock, I was so excited that for once these things didn't worry me.

The gravity of Five was so microscopic that walking was completely out of the question. We were all roped together like mountaineers and blew ourselves across the metal plain with gentle bursts from our recoil pistols. The experienced astronauts, Fulton and Groves, were at the two ends of the chain so that any unwise eagerness on the part of the people in the middle was restrained.

It took us only a few minutes to reach our objective, which we discovered to be a broad, low dome at least a kilometer in circumference. I wondered if it was a gigantic airlock, large enough to permit the entrance of whole spaceships. Unless we were very lucky, we might be unable to find a way in, since the controlling mechanisms would no longer be functioning, and even if they were, we would not know how to operate them. It would be difficult to imagine anything more tantalizing than being locked out, unable to get at the greatest archaeological find in all history.

We had made a quarter circuit of the dome when we found an opening in the metal shell. It was quite small— only about two meters across—and it was so nearly circular that for a moment we did not realize what it was. Then Tony's voice came over the radio:

"That's not artificial. We've got a meteor to thank for it."

"Impossible!" protested Professor Forster. "It's much too regular."

Tony was stubborn.

"Big meteors always produce circular holes, unless they strike very glancing blows. And look at the edges; you can see there's been an explosion of some kind. Probably the meteor and the shell were vaporized; we won't find any fragments."

"You'd expect this sort of thing to happen," put in Kingsley. "How long has this been here? Five million years? I'm surprised we haven't found any other craters."

"Maybe you're right," said the Professor, too pleased to argue. "Anyway, I'm going in first."

"Right," said Kingsley, who as captain has the last say in all such matters. "I'll give you twenty meters of rope and will sit in the hole so that we can keep radio contact. Otherwise this shell will blanket your signals."

So Professor Forster was the first man to enter Five, as he deserved to be. We crowded close to Kingsley so that he could relay news of the Professor's progress.

He didn't get very far. There was another shell just inside the outer one, as we might have expected. The Professor had room to stand upright between them, and as far as his torch could throw its beam he could see avenues of supporting struts and girders, but that was about all.

It took us about twenty-four exasperating hours before we got any farther. Near the end of that time I remember asking the Professor why he hadn't thought of bringing any explosives. He gave me a very hurt look.

"There's enough aboard the ship to blow us all to glory," he said. "But I'm not going to risk doing any damage if I can find another way."

That's what I call patience, but I could see his point of view. After all, what was another few days in a search that had already taken him twenty years?

It was Bill Hawkins, of all people, who found the way in when we had abandoned our first line of approach. Near the North Pole of the little world he discovered a really giant meteor hole—about a hundred meters across and cutting through both the outer shells surrounding Five. It had revealed still another shell below those, and by one of those chances that must happen if one waits enough eons, a second, smaller, meteor had come down inside the crater and penetrated the innermost skin. The hole was just big enough to allow entrance for a man in a spacesuit. We went through head first, one at a time.

I don't suppose I'll ever have a weirder experience than hanging from that tremendous vault, like a spider suspended beneath the dome of St. Peter's. We only knew that the space in which we floated was vast. Just *how* big it was we could not tell, for our torches gave us no sense of distance. In this airless, dustless cavern the beams were, of course, totally invisible and when we shone them on the roof above, we could see the ovals of light dancing away into the distance until they were too diffuse to be visible. If we pointed them "downward" we could see a pale smudge of illumination so far below that it revealed nothing.

Very slowly, under the minute gravity of this tiny world, we fell downward until checked by our safety ropes. Overhead I could see the tiny glimmering patch through which we had entered; it was remote but reassuring.

And then, while I was swinging with an infinitely sluggish pendulum motion at the end of my cable, with the lights of my companions glimmering like fitful stars in the darkness around me, the truth suddenly crashed into my brain. Forgetting that we were all on open circuit, I cried out involuntarily:

"Professor—I don't believe this is a planet at all! *It's a spaceship!*"

Then I stopped, feeling that I had made a fool of myself. There was a brief, tense silence, then a babble of noise as everyone else started arguing at once. Professor Forster's voice cut the confusion and I could tell that he was both pleased and surprised.

"You're quite right, Jack. This is the ship that brought Culture X to the Solar System."

I heard someone—it sounded like Eric Fulton—give a gasp of incredulity.

"It's fantastic! A ship thirty kilometers across!"

"*You* ought to know better than that," replied the Professor with surprising mildness. "Suppose a civilization wanted to cross interstellar space—how else would it attack the problem? It would build a mobile planetoid out in space, taking perhaps centuries over the task. Since the ship would have to be a self-contained world, which could support its inhabitants for generations, it would need to be as large as this. I wonder how many suns they visited before they found ours and knew that their search was ended? They must have had smaller ships that could take them down to the planets, and of course they had to leave the parent vessel somewhere in space. So they parked it here, in a close orbit near the largest planet, where it would remain safely forever—or until they needed it again. It was the logical place: if they had set it circling the Sun, in time the pulls of the planets would have disturbed its orbit so much that it might have been lost. That could never happen to it here."

"Tell me, Professor," someone asked, "did you guess all this before we started?"

"I *hoped* it. All the evidence pointed to this answer. There's always been something anomalous about Satellite Five, though no one seems to have noticed it. Why this single tiny moon so close to Jupiter, when all the other small satellites are seventy times farther away? Astronomically speaking, it didn't make sense. But enough of this chattering. We've got work to do."

That, I think, must count as the understatement of the century. There were seven of us faced with the greatest archaeological discovery of all time. Almost a whole world —a small world, an artificial one, but still a world—was waiting for us to explore. All we could perform was a swift and superficial reconnaissance: there might be material here for generations of research workers.

The first step was to lower a powerful floodlight on a power line running from the ship. This would act as a beacon and prevent our getting lost, as well as giving local illumination on the inner surface of the satellite. (Even now, I still find it hard to call Five a ship.) Then we dropped down the line to the surface below. It was a fall of about a kilometer, and in this low gravity it was quite safe to make the drop unretarded. The gentle shock of the impact could be absorbed easily enough by the spring-loaded staffs we carried for that purpose.

I don't want to take up any space here with yet another description of all the wonders of Satellite Five; there have already been enough pictures, maps, and books on the subject. (My own, by the way, is being published by Sidgwick and Jackson next summer.) What I would like to give you instead is some impression of what it was actually *like* to be the first men ever to enter that strange metal world. Yet I'm sorry to say—I know this sounds hard to believe—I simply can't remember what I was feeling when we came across the first of the great mushroom-capped entrance shafts. I suppose I was so excited and so overwhelmed by the wonder of it all that I've forgotten everything else. But I can recall the impression of sheer size, something which mere photographs can never give. The builders of this world, coming as they did from a planet of low gravity, were giants—about four times as tall as men. We were pygmies crawling among their works.

We never got below the outer levels on our first visit, so we met few of the scientific marvels which later expeditions discovered. That was just as well; the residential areas provided enough to keep us busy for several lifetimes. The globe we were exploring must once have been lit by artificial sunlight pouring down from the triple shell that surrounded it and kept its atmosphere from leaking into space. Here on the surface the Jovians (I suppose I cannot avoid adopting the popular name for the people of Culture X) had reproduced, as accurately as they could, conditions on the world they had left unknown ages ago. Perhaps they still had day and night, changing seasons, rain and mist. They had even taken a tiny sea with them into exile. The water was still there, forming a frozen lake three kilometers across. I hear that there is a plan afoot to electrolize it and provide Five with a breathable atmosphere again, as soon as the meteor holes in the outer shell have been plugged.

The more we saw of their work, the more we grew to like the race whose possessions we were disturbing for the first time in five million years. Even if they were giants from another sun, they had much in common with Man, and it is a great tragedy that our races missed each other by what is, on the cosmic scale, such a narrow margin.

We were, I suppose, more fortunate than any archaeologists in history. The vacuum of space had preserved everything from decay and—this was something which could not have been expected—the Jovians had not emptied their mighty ship of all its treasures when they had set out to colonize the Solar System. Here on the inner surface of Five everything still seemed intact, as it had been at the end of the ship's long journey. Perhaps the travelers had preserved it as a shrine in memory of their lost home, or perhaps they had thought that one day they might have to use these things again.

Whatever the reason, everything was here as its makers had left it. Sometimes it frightened me. I might be photographing, with Bill's help, some great wall carving when the sheer *timelessness* of the place would strike into my heart. I would look around nervously, half expecting to see giant shapes come stalking in through the pointed doorways, to continue the tasks that had been momentarily interrupted.

We discovered the art gallery on the fourth day. That was the only name for it; there was no mistaking its purpose. When Groves and Searle, who had been doing rapid sweeps over the southern hemisphere, reported the discovery we decided to concentrate all our forces there. For, as somebody or other has said, the art of a people reveals its soul, and here we might find the key to Culture X.

The building was huge, even by the standards of this giant race. Like all the other structures on Five, it was made of metal, yet there was nothing cold or mechanical about it. The topmost peak climbed halfway to the remote roof of the world, and from a distance—before the details were visible—the building looked not unlike a Gothic cathedral. Misled by this chance resemblance, some later writers have called it a temple; but we have never found any trace of what might be called a religion among the Jovians. Yet there seems something appropriate about the name "The Temple of Art," and it's stuck so thoroughly that no one can change it now.

It has been estimated that there are between ten and twenty million individual exhibits in this single building— the harvest garnered during the whole history of a race that may have been much older than Man. And it was here that I found a small, circular room which at first sight seemed to be no more than the meeting place of six radiating corridors. I was by myself (and thus, I'm afraid, disobeying the Professor's orders) and taking what I thought would be a short-cut back to my companions. The dark walls were drifting silently past me as glided along, the light of my torch dancing over the ceiling ahead. It was covered with deeply cut lettering, and I was so busy looking for familiar character groupings that for some time I paid no attention to the chamber's floor. Then I saw the statue and focused my beam upon it.

The moment when one first meets a great work of art has an impact that can never again be recaptured. In this case the subject matter made the effect all the more overwhelming. I was the first man ever to know what the Jovians had looked like, for here, carved with superb skill and authority, was one obviously modeled from life.

The slender, reptilian head was looking straight toward me, the sightless eyes staring into mine. Two of the hands were clasped upon the breast as if in resignation; the other two were holding an instrument whose purpose is still unknown. The long, powerful tail—which, like a kangaroo's, probably balanced the rest of the body—was stretched out along the ground, adding to the impression of rest or repose.

There was nothing human about the face or the body. There were, for example, no nostrils—only gill-like openings in the neck. Yet the figure moved me profoundly; the artist had spanned the barriers of time and culture in a way I should never have believed possible. "Not human—but humane" was the verdict Professor Forster gave. There were many things we could not have shared with the builders of this world, but all that was really important we would have felt in common.

Just as one can read emotions in the alien but familiar face of a dog or a horse, so it seemed that I knew the feelings of the being confronting me. Here was wisdom and authority—the calm, confident power that is shown, for example, in Bellini's famous portrait of the Doge Loredano. Yet there was sadness also—the sadness of a race which had made some stupendous effort, and made it in vain.

We still do not know why this single statue is the only representation the Jovians have ever made of themselves in their art. One would hardly expect to find taboos of this nature among such an advanced race; perhaps we will know the answer when we have deciphered the writing carved on the chamber walls.

Yet I am already certain of the statue's purpose. It was set here to bridge time and to greet whatever beings might one day stand in the footsteps of its makers. That, perhaps, is why they shaped it so much smaller than life. Even then they must have guessed that the future belonged to Earth or Venus, and hence to beings whom they would have dwarfed. They knew that size could be a barrier as well as time.

A few minutes later I was on my way back to the ship with my companions, eager to tell the Professor about the discovery. He had been reluctantly snatching some rest, though I don't believe he averaged more than four hours sleep a day all the time we were on Five. The golden light of Jupiter was flooding the great metal plain as we emerged through the shell and stood beneath the stars once more.

"Hello!" I heard Bill say over the radio, "the Prof's moved the ship."

"Nonsense," I retorted. "It's exactly where we left it."

Then I turned my head and saw the reason for Bill's mistake. We had visitors.

The second ship had come down a couple of kilometers away, and as far as my non-expert eyes could tell it might have been a duplicate of ours. When we hurried through the airlock, we found that the Professor, a little bleary-eyed, was already entertaining. To our surprise, though not exactly to our displeasure, one of the three visitors was an extremely attractive brunette.

"This," said Professor Forster, a little wearily, "is Mr. Randolph Mays, the science writer. I imagine you've heard of him. And this is—" He turned to Mays. "I'm afraid I didn't quite catch the names."

"My pilot, Donald Hopkins—my secretary, Marianne Mitchell."

There was just the slightest pause before the word "secretary," but it was long enough to set a little signal light flashing in my brain. I kept my eyebrows from going up, but I caught a glance from Bill that said, without any need for words: If you're thinking what I'm thinking, I'm ashamed of you.

Mays was a tall, rather cadaverous man with thinning hair and an attitude of bonhomie which one felt was only skin-deep—the protective coloration of a man who has to be friendly with too many people.

"I expect this is as big a surprise to you as it is to me," he said with unnecessary heartiness. "I certainly never expected to find anyone here before me; and I certainly didn't expect to find all *this.*"

"What brought you here?" said Ashton, trying to sound not too suspiciously inquisitive.

"I was just explaining that to the Professor. Can I have that folder please, Marianne? Thanks."

He drew out a series of very fine astronomical paintings and passed them around. They showed the planets from their satellites—a common-enough subject, of course.

"You've all seen this sort of thing before," Mays continued. "But there's a difference here. These pictures are nearly a hundred years old. They were painted by an artist named Chesley Bonestell and appeared in *Life* back in 1944—long before space-travel began, of course. Now what's happened is that *Life* has commissioned me to go around the Solar System and see how well I can match these imaginative paintings against the reality. In the centenary issue, they'll be published side by side with photographs of the real thing. Good idea, eh?"

I had to admit that it was. But it was going to make matters rather complicated, and I wondered what the Professor thought about it. Then I glanced again at Miss Mitchell, standing demurely in the corner, and decided that there would be compensations.

In any other circumstances, we would have been glad to meet another party of explorers, but here there was the question of priority to be considered. Mays would certainly be hurrying back to Earth as quickly as he could, his original mission abandoned and all his film used up here and now. It was difficult to see how we could stop him, and not even certain that we desired to do so. We wanted all the publicity and support we could get, but we would prefer to do things in our own time, after our own fashion. I wondered how strong the Professor was on tact, and feared the worst.

Yet at first diplomatic relations were smooth enough. The Professor had hit upon the bright idea of pairing each of us with one of Mays's team, so that we acted simultaneously as guides and supervisors. Doubling the number of investigating groups also greatly increased the rate at which we could work. It was unsafe for anyone to operate by himself under these conditions, and this had handicapped us a great deal.

The Professor outlined his policy to us the day after the arrival of Mays's party.

"I hope we can get along together," he said a little anxiously. "A far as I'm concerned they can go where they like and photograph what they like, as long as *they don't take anything*, and as long as they don't get back to Earth with their records before we do."

"I don't see how we can stop them," protested Ashton.

"Well, I hadn't intended to do this, but I've now registered a claim to Five. I radioed it to Ganymede last night, and it will be at The Hague by now."

"But no one can claim an astronomical body for himself. That was settled in the case of the Moon, back in the last century."

The Professor gave a rather crooked smile.

"I'm not annexing an *astronomical body,* remember. I've put in a claim for salvage, and I've done it in the name of the World Science Organization. If Mays takes anything out of Five, he'll be stealing it from them. Tomorrow I'm going to explain the situation gently to him, just in case he gets any bright ideas."

It certainly seemed peculiar to think of Satellite Five as salvage, and I could imagine some pretty legal quarrels developing when we got home. But for the present the Professor's move should have given us some safeguards and might discourage Mays from collecting souvenirs—so we were optimistic enough to hope.

It took rather a lot of organizing, but I managed to get paired off with Marianne for several trips around the interior of Five. Mays didn't seem to mind: there was no particular reason why he should. A spacesuit is the most perfect chaperon ever devised, confound it.

Naturally enough I took her to the art gallery at the first opportunity, and showed her my find. She stood looking at the statue for a long time while I held my torch beam upon it.

"It's very wonderful," she breathed at last. "Just think of it waiting here in the darkness of those millions of years! But you'll have to give it a name."

"I have. I've christened it 'The Ambassador.' "

"Why?"

"Well, because I think it's a kind of envoy, if you like, carrying a greeting to us. The people who made it knew that one day someone else was bound to come here and find this place."

"I think you're right. 'The Ambassador'—yes, that was clever of you. There's something noble about it, and something very sad, too. Don't you feel it?"

I could tell that Marianne was a very intelligent woman. It was quite remarkable the way she saw my point of view, and the interest she took in everything I showed her. But "The Ambassador" fascinated her most of all, and she kept on coming back to it.

"You know, Jack," she said (I think this was sometime the next day, when Mays had been to see it as well), "you must take that statue back to Earth. Think of the sensation it would cause."

I sighed.

"The Professor would like to, but it must weigh a ton. We can't afford the fuel. It will have to wait for a later trip."

She looked puzzled.

"But things hardly weigh anything here," she protested.

"That's different," I explained. "There's weight, and there's inertia—two quite different things. Now inertia— oh, never mind. We can't take it back, anyway. Captain Searle's told us that, definitely."

"What a pity," said Marianne.

I forgot all about this conversation until the night before we left. We had had a busy and exhausting day packing our equipment (a good deal, of course, we left behind for future use). All our photographic material had been used up. As Charlie Ashton remarked, if we met a *live* Jovian now we'd be unable to record the fact. I think we were all wanting a breathing space, an opportunity to relax and sort out our impressions and to recover from our head-on collision with an alien culture.

Mays's ship, the *Henry Luce*, was also nearly ready for takeoff. We would leave at the same time, an arrangement which suited the Professor admirably, as he did not trust Mays alone on Five.

Everything had been settled when, while checking through our records, I suddenly found that six rolls of exposed film were missing. They were photographs of a complete set of transcriptions in the Temple of Art. After a certain amount of thought I recalled that they had been entrusted to my charge, and I had put them very carefully on a ledge in the Temple, intending to collect them later.

It was a long time before takeoff, the Professor and Ashton were canceling some arrears of sleep, and there seemed no reason why I should not slip back to collect the missing material. I knew there would be a row if it was left behind, and as I remembered exactly where it was I need be gone only thirty minutes. So I went, explaining my mission to Bill just in case of accidents.

The floodlight was no longer working, of course, and the

darkness inside the shell of Five was somewhat oppressive. But I left a portable beacon at the entrance, and dropped freely until my hand torch told me it was time to break the fall. Ten minutes later, with a sigh of relief, I gathered up the missing films.

It was a natural-enough thing to pay my last respects to "The Ambassador": it might be years before I saw him again, and that calmly enigmatic figure had begun to exercise an extraordinary fascination over me.

Unfortunately, that fascination had not been confined to me alone. For the chamber was empty and the statue gone.

I suppose I could have crept back and said nothing, thus avoiding awkward explanations. But I was too furious to think of discretion, and as soon as I returned we woke the Professor and told him what had happened.

He sat on his bunk rubbing the sleep out of his eyes, then uttered a few harsh words about Mr. Mays and his companions, which it would do no good at all to repeat here.

"What I don't understand," said Searle, "is how they got the thing out—if they have, in fact. We should have spotted it."

"There are plenty of hiding places, and they could have waited until there was no one around before they took it up through the hull. It must have been quite a job, even under this gravity," remarked Eric Fulton, in tones of admiration.

"There's no time for post-mortems," said the Professor savagely. "We've got five hours to think of something. They can't take off before then, because we're only just past opposition with Ganymede. That's correct, isn't it, Kingsley?"

Searle nodded agreement.

"Yes. We must move around to the other side of Jupiter

before we can enter a transfer orbit—at least, a reasonably economical one."

"Good. That gives us a breathing space. Well, has anyone any ideas?"

Looking back on the whole thing now, it often seems to me that our subsequent behavior was, shall I say, a little peculiar and slightly uncivilized. It was not the sort of thing we could have imagined ourselves doing a few months before. But we were annoyed and overwrought, and our remoteness from all other human beings somehow made everything seem different. Since there were no other laws here, we had to make our own. . . .

"Can't we do something to stop them from taking off? Could we sabotage their rockets, for instance?" asked Bill.

Searle didn't like this idea at all.

"We mustn't do anything drastic," he said. "Besides, Don Hopkins is a good friend of mine. He'd never forgive me if I damaged his ship. There'd be the danger, too, that we might do something that couldn't be repaired."

"Then pinch their fuel," said Groves laconically.

"Of course! They're probably all asleep, there's no light in the cabin. All we've got to do is to connect up and pump."

"A very nice idea," I pointed out, "but we're two kilometers apart. How much pipeline have we got? Is it as much as a hundred meters?"

The others ignored this interruption as though it were beneath contempt and went on making their plans. Five minutes later the technicians had settled everything: we only had to climb into our spacesuits and do the work.

I never thought, when I joined the Professor's expedition, that I should end up like an African porter in one of those old adventure stories, carrying a load on my head. Especially when that load was a sixth of a spaceship (being so short, Professor Forster wasn't able to provide very effective help). Now that its fuel tanks were half empty, the weight of the ship in this gravity was about two hundred kilograms. We squeezed beneath, heaved, and up she went—very slowly, of course, because her inertia was still unchanged. Then we started marching.

It took us quite a while to make the journey, and it wasn't quite as easy as we'd thought it would be. But presently the two ships were lying side by side, and nobody had noticed us. Everyone in the *Henry Luce* was fast asleep, as they had every reason to expect us to be.

Though I was still rather short of breath, I found a certain schoolboy amusement in the whole adventure as Searle and Fulton drew the refueling pipeline out of our airlock and quietly coupled up to the other ship.

"The beauty of this plan," explained Groves to me as we stood watching, "is that they can't do anything to stop us, unless they come outside and uncouple our line. We can drain them dry in five minutes, and it will take them half that time to wake up and get into their spacesuits."

A sudden horrid fear smote me.

"Suppose they turned on their rockets and tried to get away?"

"Then we'd both be smashed up. No, they'll just have to come outside and see what's going on. Ah, there go the pumps."

The pipeline had stiffened like a fire hose under pressure, and I knew that the fuel was pouring into our tanks. Any moment now the lights would go on in the *Henry Luce* and her startled occupants would come scuttling out.

It was something of an anticlimax when they didn't. They must have been sleeping very soundly not to have felt the vibration from the pumps, but when it was all over nothing had happened and we just stood around looking rather foolish. Searle and Fulton carefully uncoupled the pipeline and put it back into the airlock.

"Well?" we asked the Professor.

He thought things over for a minute.

"Let's get back into the ship," he said.

When we had climbed out of our suits and were gathered together in the control room, or as far in as we could get, the Professor sat down at the radio and punched out the "Emergency" signal. Our sleeping neighbors would be awake in a couple of seconds as their automatic receiver sounded the alarm.

The TV screen glimmered into life. There, looking rather frightened, was Randolph Mays.

"Hello, Forster," he snapped. "What's the trouble?"

"Nothing wrong here," replied the Professor in his best deadpan manner, "but you've lost something important. Look at your fuel gauges."

The screen emptied, and for a moment there was a confused mumbling and shouting from the speaker. Then Mays was back, annoyance and alarm competing for possession of his features.

"What's going on?" he demanded angrily. "Do you know anything about this?"

The Professor let him sizzle for a moment before he replied.

"I think you'd better come across and talk things over," he said. "You won't have far to walk."

Mays glared back at him uncertainly, then retorted, "You bet I will!" The screen went blank.

"He'll have to climb down now!" said Bill gleefully. "There's nothing else he can do!"

"It's not so simple as you think," warned Fulton. "If he really wanted to be awkward, he could just sit tight and radio Ganymede for a tanker."

"What good would that do him? It would waste days and cost a fortune."

"Yes, but he'd still have the statue, if he wanted it that badly. And he'd get his money back when he sued us."

The airlock light flashed on and Mays stumped into the room. He was in a surprisingly conciliatory mood; on the way over, he must have had second thoughts.

"Well, well," he said affably. "What's all this nonsense in aid of?"

"You know perfectly well," the Professor retorted coldly. "I made it quite clear that nothing was to be taken off Five. You've been stealing property that doesn't belong to you."

"Now, let's be reasonable. Who *does* it belong to? You can't claim everything on this planet as your personal property."

"This is *not* a planet—it's a ship and the laws of salvage operate."

"Frankly, that's a very debatable point. Don't you think you should wait until you get a ruling from the lawyers?"

The Professor was being icily polite, but I could see that the strain was terrific and an explosion might occur at any moment.

"Listen, Mr. Mays," he said with ominous calm. "What you've taken is the most important single find we've made here. I will make allowances for the fact that you don't appreciate what you've done, and don't understand the viewpoint of an archaeologist like myself. Return that statue, and we'll pump your fuel back and say no more."

Mays rubbed his chin thoughtfully.

"I really don't see why you should make such a fuss about one statue, when you consider all the stuff that's still here."

It was then that the Professor made one of his rare mistakes.

"You talk like a man who's stolen the 'Mona Lisa' from the Louvre and argues that nobody will miss it because of all the other paintings. This statue's unique in a way that no terrestrial work of art can ever be. That's why I'm determined to get it back."

You should never, when you're bargaining, make it obvious that you want something really badly. I saw the greedy glint in Mays's eye and said to myself, "Uh-huh! He's going to be tough." And I remembered Fulton's remark about calling Ganymede for a tanker.

"Give me half an hour to think it over," said Mays, turning to the airlock.

"Very well," replied the Professor stiffly. "Half an hour—no more."

I must give Mays credit for brains. Within five minutes we saw his communications aerial start slewing around until it locked on Ganymede. Naturally we tried to listen in, but he had a scrambler. These newspapermen must trust each other.

The reply came back a few minutes later; that was scrambled, too. While we were waiting for the next development, we had another council of war. The Professor was now entering the stubborn, stop-at-nothing stage. He realized he'd miscalculated and that had made him fighting mad.

I think Mays must have been a little apprehensive, because he had reinforcements when he returned. Donald Hopkins, his pilot, came with him, looking rather uncomfortable.

"I've been able to fix things up, Professor," he said smugly. "It will take me a little longer, but I can get back without your help if I have to. Still, I must admit that it will save a good deal of time and money if we can come to an agreement. I'll tell you what. Give me back my fuel and I'll return the other—er—souvenirs I've collected. But I insist on keeping 'Mona Lisa,' even if it means I won't get back to Ganymede until the middle of next week."

The Professor then uttered a number of what are usually called deep-space oaths, though I can assure you they're much the same as any other oaths. That seemed to relieve his feelings a lot and he became fiendishly friendly.

"My dear Mr. Mays," he said, "You're an unmitigated crook, and accordingly I've no compunction left in dealing with you. I'm prepared to use force, knowing that the law will justify me."

Mays looked slightly alarmed, though not unduly so. We had moved to strategic positions around the door.

"Please don't be so melodramatic," he said haughtily. "This is the twenty-first century, not the Wild West back in 1800."

"In 1880," said Bill, who is a stickler for accuracy.

"I must ask you," the Professor continued, "to consider yourself under detention while we decide what is to be done. Mr. Searle, take him to Cabin B."

Mays sidled along the wall with a nervous laugh.

"Really, Professor, this is *too* childish! You can't detain me against my will." He glanced for support at the Captain of the *Henry Luce*.

Donald Hopkins dusted an imaginary speck of fluff from his uniform.

"I refuse," he remarked for the benefit of all concerned, "to get involved in vulgar brawls."

Mays gave him a venomous look and capitulated with bad grace. We saw that he had a good supply of reading matter, and locked him in.

When he was out of the way, the Professor turned to Hopkins, who was looking enviously at our fuel gauges.

"Can I take it, Captain," he said politely, "that you don't

wish to get mixed up in any of your employer's dirty business?"

"I'm neutral. My job is to fly the ship here and take her home. You can fight this out among yourselves."

"Thank you. I think we understand each other perfectly. Perhaps it would be best if you returned to your ship and explained the situation. We'll be calling you in a few minutes."

Captain Hopkins made his way languidly to the door. As he was about to leave he turned to Searle.

"By the way, Kingsley," he drawled. "Have you thought of torture? Do call me if you get around to it—I've some jolly interesting ideas." Then he was gone, leaving us with our hostage.

I think the Professor had hoped he could do a direct exchange. If so, he had not bargained on Marianne's stubbornness.

"It serves Randolph right," she said. "But I don't really see that it makes any difference. He'll be just as comfortable in your ship as in ours, and you can't do anything to him. Let me know when you're fed up with having him around."

It seemed a complete impasse. We had been too clever by half, and it had got us exactly nowhere. We'd captured Mays, but he wasn't any use to us.

The Professor was standing with his back to us, staring morosely out of the window. Seemingly balanced on the horizon, the immense bulk of Jupiter nearly filled the sky.

"We've got to convince her that we really *do* mean business," he said. Then he turned abruptly to me.

"Do you think she's actually fond of this blackguard?"

"Er—I shouldn't be surprised. Yes, I really believe so."

The Professor looked very thoughtful. Then he said to Searle, "Come into my room. I want to talk something over."

They were gone quite a while. When they returned, they both had an indefinable air of gleeful anticipation, and the Professor was carrying a piece of paper covered with figures. He went to the radio and called the *Henry Luce*.

"Hello," said Marianne, replying so promptly that she'd obviously been waiting for us. "Have you decided to call it off? I'm getting so bored."

The Professor looked at her gravely.

"Miss Mitchell," he replied. "It's apparent that you have not been taking us seriously. I'm therefore arranging a somewhat—er—drastic little demonstration for your benefit. I'm going to place your employer in a position from which he'll be only too anxious for you to retrieve him as quickly as possible."

"Indeed?" replied Marianne noncommittally—though I thought I could detect a trace of apprehension in her voice.

"I don't suppose," continued the Professor smoothly, "that you know anything about celestial mechanics. No? Too bad, but your pilot will confirm everything I tell you. Won't you, Hopkins?"

"Go ahead," came a painstakingly neutral voice from the background.

"Then listen carefully, Miss Mitchell. I want to remind you of our curious—indeed our precarious—position on this satellite. You've only got to look out of the window to see how close to Jupiter we are, and I need hardly remind you that Jupiter has by far the most intense gravitational field of all the planets. You follow me?"

"Yes," replied Marianne, no longer quite so self-possessed. "Go on."

"Very well. This little world of ours goes around Jupiter in almost exactly twelve hours. Now there's a well-known theorem stating that if a body *falls* from an orbit to the center of attraction, it will take point one seven seven of a period to make the drop. In other words, anything falling from here to Jupiter would reach the center of the planet in about two hours seven minutes. I'm sure Captain Hopkins can confirm this."

There was a long pause. Then we heard Hopkins say, "Well, of course I can't confirm the exact figures, but they're probably correct. It would be something like that, anyway."

"Good," continued the Professor. "Now I'm sure you realize," he went on with a hearty chuckle, "that a fall to the *center* of the planet is a very theoretical case. If anything really was dropped from here, it would reach the upper atmosphere of Jupiter in a considerably shorter time. I hope I'm not boring you?"

"No," said Marianne, rather faintly.

"I'm so glad to hear it. Anyway, Captain Searle has worked out the actual time for me, and it's one hour thirty-five minutes—with a few minutes either way. We can't guarantee complete accuracy, ha-ha!

"Now, it has doubtless not escaped your notice that this satellite of ours has an extremely weak gravitational field. It's escape velocity is only about ten meters a second, and anything thrown away from it at that speed would never come back. Correct, Mr. Hopkins?"

"Perfectly correct."

"Then, if I may come to the point, we propose to take Mr. Mays for a walk until he's immediately under Jupiter, remove the reaction pistols from his suit, and—ah—launch him forth. We will be prepared to retrieve him with our ship as soon as you've handed over the property you've stolen. After what I've told you, I'm sure you'll appreciate that time will be rather vital. An hour and thirty-five minutes is remarkably short, isn't it?"

"Professor!" I gasped, "You can't possibly do this!"

"Shut up!" he barked. "Well, Miss Mitchell, what about it?"

Marianne was staring at him with mingled horror and disbelief.

"You're simply bluffing!" she cried. "I don't believe you'd do anything of the kind! Your crew won't let you!"

The Professor sighed.

"Too bad," he said. "Captain Searle—Mr. Groves—will you take the prisoner and proceed as instructed."

"Aye, aye, sir," replied Searle with great solemnity.

Mays looked frightened but stubborn.

"What are you going to do now?" he said, as his suit was handed back to him.

Searle unholstered his reaction pistols. "Just climb in," he said. "We're going for a walk."

I realized then what the Professor hoped to do. The whole thing was a colossal bluff: of course he wouldn't *really* have Mays thrown into Jupiter; and in any case Searle and Groves wouldn't do it. Yet surely Marianne would see through the bluff, and then we'd be left looking mighty foolish.

Mays couldn't run away; without his reaction pistols he was quite helpless. Grasping his arms and towing him along like a captive balloon, his escorts set off toward the horizon—and toward Jupiter.

I could see, looking across the space to the other ship, that Marianne was staring out through the observation windows at the departing trio. Professor Forster noticed it too.

"I hope you're convinced, Miss Mitchell, that my men aren't carrying along an empty spacesuit. Might I suggest that you follow the proceedings with a telescope? They'll be over the horizon in a minute, but you'll be able to see Mr. Mays when he starts to—er—ascend."

There was a stubborn silence from the loudspeaker. The period of suspense seemed to last for a very long time.

Was Marianne waiting to see how far the Professor really would go?

By this time I had got hold of a pair of binoculars and was sweeping the sky beyond the ridiculously close horizon. Suddenly I saw it—a tiny flare of light against the vast yellow back-cloth of Jupiter. I focused quickly, and could just make out the three figures rising into space. As I watched, they separated: two of them decelerated with their pistols and started to fall back toward Five. The other went on ascending helplessly toward the ominous bulk of Jupiter.

I turned on the Professor in horror and disbelief.

"They've really done it!" I cried. "I thought you were only bluffing!"

"So did Miss Mitchell, I've no doubt," said the Professor calmly, for the benefit of the listening microphone. "I hope I don't need to impress upon you the urgency of the situation. As I've remarked once or twice before, the time of fall from our orbit to Jupiter's surface is ninety-five minutes. But, of course, if one waited even half that time, it would be much too late. . . ."

He let that sink in. There was no reply from the other ship.

"And now," he continued, "I'm going to switch off our receiver so we can't have any more arguments. We'll wait until you've unloaded that statue—*and* the other items Mr. Mays was careless enough to mention—before we'll talk to you again. Good-bye."

It was a very uncomfortable ten minutes. I'd lost track of Mays, and was seriously wondering if we'd better overpower the Professor and go after him before we had a murder on our hands. But the people who could fly the ship were the ones who had actually carried out the crime. I didn't know *what* to think.

Then the airlock of the *Henry Luce* slowly opened. A

couple of space-suited figures emerged, floating the cause of all the trouble between them.

"Unconditional surrender," murmured the Professor with a sigh of satisfaction. "Get it into our ship," he called over the radio, "I'll open up the airlock for you."

He seemed in no hurry at all. I kept looking anxiously at the clock; fifteen minutes had already gone by. Presently there was a clanking and banging in the airlock, the inner door opened, and Captain Hopkins entered. He was followed by Marianne, who only needed a bloodstained ax to make her look like Clytemnestra. I did my best to avoid her eyes, but the Professor seemed to be quite without shame. He walked into the airlock, checked that his property was back, and emerged rubbing his hands.

"Well, that's that," he said cheerfully. "Now let's sit down and have a drink to forget all this unpleasantness, shall we?"

I pointed indignantly at the clock.

"Have you gone crazy!" I yelled. "He's already halfway to Jupiter!"

young. I see no cause at all for hasty action."

Marianne spoke for the first time; she now looked really

Professor Forster looked at me disapprovingly.

scared.

"Impatience," he said, "is a common failing in the

"Certainly not. Everything I told you was perfectly true.

"But you promised," she whispered.

The Professor suddenly capitulated. He had had his little

"Do you mean that you lied to me?"

You simply jumped to the wrong conclusions. When I said

joke, and didn't want to prolong the agony.

"I can tell you at once, Miss Mitchell—and you too, Jack—that Mays is in no more danger than we are. We can go and collect him whenever we like."

that a body would take ninety-five minutes to fall from here to Jupiter, I omitted—not, I must confess, accidentally—a rather important phrase. I should have added '*a body at rest with respect to Jupiter.*' Your friend Mr. Mays was sharing the orbital speed of this satellite, and he's still got it. A little matter of twenty-six kilometers a second, Miss Mitchell.

"Oh, yes, we threw him completely off Five and toward Jupiter. But the velocity we gave him then was trivial. He's still moving in practically the same orbit as before. The most he can do—I've got Captain Searle to work out the figures—is to drift about a hundred kilometers inward. And in one revolution—twelve hours—*he'll be right back where he started*, without our bothering to do anything at all."

There was a long, long silence. Marianne's face was a study in frustration, relief, and annoyance at having been fooled. Then she turned on Captain Hopkins.

"You must have known all the time! Why didn't you tell me?"

Hopkins gave her a wounded expression.

"You didn't ask me," he said.

We hauled Mays down about an hour later. He was only twenty kilometers up, and we located him quickly enough by the flashing light on his suit. His radio had been disconnected, for a reason that hadn't occurred to me. He was intelligent enough to realize that he was in no danger, and if his set had been working he could have called his ship and exposed our bluff. That is, if he wanted to. Personally, I think I'd have been glad enough to call the whole thing off even if I had known that I was perfectly safe. It must have been awfully lonely up there.

To my great surprise, Mays wasn't as mad as I'd expected. Perhaps he was too relieved to be back in our snug little cabin when we drifted up to him on the merest fizzle of rockets and yanked him in. Or perhaps he felt that he'd been worsted in fair fight and didn't bear any grudge. I really think it was the latter.

There isn't much more to tell, except that we did play one other trick on him before we left Five. He had a good deal more fuel in his tanks than he really needed, now that his payload was substantially reduced. By keeping the excess ourselves, we were able to carry "The Ambassador" back to Ganymede after all. Oh, yes, the Professor gave him a check for the fuel we'd borrowed. Everything was perfectly legal.

There's one amusing sequel I must tell you, though. The day after the new gallery was opened at the British Museum I went along to see "The Ambassador," partly to discover if his impact was still as great in these changed surroundings. (For the record, it wasn't—though it's still considerable and Bloomsbury will never be quite the same to me again.) A huge crowd was milling around the gallery, and there in the middle of it were Mays and Marianne.

It ended up with us having a very pleasant lunch together in Holborn. I'll say this about Mays—he doesn't bear any grudges. But I'm still rather sore about Marianne.

And, frankly, I can't imagine *what* she sees in him.

COLLECTING TEAM

Robert Silverberg

If there is life on other worlds, no doubt explorers from Earth will go forth to collect specimens of it for the zoos of tomorrow. But Earthmen may not be the only zoologists in the universe. . . .

From fifty thousand miles up, the situation looked promising. It was a middle-sized, brown-and-green, inviting-looking planet, with no sign of cities or any other such complications. Just a pleasant sort of place, the very sort we were looking for to redeem what had been a pretty futile expedition.

I turned to Clyde Holdreth, who was staring reflectively at the thermocouple.

"Well? What do you think?"

"Looks fine to me. Temperature's about seventy down there—nice and warm, and plenty of air. I think it's worth a try."

Lee Davison came strolling out from the storage hold, smelling of animals, as usual. He was holding one of the blue monkeys we picked up on Alpheraz, and the little beast was crawling up his arm. "Have we found something, gentlemen?"

"We've found a planet," I said. "How's the storage space in the hold?"

"Don't worry about that. We've got room for a whole zooful more before we get filled up. It hasn't been a very fruitful trip."

"No," I agreed. "It hasn't. Well? Shall we go down and see what's to be seen?"

"Might as well," Holdreth said. "We can't go back to Earth with just a couple of blue monkeys and some ant-eaters, you know."

"I'm in favor of a landing too," said Davison. "You?"

I nodded. "I'll set up the charts, and you get your animals comfortable for deceleration."

Davison disappeared back into the storage hold, while Holdreth scribbled furiously in the logbook, writing down the coordinates of the planet below, its general description, and so forth. Aside from being a collecting team for the zoological department of the Bureau of Interstellar Affairs, we also double as a survey ship, and the planet down below was listed as *unexplored* on our charts.

I glanced out at the mottled brown-and-green ball spinning slowly in the viewport, and felt the warning twinge of gloom that came to me every time we made a landing on a new and strange world. Repressing it, I started to figure out a landing orbit. From behind me came the furious chatter of the blue monkeys as Davison strapped them into their acceleration cradles, and under that the deep, unmusical honking of the Rigelian anteaters, noisily bleating their displeasure.

The planet was inhabited, all right. We hadn't had the ship on the ground more than a minute before the local fauna began to congregate. We stood at the viewport and looked out in wonder.

"This is one of those things you dream about," Davison said, stroking his little beard nervously. "Look at them! There must be a thousand different species out there."

"I've never seen anything like it," said Holdreth.

I computed how much storage space we had left and how

many of the thronging creatures outside we would be able to bring back with us. "How are we going to decide what to take and what to leave behind?"

"Does it matter? Holdreth said gaily. "This is what you call an embarrassment of riches, I guess. We just grab the dozen most bizarre creatures and blast off—and save the rest for another trip. It's too bad we wasted all that time wandering around near Rigel."

"We *did* get the anteaters," Davison pointed out. They were his find, and he was proud of them.

I smiled sourly. "Yeah. We got the anteaters there." The anteaters honked at that moment, loud and clear. "You know, that's one set of beasts I think I could do without."

"Bad attitude," Holdreth said. "Unprofessional."

"Whoever said I was a zoologist, anyway? I'm just a spaceship pilot, remember. And if I don't like the way those anteaters talk—and smell—I see no reason why I—"

"Say, look at that one," Davison said suddenly.

I glanced out the viewport and saw a new beast emerging from the thick-packed vegetation in the background. I've seen some fairly strange creatures since I was assigned to the zoological department, but this one took the grand prize.

It was about the size of a giraffe, moving on long, wobbly legs and with a tiny head up at the end of a preposterous neck. Only it had six legs and a bunch of writhing snakelike tentacles as well, and its eyes, great violet globes, stood out nakedly on the ends of two thick stalks. It must have been twenty feet high. It moved with exaggerated grace through the swarm of beasts surrounding our ship, pushed its way smoothly toward the vessel, and peered gravely in at the viewport. One purple eye stared directly at me, the other at Davison. Oddly, it seemed to me as if it were trying to tell us something.

"Big one, isn't it?" Davison said finally.

"I'll bet you'd like to bring one back, too."

"Maybe we can fit a young one aboard," Davison said. "If we can find a young one." He turned to Holdreth. "How's that air analysis coming? I'd like to get out there and start collecting. God, that's a crazy-looking beast!"

The animal outside had apparently finished its inspection of us, for it pulled its head away and, gathering its legs under itself, squatted near the ship. A small doglike creature with stiff spines running along its back began to bark at the big creature, which took no notice. The other animals, which came in all shapes and sizes, continued to mill around the ship, evidently very curious about the newcomer to their world. I could see Davison's eyes thirsty with the desire to take the whole kit and caboodle back to Earth with him. I knew what was running through his mind. He was dreaming of the umpteen thousand species of extraterrestrial wildlife roaming around out there, and to each one he was attaching a neat little tag: *Something-or-other davisoni.*

"The air's fine," Holdreth announced abruptly, looking up from his test tubes. "Get your butterfly nets and let's see what we can catch."

There was something I didn't like about the place. It was just too good to be true, and I learned long ago that nothing ever is. There's always a catch someplace.

Only this seemed to be on the level. The planet was a bonanza for zoologists, and Davison and Holdreth were having the time of their lives, hip-deep in obliging specimens.

"I've never seen anything like it," Davison said for at least the fiftieth time, as he scooped up a small purplish squirrellike creature and examined it curiously. The squirrel stared back, examining Davison just as curiously.

"Let's take some of these," Davison said. "I like them."

"Carry 'em on in, then," I said, shrugging. I didn't care which specimens they chose, so long as they filled up the storage hold quickly and let me blast off on schedule. I watched as Davison grabbed a pair of the squirrels and brought them into the ship.

Holdreth came over to me. He was carrying a sort of dog with insect-faceted eyes and gleaming furless skin. "How's this one Gus?"

"Fine," I said bleakly. "Wonderful."

He put the animal down—it didn't scamper away, just sat there smiling at us—and looked at me. He ran a hand through his fast-vanishing hair. "Listen, Gus, you've been gloomy all day. What's eating you?"

"I don't like this place," I said.

"Why? Just on general principles?"

"It's too *easy,* Clyde. Much too easy. These animals just flock around here waiting to be picked up."

Holdreth chuckled. "And you're used to a struggle, aren't you? You're just angry at us because we have it so simple here!"

"When I think of the trouble we went through just to get a pair of miserable vile-smelling anteaters, and—"

"Come off it, Gus. We'll load up in a hurry, if you like. But this place is a zoological gold mine!"

I shook my head. "I don't like it, Clyde. Not at all."

Holdreth laughed again and picked up his faceted-eyed dog. "Say, know where I can find another of these, Gus?"

"Right over there," I said, pointing. "By that tree. With its tongue hanging out. It's just waiting to be carried away."

Holdreth looked and smiled. "What do you know about that!" He snared his specimen and carried both of them inside.

I walked away to survey the grounds. The planet was too flatly incredible for me to accept at face value, without at least a look-see, despite the blithe way my two companions were snapping up specimens.

For one thing, animals just don't exist this way—in big

miscellaneous quantities, living all together happily. I hadn't noticed more than a few of each kind, and there must have been five hundred different species, each one stranger-looking than the next. Nature doesn't work that way.

For another, they all seemed to be on friendly terms with one another, though they acknowledged the unofficial leadership of the giraffelike creature. Nature doesn't work *that* way, either. I hadn't seen one quarrel between the animals yet. That argued that they were all herbivores, which didn't make sense ecologically.

I shrugged my shoulders and walked on.

Half an hour later, I knew a little more about the geography of our bonanza. We were on either an immense island or a peninsula of some sort, because I could see a huge body of water bordering the land some ten miles off. Our vicinity was fairly flat, except for a good-sized hill from which I could see the terrain.

There was a thick, heavily wooded jungle not too far from the ship. The forest spread out all the way toward the water in one direction, but ended abruptly in the other. We had brought the ship down right at the edge of the clearing. Apparently most of the animals we saw lived in the jungle.

On the other side of our clearing was a low, broad plain that seemed to trail away into a desert in the distance; I could see an uninviting stretch of barren sand that contrasted strangely with the fertile jungle to my left. There was a small lake to the side. It was, I saw, the sort of country likely to attract a varied fauna, since there seemed to be every sort of habitat within a small area.

And the fauna! Although I'm a zoologist only by osmosis, picking up both my interest and my knowledge second-hand from Holdreth and Davison, I couldn't help but be astonished by the wealth of strange animals. They came in all different shapes and sizes, colors and odors, and the only thing they all had in common was their friendliness. During the course of my afternoon's wanderings a hundred animals must have come marching boldly right up to me, given me the once-over, and walked away. This included half a dozen kinds that I hadn't seen before, plus one of the eye-stalked, intelligent-looking giraffes and a furless dog. Again, I had the feeling that the giraffe seemed to be trying to communicate.

I didn't like it. I didn't like it at all.

I returned to our clearing, and saw Holdreth and Davison still buzzing madly around, trying to cram as many animals as they could into our hold.

"How's it going?" I asked.

"Hold's all full," Davison said. "We're busy making our alternate selections now." I saw him carrying out Holdreth's two furless dogs and picking up instead a pair of eight-legged penguinish things that uncomplainingly allowed themselves to be carried in. Holdreth was frowning unhappily.

"What do you want *those* for, Lee? Those doglike ones seem much more interesting, don't you think?"

"No," Davison said, "I'd rather bring along these two. They're curious beasts, aren't they? Look at the muscular network that connects the—"

"Hold it, fellows," I said. I peered at the animal in Davison's hands and glanced up. "This *is* a curious beast," I said. "It's got eight legs."

"You becoming a zoologist?" Holdreth asked, amused.

"No—but I am getting puzzled. Why should this one have eight legs, some of the others here six, and some of the others only four?"

They looked at me blankly, with the scorn of professionals.

"I mean, there ought to be some sort of logic to evolution

here, shouldn't there? On Earth we've developed a four-legged pattern of animal life; on Venus, they usually run to six legs. But have you ever seen an evolutionary hodgepodge like this place before?"

"There are stranger setups," Holdreth said. "The symbiotes on Sirius Three, the burrowers of Mizar—but you're right, Gus. This *is* a peculiar evolutionary dispersal. I think we ought to stay and investigate it fully."

Instantly I knew from the bright expression on Davison's face that I had blundered, had made things worse than ever. I decided to take a new tack.

"I don't agree," I said. "I think we ought to leave with what we've got, and come back with a larger expedition later."

Davison chuckled. "Come on, Gus, don't be silly! This is a chance of a lifetime for us—why should we call in the whole zoological department on it?"

I didn't want to tell them I was afraid of staying longer. I crossed my arms. "Lee, I'm the pilot of this ship, and you'll have to listen to me. The schedule calls for a brief stopover here, and we have to leave. Don't tell me I'm being silly."

"But you are, man! You're standing blindly in the path of scientific investigation, of—"

"Listen to me, Lee. Our food is calculated on a pretty narrow margin, to allow you fellows more room for storage. And this is strictly a collecting team. There's no provision for extended stays on any one planet. Unless you want to wind up eating your own specimens, I suggest you allow us to get out of here."

They were silent for a moment. Then Holdreth said, "I guess we can't argue with that, Lee. Let's listen to Gus and go back now. There's plenty of time to investigate this place later when we can take longer."

"But—oh, all right," Davison said reluctantly. He picked

up the eight-legged penguins. "Let me stash these things in the hold, and we can leave." He looked strangely at me, as if I had done something criminal.

As he started into the ship, I called to him.

"What is it, Gus?"

"Look here, Lee. I don't *want* to pull you away from here. It's simply a matter of food," I lied, masking my nebulous suspicions.

"I know how it is, Gus." He turned and entered the ship.

I stood there thinking about nothing at all for a moment, then went inside myself to begin setting up the blastoff orbit.

I got as far as calculating the fuel expenditure when I noticed something. Feed wires were dangling crazily down from the control cabinet. Somebody had wrecked our drive mechanism, but thoroughly.

For a long moment, I stared stiffly at the sabotaged drive. Then I turned and headed into the storage hold.

"Davison?"

"What is it, Gus?"

"Come out here a second, will you?"

I waited, and a few minutes later he appeared, frowning impatiently. "What do you want, Gus? I'm busy and I—" His mouth dropped open. *"Look at the drive!"*

"You look at it," I snapped. "I'm sick. Go get Holdreth, on the double."

While he was gone I tinkered with the shattered mechanism. Once I had the cabinet panel off and could see the inside, I felt a little better; the drive wasn't damaged beyond repair, though it had been pretty well scrambled. Three or four days of hard work with a screwdriver and solderbeam might get the ship back into functioning order.

But that didn't make me any less angry. I heard Holdreth and Davison entering behind me, and I whirled to face them.

"All right, you idiots. Which one of you did this?"

They opened their mouths in protesting squawks at the same instant. I listened to them for a while, then said, "One at a time!"

"If you're implying that one of us deliberately sabotaged the ship," Holdreth said, "I want you to know—"

"I'm not implying anything. But the way it looks to me, you two decided you'd like to stay here a while longer to continue your investigations, and figured the easiest way of getting me to agree was to wreck the drive." I glared hotly at them. "Well, I've got news for you. I can fix this, and I can fix it in a couple of days. So go on—get about your business! Get all the zoologizing you can in, while you still have time. I—"

Davison laid a hand gently on my arm. "Gus," he said quietly, *"We didn't do it.* Neither of us."

Suddenly all the anger drained out of me and was replaced by raw fear. I could see that Davison meant it.

"If you didn't do it, and Holdreth didn't do it, and *I* didn't do it—then who did?"

Davison shrugged.

"Maybe it's one of us who doesn't know he's doing it," I suggested. "Maybe—" I stopped. "Oh, that's nonsense. Hand me that tool kit, will you, Lee?"

They left to tend to the animals, and I set to work on the repair job, dismissing all further speculations and suspicions from my mind, concentrating solely on joining Lead A to Input A and Transistor F to Potentiometer K, as indicated. It was slow, nerve-harrowing work, and by mealtime I had accomplished only the barest preliminaries. My fingers were starting to quiver from the strain of small-scale work, and I decided to give up the job for the day and get back to it tomorrow.

I slept uneasily, my nightmares punctuated by the moaning of the accursed anteaters and the occasional squeals, chuckles, bleats, and hisses of the various other creatures in the hold. It must have been four in the morning before I dropped off into a really sound sleep, and what was left of the night passed swiftly. The next thing I knew, hands were shaking me, and I was looking up into the pale, tense faces of Holdreth and Davison.

I pushed my sleep-stuck eyes open and blinked. "Huh? What's going on?"

Holdreth leaned down and shook me savagely. "Get up, Gus!"

I struggled to my feet slowly. "Hell of a thing to do, wake a fellow up in the middle of the—"

I found myself being propelled from my cabin and led down the corridor to the control room. Blearily, I followed where Holdreth pointed, and then I woke up in a hurry.

The drive was battered again. Someone—or *something*—had completely undone my repair job of the night before.

If there had been bickering among us, it stopped. This was past the category of a joke now; it couldn't be laughed off, and we found ourselves working together as a tight unit again, trying desperately to solve the puzzle before it was too late.

"Let's review the situation," Holdreth said, pacing nervously up and down the control cabin. "The drive has been sabotaged twice. None of us knows who did it, and on a conscious level each of us is convinced *he* didn't do it."

He paused. "That leaves us with two possibilities. Either, as Gus suggested, one of us is doing it unaware of it even himself, or someone else is doing it while we're not looking. Neither possibility is a very cheerful one."

"We can stay on guard, though," I said. "Here's what I propose: first, have one of us awake at all times—sleep in shifts, that is, with somebody guarding the drive until

I get it fixed. Two—jettison all the animals aboard ship."

"What?"

"He's right," Davison said. "We don't know what we may have brought aboard. They don't seem to be intelligent, but we can't be sure. That purple-eyed baby giraffe, for instance—suppose he's been hypnotizing us into damaging the drive ourselves? How can we tell?"

"Oh, but—" Holdreth started to protest, then stopped and frowned soberly. "I suppose we'll have to admit the possibility," he said, obviously unhappy about the prospect of freeing our captives. "We'll empty out the hold, and you see if you can get the drive fixed. Maybe later we'll recapture them all, if nothing further develops."

We agreed to that, and Holdreth and Davison cleared the ship of its animal cargo while I set to work determinedly at the drive mechanism. By nightfall, I had managed to accomplish as much as I had the day before.

I sat up as watch the first shift, aboard the strangely quiet ship. I paced around the drive cabin, fighting the great temptation to doze off, and managed to last through until the time Holdreth arrived to relieve me.

Only—when he showed up, he gasped and pointed at the drive. It had been ripped apart a third time.

Now we had no excuse, no explanation. The expedition had turned into a nightmare.

I could only protest that I had remained awake my entire spell on duty, and that I had seen no one and no thing approach the drive panel. But that was hardly a satisfactory explanation, since it either cast guilt on me as the saboteur or implied that some unseen external power was repeatedly wrecking the drive. Neither hypothesis made sense, at least to me.

By now we had spent four days on the planet, and food

was getting to be a major problem. My carefully budgeted flight schedule called for us to be two days out on our return journey to Earth by now. But we still were no closer to departure than we had been four days ago.

The animals continued to wander around outside, nosing up against the ship, examining it, almost fondling it, with those damned pseudo-giraffes staring soulfully at us always. The beasts were as friendly as ever, little knowing how the tension was growing within the hull. The three of us walked around like zombies, eyes bright and lips clamped. We were scared—all of us.

Something was keeping us from fixing the drive.

Something didn't want us to leave this planet.

I looked at the bland face of the purple-eyed giraffe staring through the viewport, and it stared mildly back at me. Around it was grouped the rest of the local fauna, the same incredible hodgepodge of improbable genera and species.

That night, the three of us stood guard in the control room together. The drive was smashed anyway. The wires were soldered in so many places by now that the control panel was a mass of shining alloy, and I knew that a few more such sabotagings and it would be impossible to patch it together any more—if it wasn't so already.

The next night, I just didn't knock off. I continued soldering right on after dinner (and a pretty skimpy dinner it was, now that we were on close rations) and far on into the night.

By morning, it was as if I hadn't done a thing.

"I give up," I announced, surveying the damage. "I don't see any sense in ruining my nerves trying to fix a thing that won't stay fixed."

Holdreth nodded. He looked terribly pale. "We'll have to find some new approach."

"Yeah. Some new approach."

I yanked open the food closet and examined our stock. Even figuring in the synthetics we would have fed to the animals if we hadn't released them, we were low on food. We had overstayed even the safety margin. It would be a hungry trip back—if we ever did get back.

I clambered through the hatch and sprawled down on a big rock near the ship. One of the furless dogs came over and nuzzled in my shirt. Davison stepped to the hatch and called down to me.

"What are you doing out there, Gus?"

"Just getting a little fresh air. I'm sick of living aboard that ship." I scratched the dog behind his pointed ears, and looked around.

The animals had lost most of their curiosity about us, and didn't congregate the way they used to. They were meandering all over the plain, nibbling at little deposits of a white doughy substance. It precipitated every night. "Manna," we called it. All the animals seemed to live on it.

I folded my arms and leaned back.

We were getting to look awfully lean by the eighth day. I wasn't even trying to fix the ship any more; the hunger was starting to get me. But I saw Davison puttering around with my solderbeam.

"What are you doing?"

"I'm going to repair the drive," he said. "You don't want to, but we can't just sit around, you know." His nose was deep in my repair guide, and he was fumbling with the release on the solderbeam.

I shrugged. "Go ahead, if you want to." I didn't care what he did. All I cared about was the gaping emptiness in my stomach, and about the dimly grasped fact that somehow we were stuck here for good.

"Gus?"

"Yeah?"

"I think it's time I told you something. I've been eating the manna for four days. It's good. It's nourishing stuff."

"You've been eating—the manna? Something that grows on an alien world? You crazy?"

"What else can we do? Starve?"

I smiled feebly, admitting that he was right. From somewhere in the back of the ship came the sounds of Holdreth moving around. Holdreth had taken this thing worse than any of us. He had a family back on Earth, and he was beginning to realize that he wasn't ever going to see them again.

"Why don't you get Holdreth?" Davison suggested. "Go out there and stuff yourselves with the manna. You've got to eat something."

"Yeah. What can I lose?" Moving like a mechanical man, I headed toward Holdreth's cabin. We would go out and eat the manna and cease being hungry, one way or another.

"Clyde?" I called. "Clyde?"

I entered his cabin. He was sitting at his desk, shaking convulsively, staring at the two streams of blood that trickled in red spurts from his slashed wrists.

"Clyde!"

He made no protest as I dragged him toward the infirmary cabin and got tourniquets around his arms, cutting off the bleeding. He just stared dully ahead, sobbing.

I slapped him and he came around. He shook his head dizzily, as if he didn't know where he was.

"I—I—"

"Easy, Clyde. Everything's all right."

"It's *not* all right," he said hollowly. "I'm still alive. Why didn't you let me die? Why didn't you—"

Davison entered the cabin. "What's been happening, Gus?"

"It's Clyde. The pressure's getting him. He tried to kill himself, but I think he's all right now. Get him something to eat, will you?"

We had Holdreth straightened around by evening. Davison gathered as much of the manna as he could find, and we held a feast.

"I wish we had nerve enough to kill some of the local fauna," Davison said. "Then we'd have a feast—steaks and everything!"

"The bacteria." Holdreth pointed out quietly. "We don't dare."

"I know. But it's a thought."

"No more thoughts," I said sharply. "Tomorrow morning we start work on the drive panel again. Maybe with some food in our bellies we'll be able to keep awake and see what's happening here."

Holdreth smiled. "Good. I can't wait to get out of this ship and back to a normal existence. God, I just can't wait!"

"Let's get some sleep," I said. "Tomorrow we'll give it another try. We'll get back," I said with a confidence I didn't feel.

The following morning I rose early and got my tool kit. My head was clear, and I was trying to put the pieces together without much luck. I started toward the control cabin.

And stopped.

And looked out the viewport.

I went back and awoke Holdreth and Davison. "Take a look out the port," I said hoarsely.

They looked. They gaped.

"It looks just like. my house," Holdreth said. "My house on Earth."

"With all the comforts of home inside, I'll bet." I walked forward uneasily and lowered myself through the hatch. "Let's go look at it."

We approached it, while the animals frolicked around us. The big giraffe came near and shook its head gravely. The house stood in the middle of the clearing, small and neat and freshly painted.

I saw it now. During the night, invisible hands had put it there. Had assembled and built a cozy little Earth-type house and dropped it next to our ship for us to live in.

"Just like my house," Holdreth repeated in wonderment.

"It should be," I said. "They grabbed the model from your mind, as soon as they found out we couldn't live on the ship indefinitely."

Holdreth and Davison asked as one, "What do you mean?"

"You mean you haven't figured this place out yet?" I licked my lips, getting myself used to the fact that I was going to spend the rest of my life here. "You mean you don't realize what this house is intended to be?"

They shook their heads, baffled. I glanced around, from the house to the useless ship to the jungle to the plain to the little pond. It all made sense now.

"They want to keep us happy," I said. "They knew we weren't thriving aboard the ship, so they—they built us something a little more like home."

"*They?* The giraffes?"

"Forget the giraffes. They tried to warn us, but it's too late. They're intelligent beings, but they're prisoners just like us. I'm talking about the ones who run this place. The super-aliens who make us sabotage our own ship and not even know we're doing it, who stand someplace up there and gape at us. The ones who dredged together this motley assortment of beasts from all over the galaxy. Now we've been collected too. This whole damned place is just a zoo— a zoo for aliens so far ahead of us we don't dare dream what they're like."

I looked up at the shimmering blue-green sky, where invisible bars seemed to restrain us, and sank down dismally on the porch of our new home. I was resigned. There wasn't any sense in struggling against *them*.

I could see the neat little placard now:

EARTHMEN. Native Habitat, Sol III.

EACH AN EXPLORER

Isaac Asimov

So many stories have been written about the ferocious perils humanity will encounter in space—the bug-eyed monsters, the purple-tusked flesh-eaters—that if they were all laid end to end, they would stretch from Brooklyn to the Crab Nebula. Isaac Asimov is no man to traffic in melodramatic cliches; and so he has provided this sly story of a dread intergalactic menace in which the deadliest creatures have neither fangs nor tentacles nor throbbing, twitching antennae, nor any of the other standard equipment of bang-bang space opera, but are none the less menacing for it.

Herman Chouns was a man of hunches. Sometimes he was right; sometimes he was wrong—about fifty-fifty. Still, considering that one has the whole universe of possibilities from which to pull a right answer, fifty-fifty begins to look pretty good.

Chouns wasn't always as pleased with the matter as might be expected. It put too much of a strain on him. People would huddle around a problem, making nothing of it, then turn to him and say, "What do you think, Chouns? Turn on the old intuition."

And if he came up with something that fizzled, the responsibility for that was made clearly his.

His job, as Field Explorer, rather made things worse.

"Think that planet's worth a closer look?" they would say. "What do you think, Chouns?"

So it was a relief to draw a two-man spot for a change (meaning that the next trip would be to some low-priority spot, and the pressure would be off) and on top of it, to get Allen Smith as partner.

Smith was as matter-of-fact as his name. He said to Chouns the first day out, "The thing about you is that the memory files in your brain are on extra-special call. Faced with a problem, you remember enough little things that maybe the rest of us don't come up with to make a decision. Calling it a hunch just makes it mysterious, and it isn't."

He rubbed his hair slickly back as he said that. He had light hair that lay down like a skullcap.

Chouns, whose hair was very unruly, and whose nose was snub and a bit off-center, said softly (as was his way), "I think maybe it's telepathy."

"What!"

"Just a trace of it."

"Nuts!" said Smith, with loud derision (as was *his* way). "Scientists have been tracking psionics for a thousand years and gotten nowhere. There's no such thing: no precognition; no telekinesis; no clairvoyance; *and* no telepathy."

"I admit that, but consider this. If I get a picture of what each of a group of people are thinking—even though I might not be aware of what was happening—I could integrate the information and come up with an answer. I would know more than any single individual in the group, so I could make a better judgment than the others—sometimes."

"Do you have any evidence at all for that?"

Chouns turned his mild brown eyes on the other. "Just a hunch."

They got along well. Chouns welcomed the other's refreshing practicality, and Smith patronized the other's speculations. They often disagreed but never quarreled.

Even when they reached their objective, which was a globular cluster that had never felt the energy thrusts of a human-designed nuclear reactor before, increasing tension did not worsen matters.

Smith said, "Wonder what they do with all this data back on Earth. Seems a waste sometimes."

Chouns said, "Earth is just beginning to spread out. No telling how far humanity will move out into the Galaxy, given a million years or so. All the data we can get on any world will come in handy some day."

"You sound like a recruiting manual for the Exploration Teams. Think there'll be anything interesting in that thing?" He indicated the visi-plate on which the no-longer distant cluster was centered like spilled talcum powder.

"Maybe. I've got a hunch—" Chouns stopped, gulped, blinked once or twice, and then smiled weakly.

Smith snorted. "Let's get a fix on the nearest star groups and make a random pass through the thickest of it. One gets you ten, we find a McKomin ratio under O.2."

"You'll lose," murmured Chouns. He felt the quick stir of excitement that always came when new worlds were about to be spread beneath them. It was a most contagious feeling, and it caught hundreds of youngsters each year. Youngsters, such as he had been once, flocked to the Teams, eager to see the worlds their descendants some day would call their own, each an explorer—

They got their fix, made their first close-quarters hyper-spatial jump into the cluster, and began scanning stars for planetary systems. The computers did their work; the infor-mation files grew steadily, and all proceeded in satisfactory routine—until at system 23, shortly after completion of the jump, the ship's hyperatomic motors failed.

Chouns muttered, "Funny. The analyzers don't say what's wrong."

He was right. The needles wavered erratically, never stop-ping once for a reasonable length of time, so that no diag-nosis was indicated. And, as a consequence, no repairs could be carried through.

"Never saw anything like it," growled Smith. "We'll have to shut everything off and diagnose manually."

"We might as well do it comfortably," said Chouns, who was already at the telescopes. "Nothing's wrong with the ordinary space-drive, and there are two decent planets in this system."

"Oh? How decent and which ones?"

"The first and second out of four: Both water-oxygen. The first is a bit warmer and larger than Earth; the second a bit colder and smaller. Fair enough?"

"Life?"

"Both. Vegetation, anyway."

Smith grunted. There was nothing in that to surprise anyone; vegetation occurred more often than not on water-oxygen worlds. And unlike animal life, vegetation could be seen telescopically—or, more precisely, spectroscopically. Only four photochemical pigments had ever been found in any plant form, and each could be detected by the nature of the light it reflected.

Chouns said, "Vegetation on both planets is chlorophyll-type, no less. It'll be just like Earth; real homey."

Smith said, "Which is closer?"

"Number two, and we're on our way. I have a feeling it's going to be a nice planet."

"I'll judge that by the instruments, *if* you don't mind," said Smith.

But this seemed to be one of Chouns's correct hunches. The planet was a tame one with an intricate ocean network that ensured a climate of small temperature range. The mountain ranges were low and rounded, and the distribution of vegetation indicated high and widespread fertility.

Chouns was at the controls for the actual landing.

Smith grew impatient. "What are you picking and choosing for? One place is like another."

"I'm looking for a bare spot," said Chouns. "No use burning up an acre of plant life."

"What if you do?"

"What if I don't?" said Chouns, and found his bare spot.

It was only then, after landing, that they realized a small part of what they had tumbled into.

"Jumping space-warps," said Smith.

Chouns felt stunned. Animal life was much rarer than vegetation, and even the glimmerings of intelligence were far rarer still; yet here, not half a mile away from landing point, was a clustering of low, thatched huts that were obviously the product of a primitive intelligence.

"Careful," said Smith, dazedly.

"I don't think there's any harm," said Chouns. He stepped out onto the surface of the planet with firm confidence; Smith followed.

Chouns controlled his excitement with difficulty. "This is terrific. No one's ever reported anything better than caves or woven tree branches before."

"I hope they're harmless."

"It's too peaceful for them to be anything else. Smell the air."

Coming down to landing, the terrain—to all points of horizon, except where a low range of hills broke the even line—had been colored a soothing pale pink, dappled against the chlorophyll-green. At closer quarters the pale pink broke up into individual flowers, fragile and fragrant. Only the areas in the immediate neighborhood of the huts were amber with something that looked like a cereal grain.

Creatures were emerging from the huts, moving closer to the ship with a kind of hesitating trust. They had four legs and a sloping body which stood three feet high at the shoulders. Their heads were set firmly on those shoulders, with bulging eyes (Chouns counted six) set in a circle and capable of the most disconcertingly independent motion. *(That makes up for the immovability of the head,* thought Chouns.)

Each animal had a tail that forked at the end, forming two sturdy fibrils that each animal held high. The fibrils maintained a rapid tremor that gave them a hazy, blurred look.

"Come on," said Chouns. "They won't hurt us; I'm sure of it."

The animals surrounded the men at a cautious distance. Their tails made a modulated humming noise.

"They might communicate that way," said Chouns. "And I think it's obvious they're vegetarians." He pointed toward one of the huts, where a small member of the species sat on its haunches, plucking at the amber grain with his tails, and flicking an ear of it through his mouth like a man sucking a series of maraschino cherries off a toothpick.

"Human beings eat lettuce," said Smith, "but that doesn't prove anything."

More of the tailed creatures emerged, hovered about the men for a moment, then vanished off into the pink and green.

"Vegetarians," said Chouns firmly. "Look at the way they cultivate the main crop."

The main crop, as Chouns called it, consisted of a coronet of soft green spikes, close to the ground. Out of the center of the coronet grew a hairy stem which, at two-inch intervals, shot out fleshy veined buds that almost pulsated, they seemed so vitally alive. The stem ended at the tip with the pale-pink blossoms that, except for the color, was the most Earthly thing about the plants.

The plants were laid out in rows and files with geometric precision. The soil about each was well loosened and powdered with a foreign substance that could be nothing but fertilizer. Narrow passageways, just wide enough for an animal to pass along, crisscrossed the field and each passageway was lined with narrow sluiceways, obviously for water.

The animals were spread through the fields now, working diligently, heads bent. Only a few remained in the neighborhood of the two men.

Chouns nodded. "They're good farmers."

"Not bad," agreed Smith. He walked briskly toward the nearest of the pale-pink blooms and reached for one; but six inches short of it he was stopped by the sound of tail-vibrations keening to shrillness, and by the actual touch of a tail upon his arm. The touch was delicate but firm, interposing itself between Smith and the plants.

Smith fell back, "What in Space—"

He had half reached for his blaster when Chouns said, "No cause for excitement; take it easy."

Half a dozen of the creatures were now gathering about the two, offering stalks of grain humbly and gently, some using their tails, some nudging it forward with their muzzles.

Chouns said, "They're friendly enough. Picking a bloom might be against their customs; the plants probably have to be treated according to rigid rules. Any culture that has agriculture probably has fertility rites, and Lord knows what that involves. The rules governing the cultivation of the plants must be strict, or there wouldn't be those accurate measured rows. . . . Space, won't they sit up back home when they hear this?"

The tail-humming shot up in pitch again, and the creatures near them fell back. Another member of the species was emerging from a larger hut in the center of the group.

"The chief, I suppose," muttered Chouns.

The new one advanced slowly, tail high, each fibril encircling a small black object. At a distance of five feet, its tail arched forward.

"He's giving it to us," said Smith, in astonishment, "and Chouns, for God's sake, *look* at it."

Chouns was doing so, feverishly. He choked out, "They're Gamow hyperspatial sighters. Those are ten-thousand-dollar instruments."

Smith emerged from the ship again, after an hour within. He shouted from the ramp in high excitement. "They work. They're perfect. We're rich."

Chouns called back. "I've been checking through their huts. I can't find any more."

"Don't sneeze at just two. Good Lord, these are as negotiable as a handful of cash."

But Chouns still looked about, arms akimbo, exasperated. Three of the tailed creatures had dogged him from hut to hut—patiently, never interfering, but remaining always between him and the geometrically cultivated pale-pink blossoms. Now they stared multiply at him.

Smith said, "It's the latest model, too. Look here." He pointed to the raised lettering which said *Model X-20, Gamow Products, Warsaw, European Sector.*

Chouns glanced at it and said impatiently, "What interests me is getting more. I *know* there are more Gamow sighters somewhere, and I want them." His cheeks were flushed and his breathing heavy.

The sun was setting; the temperature dropped below the comfortable point. Smith sneezed twice, then Chouns.

"We'll catch pneumonia," snuffled Smith.

"I've got to make them understand," said Chouns stubbornly. He had eaten hastily through a can of pork sausage, had gulped down a can of coffee, and was ready to try again.

He held the sighter high. "More," he said, "more," making encircling movements with his arms. He pointed to one sighter, then to the other, then to the imaginary additional ones lined up before him. "More."

Then, as the last of the sun dipped below the horizon, a vast hum arose from all parts of the field as every creature in sight ducked its head, lifted its forked tail, and vibrated it into screaming invisibility in the twilight.

"What in Space," muttered Smith uneasily. "Hey, look at the blooms!" He sneezed again.

The pale-pink flowers were shriveling visibly.

Chouns shouted to make himself heard above the hum. "It may be a reaction to sunset. You know, the blooms close at night. The noise may be a religious observance of the fact."

A soft flick of a tail across his wrist attracted Chouns's instant attention. The tail he had felt belonged to the nearest creature; and now it was raised to the sky, toward a bright object low on the western horizon. The tail bent downward to point to the sighter, then up again to the star.

Chouns said excitedly, "Of course—the inner planet; the other habitable one. These must have come from there." Then, reminded by the thought, he cried in sudden shock, "Hey, Smith, the hyperatomic motors are still out."

Smith looked shocked, as though he had forgotten, too; then he mumbled, "Meant to tell you— They're all right."

"You fixed them?"

"Never touched them. But when I was testing the sighters, I used the hyperatomics and they worked. I didn't pay any attention at the time; I forgot there was anything wrong. Anyway, they worked."

"Then let's go," said Chouns at once. The thought of sleep never occurred to him.

Neither one slept through the six-hour trip. They remained at the controls in an almost drug-fed passion. Once again they chose a bare spot on which to land.

It was hot with an afternoon subtropical heat; and a broad, muddy river moved placidly by them. The near bank was of hardened mud, riddled with large cavities.

The two men stepped out onto planetary surface and Smith cried hoarsely, "Chouns, look at that!"

Chouns shook off the other's grasping hand. He said, "The same plants! I'll be damned."

There was no mistaking the pale-pink blossoms, the stalk with its veined buds, and the coronet of spikes below. Again there was the geometric spacing, the careful planting and fertilization, the irrigation canals.

Smith said, "We haven't made a mistake and circled—"

"Oh, look at the sun; it's twice the diameter it was before. And look there."

Out of the nearest burrows in the riverbank, smoothly tan and sinuous objects, as limbless as snakes, emerged. They were a foot in diameter, ten feet in length. The two ends were equally featureless, equally blunt. Midway along their upper portions were bulges. All the bulges, as though on signal, grew before their eyes to fat ovals, split in two to form lipless, gaping mouths that opened and closed with a sound like a forest of dry sticks clapping together.

Then, just as on the outer planet, once their curiosities were satisfied and their fears calmed, most of the creatures drifted away toward the carefully cultivated field of plants.

Smith sneezed. The force of expelled breath against the sleeve of his jacket raised a powdering of dust.

He stared at that with amazement, then slapped himself and said, "Damn it, I'm dusty." The dust rose, like a pale-pink fog. "You, too," he added, slapping Chouns.

Both men sneezed with abandon.

"Picked it up on the other planet, I suppose," said Chouns.

"We can work up an allergy."

"Impossible." Chouns held up one of the sighters and shouted at the snake-things, "Do you have any of these?"

For a while there was nothing in answer but the splashing of water, as some of the snake-things slid into the river and emerged with silvery clusters of water-life, which they tucked beneath their bodies toward some hidden mouth.

But then one snake-thing, longer than the others, came thrusting along the ground, one blunt end raised questingly some two inches, weaving blindly side to side. The bulb in its center swelled gently at first, then alarmingly, splitting in two with an audible pop. There, nestling within the two halves were two more sighters, the duplicates of the first two.

Chouns said ecstatically, "Lord in Heaven, isn't that beautiful?"

He stepped hastily forward, reaching out for the objects. The swelling that held them thinned and lengthened, forming what were almost tentacles. They reached out toward him.

Chouns was laughing. They were Gamow sighters all right; duplicates, absolute duplicates, of the first two. Chouns fondled them.

Smith was shouting, "Don't you hear me? Chouns, damn it, listen to me."

Chouns said, "What?" He was dimly aware that Smith had been yelling at him for over a minute.

"Look at the flowers, Chouns."

They were closing, as had those on the other planet, and among the rows, the snake-things reared upward, balancing on one end and swaying with a queer, broken rhythm. Only the blunt ends of them were visible above the pale pink.

Smith said, "You can't say they're closing up because of nightfall. It's broad day."

Chouns shrugged. "Different planet, different plant. Come on! We've only got two sighters here; there must be more."

"Chouns, let's go home." Smith firmed his legs into two stubborn pillars and the grip he held on Chouns's collar tightened.

Chouns's reddened face turned back toward him indignantly. "What are you doing?"

"I'm getting ready to knock you out if you don't come back with me at once into the ship."

For a moment, Chouns stood irresolute; then a certain wildness about him faded, a certain slackening took place, and he said, "All right."

They were half out of the star cluster. Smith said, "How are you?"

Chouns sat up in his bunk and rumpled his hair. "Normal, I guess; sane again. How long have I been sleeping?"

"Twelve hours."

"What about you?"

"I've catnapped." Smith turned ostentatiously to the instruments and made some minor adjustments. He said self-consciously, "Do you know what happened back there on those planets?"

Chouns said slowly, "Do you?"

"I think so."

"Oh? May I hear?"

Smith said, "It was the same plant on both planets. You'll grant that?"

"I most certainly do."

"It was transplanted from one planet to the other somehow. It grows on both planets perfectly well; but occasionally—to maintain vigor, I imagine—there must be cross-fertilization, the two strains mingling. That sort of thing happens on Earth often enough."

"Cross-fertilization for vigor? Yes."

"But *we* were the agents that arranged for the mingling.

We landed on one planet and were coated with pollen. Remember the blooms closing? That must have been just after they released their pollen; and that's what was making us sneeze, too. Then we landed on the other planet and knocked the pollen off our clothes. A new hybrid strain will start up. We were just a pair of two-legged bees, Chouns, doing our duty by the flowers."

Chouns smiled tentatively, "An inglorious role, in a way."

"Hell, that's not it. Don't you see the danger? Don't you see why we have to get back home *fast?*"

"Why?"

"Because organisms don't adapt themselves to nothing. Those plants seem to be adapted to interplanetary fertilization. We even got paid off, the way bees are; not with nectar, but with Gamow sighters."

"Well?"

"Well, you can't have interplanetary fertilization unless something or someone is there to do the job. *We* did it this time, but we were the first humans ever to enter the cluster. So, before this, it must be non-humans who did it; maybe the same non-humans who transplanted the blooms in the first place. That means that somewhere in this cluster there is an intelligent race of beings; intelligent enough for space travel. And Earth must know about that."

Slowly Chouns shook his head.

Smith frowned. "You find flaws somewhere in the reasoning?"

Chouns put his head between his own palms and looked miserable. "Let's say you've missed almost everything."

"What have I missed?" demanded Smith, angrily.

"Your cross-fertilization theory is good, as far as it goes, but you haven't considered a few points. When we approached that stellar system, our hyperatomic motor went out of order in a way the automatic controls could neither diagnose nor correct. After we landed, we made no effort to adjust them. We forgot about them, in fact; and when you handled them later you found they were in perfect order, and were so unimpressed by that that you didn't even mention it to me for another few hours.

"Take something else: How conveniently we chose the landing spots near a grouping of animal life on both planets. Just luck? And our incredible confidence in the goodwill of the creatures. We never even bothered checking atmospheres for trace poisons before exposing ourselves.

"And what bothers me most of all is that I went completely crazy over the Gamow sighters. Why? They're valuable, yes, but not *that* valuable—and I don't generally go overboard for a quick buck."

Smith had kept an uneasy silence during all that. Now he said, "I don't see that any of that adds up to anything."

"Get off it, Smith; you know better than that. Isn't it obvious to you that we were under mental control from the outside?"

Smith's mouth twisted and caught halfway between derision and doubt. "Are you on the psionic kick again?"

"Yes; facts are facts. I told you that my hunches might be a form of rudimentary telepathy."

"Is that a fact, too? You didn't think so a couple of days ago."

"I think so now. Look, I'm a better receiver than you, and I was more strongly affected. Now that it's over, I understand more about what happened because I received more. Understand?"

"No," said Smith harshly.

"Then listen further. You said yourself the Gamow sighters were the nectar that bribed us into pollination. *You* said that."

"All right."

"Well, then, where did they come from? They were Earth products; we even read the manufacturer's name and model on them, letter by letter. Yet, if no human beings have ever been in the cluster, where did the sighters come from? Neither one of us worried about that, then; and you don't seem to worry about it even now."

"Well—"

"What did you do with the sighters after we got on board ship, Smith? You took them from me; I remember that."

"I put them in the safe," said Smith defensively.

"Have you touched them since?"

"No."

"Have I?"

"Not as far as I know."

"You have my word I didn't. Then why not open the safe now?"

Smith stepped slowly to the safe. It was keyed to his fingerprints, and it opened. Without looking, he reached in. His expression altered and with a sharp cry he first stared at the contents, then scrabbled them out.

He held four rocks of assorted color, each of them roughly rectangular.

"They used our own emotions to drive us," said Chouns softly, as though insinuating the words into the other's stubborn skull one at a time. "They made us think the hyperatomics were wrong so we could land on one of the planets; it didn't matter which, I suppose. They made us think we had precision instruments in our hand after we landed on one so we would race to the other."

"Who are they?" groaned Smith. "The tails or the snakes? Or both?"

"Neither," said Chouns. "It was the plants."

"The plants? The *flowers?*"

"Certainly. We saw two different sets of animals tending

the same species of plant. Being animals ourselves, we assumed the animals were the masters. But why should we assume that? It was the plants that were being taken care of."

"We cultivate plants on Earth, too, Chouns."

"But we eat those plants," said Chouns.

"And maybe those creatures eat their plants, too."

"Let's say I know they don't," said Chouns. "They maneuvered us well enough. Remember how careful I was to find a bare spot on which to land."

"*I* felt no such urge."

"You weren't at the controls; they weren't worried about you. Then, too, remember that we never noticed the pollen, though we were covered with it—not till we were safely on the second planet. Then we dusted the pollen off, on order."

"I never heard anything so impossible."

"Why is it impossible? We don't associate intelligence with plants, because plants have no nervous systems; but these might have. Remember the fleshy buds on the stems? Also, plants aren't free-moving; but they don't have to be if they develop psionic powers and can make use of free-moving animals. They get cared for, fertilized, irrigated, pollinated, and so on. The animals tend them with single-minded devotion and are happy over it because the plants make them feel happy."

"I'm sorry for you," said Smith, in a monotone. "If you try to tell this story back on Earth, I'm sorry for you."

"I have no illusions," muttered Chouns, "yet—what can I do but try to warn Earth. You see what they do to animals."

"They make slaves of them, according to you."

"Worse than that. Either the tailed creatures, or the snake-things, or both, must have been civilized enough to have developed space travel once; otherwise, the plants couldn't be on both planets. But once the plants developed psionic powers (a mutant strain perhaps) that came to an end. Animals at the atomic stage are dangerous. So they were made to forget; they were reduced to what they are. Damn it, Smith, those plants are the most dangerous things in the Universe. Earth must be informed about them, because some day Earthmen may be entering that cluster."

Smith laughed. "You know, you're completely off base. If those plants really had us under control, why would they let us get away to warn the others?"

Chouns paused. "I don't know."

Smith's good humor was restored. He said, "For a minute, you had me going, I don't mind telling you."

Chouns rubbed his skull violently. Why *were* they let go? And for that matter, why did he feel this horrible urgency to warn Earth about a matter with which Earthmen would not come into contact for millennia perhaps?

He thought desperately and something came glimmering. He fumbled for it, but it drifted away. For a moment he thought desperately that it was as though the thought had been *pushed* away; but then that feeling, too, left.

He knew only that the ship had to remain at full thrust; that they had to hurry.

So, after uncounted years, the proper conditions had come about again. The protospores from two planetary strains of the mother plant met and mingled, sifting together into the clothes and hair and ship of the new animals. Almost at once, the hybrid spores formed; the hybrid spores that alone had all the capacity and potentiality of adapting themselves to a new planet.

The spores waited quietly, now, on the ship which, with the last impulse of the mother plant upon the minds of the creatures aboard, was hurtling them at top thrust toward a new and ripe world where free-moving creatures would tend their needs.

The spores waited with the patience of the plant (the all-conquering patience no animal can ever know) for their arrival on a new world—each, in its own tiny way, an explorer—

VASTER THAN EMPIRES, AND MORE SLOW

Ursula K. Le Guin

When Ursula K. Le Guin's novel The Farthest Shore *received the 1972 National Book Award for Children's Literature, the world of general publishing thereby confirmed what had been recognized for some years within the smaller world of science fiction: that Mrs. Le Guin is a writer of soaring vision and extraordinary accomplishment. Her stories had been appearing in science-fiction magazines since 1962, and, after publishing several well-received novels, she carried off both the Hugo and Nebula trophies for her 1969 book,* The Left Hand of Darkness, *now considered a modern science-fiction classic. Her work is marked not only by eloquent prose and sensitive insight into character but also by a strong grasp of the forces that shape and change a culture—not so surprising when one considers that her father, Alfred Kroeber, was perhaps the greatest of American anthropologists, and that her mother, Theodora Kroeber, wrote that superb portrait of the vanishing Indians of California,* Ishi in Two Worlds.

The story reprinted here takes its title from a poem by Andrew Marvell (1621–1678), To His Coy Mistress:

> *My vegetable love should grow*
> *Vaster than empires, and more slow.*

Rarely has the familiar theme of planetary exploration been handled with such imagination and with such grace of style.

You're looking at a clock. It has hands, and figures arranged in a circle. The hands move. You can't tell if they move at the same rate, or if one moves faster than the other. What does *than* mean? There is a relationship between the hands and the circle of figures, and the name of this relationship is on the tip of your tongue; the hands are . . . something-or-other, at the figures. Or is it the figures that . . . at the hands? What does *at* mean? They are figures—your vocabulary hasn't shrunk at all— and of course you can count, one two three four etc., but the trouble is you can't tell which one is one. Each one is one: itself. Where do you begin? Each one being one, there is no, what's the word, I had it just now, something-ship, between the ones. There is no between. There is only here and here, one and one. There is no there. Maya has fallen. All is here now one. But if all is now and all here and one all, there is no end. It did not begin so it cannot end. Oh God, here now One get me out of this—

I'm trying to describe the sensations of the average person in NAFAL flight. It can be much worse than this for some, whose time-sense is acute. For others it is restful, like a drug-haze freeing the mind from the tyranny of hours. And for a few the experience is certainly mystical; the collapse of time and relation leading them directly to intuition of the eternal. But the mystic is a rare bird, and the nearest most people get to God in paradoxical time is by inarticulate and anguished prayer for release.

They used to drug people for the long jumps, but stopped the practice when they realized its effects. What happens to a drugged, or ill, or wounded person during near light-speed flight is, of course, indeterminable. A jump of ten light-years should logically make no difference to a victim of measles or gunshot. The body ages only a few minutes; why is the measles patient carried out of the ship a leper, and the wounded man a corpse? Nobody knows, except perhaps the body, which keeps the logic of the flesh, and knows it has lain festering, bleeding, or drugged into mindlessness, for ten years. Many imbeciles having been produced, the Fisher King Effect was established as fact, and they stopped using drugs and transporting the ill, the damaged, and the pregnant. You have to be in common health to go NAFAL, and you have to take it straight.

But you don't have to be sane.

It was only during the earliest decades of the League that Earthmen, perhaps trying to bolster their battered collective ego, sent out ships on enormously long voyages, beyond the pale, over the stars and far away. They were seeking for worlds that had not, like all the known worlds, been settled or seeded by the Founders on Hain, truly alien worlds; and all the crews of these Extreme Surveys were of unsound mind. Who else would go out to collect information that wouldn't be received for four, or five, or six centuries? Received by whom? This was before the invention of the instantaneous communicator; they would be isolated both in space and time. No sane person who has experienced time-slippage of even a few decades between near worlds would volunteer for a round trip of a half millennium. The Surveyors were escapists, misfits, nuts.

Ten of them climbed aboard the ferry at Smeming Port on Pesm, and made varyingly inept attempts to get to know one another during the three days the ferry took getting to their ship, *Gum*. Gum is a Low Cetian nickname, on the order of Baby or Pet. There was one Low Cetian on the team, one Hairy Cetian, two Hainishmen, one Beldene, and five Terrans; the ship was Cetian-built, but chartered by the Government of Earth. Her motley crew came aboard wriggling through the coupling-tube one by one like apprehensive spermatozoa fertilizing the universe. The ferry left, and the navigator put *Gum* under way. She flittered for some hours on the edge of space a few hundred million miles from Pesm, and then abruptly vanished.

When, after ten hours twenty-nine minutes, or 256 years, *Gum* reappeared in normal space, she was supposed to be in the vicinity of Star KG-E-96651. Sure enough, there was the cheerful gold pinhead of the star. Somewhere within a 400-million-kilometer sphere there was also a greenish planet, World 4470, as charted by a Cetian mapmaker long ago. The ship now had to find the planet. This was not quite so easy as it might sound, given a 400-million-kilometer haystack. And *Gum* couldn't bat about in planetary space at near lightspeed; if she did, she and Star KG-E-96651 and World 4470 might all end up going bang. She had to creep, using rocket propulsion, at a few hundred thousand miles an hour. The Mathematician/Navigator, Asnanifoil, knew pretty well where the planet ought to be, and thought they might raise it within ten E-days. Meanwhile the members of the Survey team got to know one another still better.

"I can't stand him," said Porlock, the Hard Scientist (chemistry, plus physics, astronomy, geology, etc.), and little blobs of spittle appeared on his mustache. "The man is insane. I can't imagine why he was passed as fit to join a Survey team, unless this is a deliberate experiment in non-compatibility, planned by the Authority, with us as guinea pigs."

"We generally use hamsters and Hainish gholes," said Mannon, the Soft Scientist (psychology, plus psychiatry, anthropology, ecology, etc.), politely; he was one of the Hainishmen. "Instead of guinea pigs. Well, you know, Mr. Osden is really a very rare case. In fact, he's the first fully cured case of Render's Syndrome—a variety of infantile autism which was thought to be incurable. The great Terran analyst Hammergeld reasoned that the cause of the autistic condition in this case is a supernormal emphatic capacity, and developed an appropriate treatment. Mr. Osden is the first patient to undergo that treatment, in fact he lived with Dr. Hammergeld until he was eighteen. The therapy was completely successful."

"Successful?"

"Why, yes. He certainly is not autistic."

"No, he's intolerable!"

"Well, you see," said Mannon, gazing mildly at the saliva flecks on Porlock's mustache, "the normal defensive-aggressive reaction between strangers meeting—let's say you and Mr. Osden just for example—is something you're scarcely aware of; habit, manners, inattention get you past it; you've learned to ignore it, to the point where you might even deny it exists. However, Mr. Osden, being an empath, feels it. Feels his feelings, and yours, and is hard put to say which is which. Let's say that there's a normal element of hostility towards any stranger in your emotional reaction to him when you meet him, plus a spontaneous dislike of his looks, or clothes, or handshake—it doesn't matter what. He feels that dislike. As his autistic defense has been unlearned, he resorts to an aggressive-defense mechanism, a response in kind to the aggression which you have unwittingly projected onto him." Mannon went on for quite a long time.

"Nothing gives a man the right to be such a bastard," Porlock said.

"He can't tune us out?" asked Harfex, the Biologist, another Hainishman.

"It's like hearing," said Olleroo, Assistant Hard Scientist, stooping over to paint her toenails with fluorescent lacquer. "No eyelids on your ears. No Off switch on empathy. He hears our feelings whether he wants to or not."

"Does he know what we're *thinking*?" asked Eskwana,

the Engineer, looking around at the others in real dread.

"No," Porlock snapped. "Empathy's not telepathy! Nobody's got telepathy."

"Yet," said Mannon, with his little smile. "Just before I left Hain there was a most interesting report in from one of the recently rediscovered worlds, a hilfer named Rocannon reporting what appears to be a teachable telepathic technique existent among a mutated hominid race; I only saw a synopsis of the HILF *Bulletin,* but—" He went on. The others had learned that they could talk while Mannon went on talking; he did not seem to mind, nor even to miss much of what they said.

"Then why does he hate us?" Eskwana asked.

"Nobody hates you, Ander honey," said Olleroo, daubing Eskwana's left thumbnail with fluorescent pink. The engineer flushed and smiled vaguely.

"He acts as if he hated us," said Haito, the Coordinator. She was a delicate-looking woman of pure Asian descent, with a surprising voice, husky, deep, and soft, like a young bullfrog. "Why, if he suffers from our hostility, does he increase it by constant attacks and insults? I can't say I think much of Dr. Hammergeld's cure, really, Mannon; autism might be preferable . . ."

She stopped. Osden had come into the main cabin.

He looked flayed. His skin was unnaturally white and thin, showing the channels of his blood like a faded road map in red and blue. His Adam's apple, the muscles that circled his mouth, the bones and ligaments of his wrists and hands, all stood out distinctly as if displayed for an anatomy lesson. His hair was pale rust, like long-dried blood. He had eyebrows and lashes, but they were visible only in certain lights; what one saw was the bones of the eyesockets, the veining of the lids, and the colorless eyes. They were not red eyes, for he was not really an albino, but they were not blue or gray; colors had canceled out in Osden's eyes, leaving a cold waterlike clarity, infinitely penetrable. He never looked directly at one. His face lacked expression, like an anatomical drawing, or a skinned face.

"I agree," he said in a high, harsh tenor, "that even autistic withdrawal might be preferable to the smog of cheap secondhand emotions with which you people surround me. What are you sweating hate for now, Porlock? Can't stand the sight of me? Go practice some autoeroticism the way you were doing last night, it improves your vibes. Who the devil moved my tapes, here? Don't touch my things, any of you. I won't have it."

"Osden," said Asnanifoil, the Hairy Cetian, in his large slow voice, "why *are* you such a bastard?"

Ander Eskwana cowered down and put his hands in front of his face. Contention frightened him. Olleroo looked up with a vacant yet eager expression, the eternal spectator.

"Why shouldn't I be?" said Osden. He was not looking at Asnanifoil, and was keeping physically as far away from all of them as he could in the crowded cabin. "None of you constitute, in yourselves, any reason for my changing my behavior."

Asnanifoil shrugged; Cetians are seldom willing to state the obvious. Harfex, a reserved and patient man, said, "The reason is that we shall be spending several years together. Life will be better for all of us if—"

"Can't you understand that I don't give a damn for all of you?" Osden said, took up his microtapes, and went out. Eskwana had suddenly gone to sleep. Asnanifoil was drawing slipstreams in the air with his finger and muttering the Ritual Primes. "You cannot explain his presence on the team except as a plot on the part of the Terran Authority. I saw this almost at once. This mission is meant to fail," Harfex whispered to the Coordinator, glancing over his shoulder. Porlock was fumbling with his fly-button; there were tears in his eyes. I did tell you they were all crazy, but you thought I was exaggerating.

All the same, they were not unjustified. Extreme Surveyors expected to find their fellow team members intelligent, well trained, unstable, and personally sympathetic. They had to work together in close quarters and nasty places, and could expect one another's paranoias, depressions, manias, phobias, and compulsions to be mild enough to admit of good personal relationships, at least most of the time. Osden might be intelligent, but his training was sketchy and his personality was disastrous. He had been sent only on account of his singular gift, the power of empathy: properly speaking, of wide-range bioempathic receptivity. His talent wasn't species-specific; he could pick up emotion or sentience from anything that felt. He could share lust with a white rat, pain with a squashed cockroach, and phototrophy with a moth. On an alien world, the Authority had decided, it would be useful to know if anything nearby is sentient, and if so, what its feelings towards you are. Osden's title was a new one; he was the team's Sensor.

"What is emotion, Osden?" Haito Tomiko asked him one day in the main cabin, trying to make some rapport with him for once. "What is it, exactly, that you pick up with your empathic sensitivity?"

"Muck," the man answered in his high, exasperated voice. "The psychic excreta of the animal kingdom. I wade through your feces."

"I was trying," she said, "to learn some facts." She thought her tone was admirably calm.

"You weren't after facts. You were trying to get at me. With some fear, some curiosity, and a great deal of distaste. The way you might poke a dead dog, to see the maggots crawl. Will you understand once and for all that I don't want to be got at, that I want to be left alone?" His skin was mottled with red and violet, his voice had risen. "Go roll in your own dung, you yellow bitch!" he shouted at her silence.

"Calm down," she said, still quietly, but she left him at once and went to her cabin. Of course he had been right about her motives; her question had been largely a pretext, a mere effort to interest him. But what harm in that? Did not that effort imply respect for the other? At the moment of asking the question she had felt at most a slight distrust of him; she had mostly felt sorry for him, the poor arrogant venomous bastard, Mr. No-Skin, as Olleroo called him. What did he expect, the way he acted? Love?

"I guess he can't stand anybody feeling sorry for him," said Olleroo, lying on the lower bunk, gilding her nipples.

"Then he can't form any human relationship. All his Dr. Hammergeld did was turn an autism inside out. . . ."

"Poor frot," said Olleroo. "Tomiko, you don't mind if Harfex comes in for a while tonight, do you?"

"Can't you go to his cabin? I'm sick of always having to sit in Main with that damned peeled turnip."

"You do hate him, don't you? I guess he feels that. But I slept with Harfex last night too, and Asnanifoil might get jealous, since they share the cabin. It would be nicer here."

"Service them both," Tomiko said with the coarseness of offended modesty. Her Terran subculture, the East Asian, was a puritanical one; she had been brought up chaste.

"I only like one a night," Olleroo replied with innocent serenity. Beldene, the Garden Planet, had never discovered chastity, or the wheel.

"Try Osden, then," Tomiko said. Her personal instability was seldom so plain as now: a profound self-distrust manifesting itself as destructivism. She had volunteered for this job because there was, in all probability, no use in doing it.

The little Beldene looked up, paintbrush in hand, eyes wide. "Tomiko, that was a dirty thing to say."

"Why?"

"It would be vile! I'm not attracted to Osden!"

"I didn't know it mattered to you," Tomiko said indifferently, though she did know. She got some papers together and left the cabin, remarking, "I hope you and Harfex or whoever it is finish by last bell; I'm tired."

Olleroo was crying, tears dripping on her little gilded nipples. She wept easily. Tomiko had not wept since she was ten years old.

It was not a happy ship; but it took a turn for the better when Asnanifoil and his computer raised World 4470. There it lay, a dark-green jewel, like the truth at the bottom of a gravity well. As they watched the jade disk grow, a sense of mutuality grew among them. Osden's selfishness, his accurate cruelty, served now to draw the others together. "Perhaps," Mannon said, "he was sent as a beating-gron. What Terrans call a scapegoat. Perhaps his influence will be good after all." And no one, so careful were they to be kind to one another, disagreed.

They came into orbit. There were no lights on nightside, on the continents none of the lines and clots made by animals who build.

"No men," Harfex murmured.

"Of course not," snapped Osden, who had a viewscreen to himself, and his head inside a polythene bag. He claimed that the plastic cut down on the empathic noise he received from the others. "We're two light-centuries past the limit of the Hainish Expansion, and outside that there are no men. Anywhere. You don't think Creation would have made the same hideous mistake twice?"

No one was paying him much heed; they were looking with affection at that jade immensity below them, where there was life, but not human life. They were misfits among men, and what they saw there was not desolation, but peace. Even Osden did not look quite so expressionless as usual; he was frowning.

Descent in fire on the sea; air reconnaissance; landing. A plain of something like grass, thick, green, bowing stalks, surrounded the ship, brushed against extended view-cameras, smeared the lenses with a fine pollen.

"It looks like a pure phytosphere," Harfex said. "Osden, do you pick up anything sentient?"

They all turned to the Sensor. He had left the screen and was pouring himself a cup of tea. He did not answer. He seldom answered spoken questions.

The chitinous rigidity of military discipline was quite inapplicable to these teams of Mad Scientists; their chain of command lay somewhere between parliamentary procedure and peck-order, and would have driven a regular service officer out of his mind. By the inscrutable decision of the Authority, however, Dr. Haito Tomiko had been given the title of Coordinator, and she now exercised her prerogative for the first time. "Mr. Sensor Osden," she said, "please answer Mr. Harfex."

"How could I 'pick up' anything from outside," Osden said without turning, "with the emotions of nine neurotic hominids pullulating around me like worms in a can? When I have anything to tell you, I'll tell you. I'm aware of my responsibility as Sensor. If you presume to give me an order again, however, Coordinator Haito, I'll consider my responsibility void."

"Very well, Mr. Sensor. I trust no orders will be needed henceforth." Tomiko's bullfrog voice was calm, but Osden seemed to flinch slightly as he stood with his back to her: as if the surge of her suppressed rancor had struck him with physical force.

The Biologist's hunch proved correct. When they began field analyses they found no animals even among the micro-biota. Nobody here ate anybody else. All life-forms were photosynthesizing or saprophagous, living off light or death, not off life. Plants: infinite plants, not one species known to the visitors from the house of Man. Infinite shades and intensities of green, violet, purple, brown, red. Infinite silences. Only the wind moved, swaying leaves and fronds, a warm soughing wind laden with spores and pollens, blowing the sweet pale-green dust over prairies of great grasses, heaths that bore no heather, flowerless forests where no foot had ever walked, no eye had ever looked. A warm, sad world, sad and serene. The Surveyors, wandering like pic-nickers over sunny plains of violet filicaliformes, spoke softly to each other. They knew their voices broke a silence of a thousand million years, the silence of wind and leaves, leaves and wind, blowing and ceasing and blowing again. They talked softly; but being human, they talked.

"Poor old Osden," said Jenny Chong, Bio and Tech, as she piloted a helijet on the North Polar Quadrating run. "All that fancy hi-fi stuff in his brain and nothing to receive. What a bust."

"He told me he hates plants," Olleroo said with a giggle. "You'd think he'd like them, since they don't bother him like we do."

"Can't say I much like these plants myself," said Porlock, looking down at the purple undulations of the North Cir-cumpolar Forest. "All the same. No mind. No change. A man alone in it would go right off his head."

"But it's all alive," Jenny Chong said. "And if it lives, Osden hates it."

"He's not really so bad," Olleroo said, magnanimous. Porlock looked at her sidelong and asked, "You ever slept with him, Olleroo?"

Olleroo burst into tears and cried, "You Terrans are obscene!"

"No she hasn't," Jenny Chong said, prompt to defend. "Have you, Porlock?"

The Chemist laughed uneasily: Ha, ha, ha. Flecks of spittle appeared on his mustache.

"Osden can't bear to be touched," Olleroo said shakily. "I just brushed against him once by accident and he knocked me off like I was some sort of dirty . . . thing. We're all just things, to him."

"He's evil," Porlock said in a strained voice, startling the two women. "He'll end up shattering this team, sabotaging it, one way or another. Mark my words. He's not fit to live with other people!"

They landed on the North Pole. A midnight sun smoldered over low hills. Short, dry, greenish-pink bryoform grasses stretched away in every direction, which was all one direction, south. Subdued by the incredible silence, the three Surveyors set up their instruments and collected their samples, three viruses twitching minutely on the hide of an unmoving giant.

Nobody asked Osden along on runs as pilot or photographer or recorder, and he never volunteered, so he seldom left base camp. He ran Harfex's botanical taxonomic data through the on-ship computers and served as assistant to Eskwana, whose job here was mainly repair and maintenance. Eskwana had begun to sleep a great deal, twenty-five hours or more out of the thirty-two-hour day, dropping off in the middle of repairing a radio or checking the guidance circuits of a helijet. The Coordinator stayed at base one day to observe. No one else was home except Poswet To, who was subject to epileptic fits; Mannon had plugged her into a therapy-circuit today in a state of preventive catatonia. Tomiko spoke reports into the storage banks, and kept an eye on Osden and Eskwana. Two hours passed.

"You might want to use the 860 microwaldoes in sealing that connection," Eskwana said in his soft, hesitant voice.

"Obviously!"

"Sorry. I just saw you had the 840's there—"

"And will replace them when I take the 860's out. When I don't know how to proceed, Engineer, I'll ask your advice."

After a minute Tomiko looked around. Sure enough, there was Eskwana sound asleep, head on the table, thumb in his mouth.

"Osden!"

The white face did not turn, he did not speak, but conveyed impatiently that he was listening.

"You can't be unaware of Eskwana's vulnerability."

"I am not responsible for his psychopathic reactions."

"But you are responsible for your own. Eskwana is essential to our work here, and you're not. If you can't control your hostility, you must avoid him altogether."

Osden put down his tools and stood up. "With pleasure!" he said in his vindictive, scraping voice. "You could not possibly imagine what it's like to *experience* Eskwana's irrational terrors. To have to share his horrible cowardice, to have to cringe with him at everything!"

"Are you trying to justify your cruelty towards him? I thought you had more self-respect." Tomiko found herself shaking with spite. "If your empathic power really makes you share Ander's misery, why does it never induce the least compassion in you?"

"Compassion," Osden said. "Compassion. What do you know about compassion?"

She stared at him, but he would not look at her.

"Would you like me to verbalize your present emotional affect regarding myself?" he said. "I can do so more precisely than you can. I'm trained to analyze such responses as I receive them. And I do receive them."

"But how can you expect me to feel kindly towards you when you behave as you do?"

"What does it matter how I *behave*, you stupid sow, do you think it makes any difference? Do you think the average human is a well of loving kindness? My choice is to be hated or to be despised. Not being a woman or a coward, I prefer to be hated."

"That's rot. Self-pity. Every man has—"

"But I am not a man," Osden said. "There are all of you. And there is myself. I am *one*."

Awed by that glimpse of abysmal solipsism, she kept silent a while; finally she said with neither spite nor pity, clinically, "You could kill yourself, Osden."

"That's your way, Haito," he jeered. "I'm not depressive and *seppuku* isn't my bit. What do you want me to do here?"

"Leave. Spare yourself and us. Take the aircar and a data-feeder and go do a species count. In the forest; Harfex hasn't even started the forests yet. Take a hundred-square-meter forested area inside radio range. But outside empathy range. Report in at eight and twenty-four o'clock daily."

Osden went, and nothing was heard from him for five days but laconic all-well signals twice daily. The mood at base camp changed like a stage set. Eskwana stayed awake up to eighteen hours a day. Poswet To got out her stellar lute and chanted the celestial harmonies (music had driven Osden into a frenzy). Mannon, Harfex, Jenny Chong, and Tomiko all went off tranquilizers. Porlock distilled something in his laboratory and drank it all by himself. He had a hangover. Asnanifoil and Poswet To held an all-night Numerical Epiphany, that mystical orgy of higher mathematics which is the chiefest pleasure of the religious Cetian soul. Olleroo slept with everybody. Work went well.

The Hard Scientist came towards base at a run, laboring through the high, fleshy stalks of the graminiformes. "Something—in the forest—" His eyes bulged, he panted, his mustache and fingers trembled. "Something big. Moving, behind me. I was putting in a benchmark, bending down. It came at me. As if it was swinging down out of the trees. Behind me." He stared at the others with the opaque eyes of terror or exhaustion.

"Sit down, Porlock. Take it easy. Now wait, go through this again. You *saw* something—"

"Not clearly. Just the movement. Purposive. A—an—I don't know what it could have been. Something self-moving. In the trees, the arboriformes, whatever you call 'em. At the edge of the woods."

Harfex looked grim. "There is nothing here that could attack you, Porlock. There are not even microzoa. There *could not* be a large animal."

"Could you possibly have seen an epiphyte drop suddenly, a vine come loose behind you?"

"No," Porlock said. "It was coming down at me, through the branches, fast. When I turned it took off again, away and upward. It made a noise, a sort of crashing. If it wasn't an animal, God knows what it could have been! It was big—as big as a man, at least. Maybe a reddish color. I couldn't see, I'm not sure."

"It was Osden," said Jenny Chong, "doing a Tarzan act." She giggled nervously, and Tomiko repressed a wild feckless laugh. But Harfex was not smiling.

"One gets uneasy under the arboriformes," he said in his polite, repressed voice. "I've noticed that. Indeed that may be why I've put off working in the forest. There's a hypnotic quality in the colors and spacing of the stems and branches, especially the helically arranged ones; and the spore-throwers grow so regularly spaced that it seems unnatural. I find it quite disagreeable, subjectively speaking. I wonder if a stronger effect of that sort mightn't have produced a hallucination . . . ?"

Porlock shook his head. He wet his lips. "It was there," he said. "Something. Moving with purpose. Trying to attack me from behind."

When Osden called in, punctual as always, at twenty-four o'clock that night, Harfex told him Porlock's report. "Have you come on anything at all, Mr. Osden, that could substantiate Mr. Porlock's impression of a motile, sentient life-form, in the forest?"

Ssss, the radio said sardonically. "No. Bullshit," said Osden's unpleasant voice.

"You've been actually inside the forest longer than any of us," Harfex said with unmitigable politeness. "Do you agree with my impression that the forest ambiance has a rather troubling and possibly hallucinogenic effect on the perceptions?"

Ssss. "I'll agree that Porlock's perceptions are easily troubled. Keep him in his lab, he'll do less harm. Anything else?"

"Not at present," Harfex said, and Osden cut off.

Nobody could credit Porlock's story, and nobody could discredit it. He was positive that something, something big, had tried to attack him by surprise. It was hard to deny this, for they were on an alien world, and everyone who had entered the forest had felt a certain chill and foreboding under the "trees." ("Call them trees, certainly," Harfex had said. "They really are the same thing, only, of course, altogether different.") They agreed that they had felt uneasy, or had had the sense that something was watching them from behind.

"We've got to clear this up," Porlock said, and he asked to be sent as a temporary Biologist's Aide, like Osden, into the forest to explore and observe. Olleroo and Jenny Chong volunteered if they could go as a pair. Harfex sent them all off into the forest near which they were encamped, a vast tract covering four-fifths of Continent D. He forbade side arms. They were not to go outside of fifty-kilo half-circle, which included Osden's current site. They all reported in twice daily, for three days. Porlock reported a glimpse of what seemed to be a large semi-erect shape moving through the trees across the river; Olleroo was sure she had heard something moving near the tent the second night.

"There are no animals on this planet," Harfex said, dogged.

Then Osden missed his morning call.

Tomiko waited less than an hour, then flew with Harfex to the area where Osden had reported himself the night before. But as the helijet hovered over the sea of purplish leaves, illimitable, impenetrable, she felt a panic despair. "How can we find him in this?"

"He reported landing on the riverbank. Find the aircar; he'll be camped near it, and he can't have gone far from his camp. Species-counting is slow work. There's the river."

"There's his car," Tomiko said, catching the bright foreign glint among the vegetable colors and shadows. "Here goes, then."

She put the ship in hover and pitched out the ladder. She and Harfex descended. The sea of life closed over their heads.

As her feet touched the forest floor, she unsnapped the flap of her holster; then glancing at Harfex, who was unarmed, she left the gun untouched. But her hand kept coming back up to it. There was no sound at all, as soon as they were a few meters away from the slow, brown river, and the light was dim. Great boles stood well apart, almost regularly, almost alike; they were soft-skinned, some appearing smooth and others spongy, gray or greenish-brown or brown, twined with cablelike creepers and festooned with epiphytes, extending rigid, entangled armfuls of big, saucer-shaped, dark leaves that formed a roof-layer twenty to thirty meters thick. The ground underfoot was springy as a mattress, every inch of it knotted with roots and peppered with small, fleshy-leaved growths.

"Here's his tent," Tomiko said, cowed at the sound of her voice in that huge community of the voiceless. In the tent was Osden's sleeping bag, a couple of books, a box of rations. We should be calling, shouting for him, she thought, but did not even suggest it; nor did Harfex. They circled out from the tent, careful to keep each other in sight through the thick-standing presences, the crowding gloom. She stumbled over Osden's body, not thirty meters from the tent, led to it by the whitish gleam of a dropped notebook. He lay face down between two huge-rooted trees. His head and hands were covered with blood, some dried, some still oozing red.

Harfex appeared beside her, his pale Hainish complexion quite green in the dusk. "Dead?"

"No. He's been struck. Beaten. From behind." Tomiko's fingers felt over the bloody skull and nape and temples. "A weapon or a tool . . . I don't find a fracture."

As she turned Osden's body over so they could lift him, his eyes opened. She was holding him, bending close to his face. His pale lips writhed. A deathly fear came into her. She screamed aloud two or three times and tried to run away, shambling and stumbling into the terrible dusk. Harfex caught her, and at his touch and the sound of his voice, her panic decreased. "What is it? What is it?" he was saying.

"I don't know," she sobbed. Her heartbeat still shook her, and she could not see clearly. "The fear—the . . . I panicked. When I saw his eyes."

"We're both nervous. I don't understand this—"

"I'm all right now, come on, we've got to get him under care."

Both working with senseless haste, they lugged Osden to the riverside and hauled him up on a rope under his armpits; he dangled like a sack, twisting a little, over the glutinous dark sea of leaves. They pulled him into the helijet and took off. Within a minute they were over open prairie. Tomiko locked onto the homing beam. She drew a deep breath, and her eyes met Harfex's.

"I was so terrified I almost fainted. I have never done that."

"I was . . . unreasonably frightened also," said the Hainishman, and indeed he looked aged and shaken. "Not so badly as you. But as unreasonably."

"It was when I was in contact with him, holding him. He seemed to be conscious for a moment."

"Empathy? . . . I hope he can tell us what attacked him."

Osden, like a broken dummy covered with blood and mud, half-lay as they had bundled him into the rear seats in their frantic urgency to get out of the forest.

More panic met their arrival at base. The ineffective brutality of the assault was sinister and bewildering. Since Harfex stubbornly denied any possibility of animal life they began speculating about sentient plants, vegetable monsters, psychic projections. Jenny Chong's latent phobia reasserted itself and she could talk about nothing except the Dark Egos which followed people around behind their backs. She and Olleroo and Porlock had been summoned back to base; and nobody was much inclined to go outside.

Osden had lost a good deal of blood during the three or

four hours he had lain alone, and concussion and severe contusions had put him in shock and semi-coma. As he came out of this and began running a low fever he called several times for "Doctor," in a plaintive voice: "Doctor Hammergeld . . ." When he regained full consciousness, two of those long days later, Tomiko called Harfex into his cubicle.

"Osden, can you tell us what attacked you?"

The pale eyes flickered past Harfex's face.

"You were attacked," Tomiko said gently. The shifty gaze was hatefully familiar, but she was a physician, protective of the hurt. "You may not remember it yet. Something attacked you. You were in the forest—"

"Ah!" he cried out, his eyes growing bright and his features contorting. "The forest—in the forest—"

"What's in the forest?"

He gasped for breath. A look of clearer consciousness came into his face. After a while he said, "I don't know."

"Did you see what attacked you?" Harfex asked.

"I don't know."

"You remember it now."

"I don't know."

"All our lives may depend on this. You must tell us what you saw!"

"I don't know," Osden said, sobbing with weakness. He was too weak to hide the fact that he was hiding the answer, yet he would not say it. Porlock, nearby, was chewing his pepper-colored mustache as he tried to hear what was going on in the cubicle. Harfex leaned over Osden and said, "You *will* tell us—" Tomiko had to interfere bodily.

Harfex controlled himself with an effort that was painful to see. He went off silently to his cubicle, where no doubt he took a double or triple dose of tranquilizers. The other men and women, scattered about the big frail building, a long main hall and ten sleeping-cubicles, said nothing, but looked depressed and edgy. Osden, as always, even now, had them all at his mercy. Tomiko looked down at him with a rush of hatred that burned in her throat like bile. This monstrous egotism that fed itself on others' emotions, this absolute selfishness, was worse than any hideous deformity of the flesh. Like a congenital monster, he should not have lived. Should not be alive. Should have died. Why had his head not been split open?

As he lay flat and white, his hands helpless at his sides, his colorless eyes were wide open, and there were tears running from the corners. Tomiko moved towards him suddenly. He tried to flinch away. "Don't," he said in a weak hoarse voice, and tried to raise his hands to protect his head. "Don't!"

She sat down on the folding stool beside the cot, and after a while put her hand on his. He tried to pull away, but lacked the strength.

A long silence fell between them.

"Osden," she murmured, "I'm sorry. I'm very sorry. I will you well. Let me will you well, Osden. I don't want to hurt you. Listen, I do see now. It was one of us. That's right, isn't it? No, don't answer, only tell me if I'm wrong; but I'm not. . . . Of course there are animals on this planet: Ten of them. I don't care who it was. It doesn't matter, does it? It could have been me, just now. I realize that. I didn't understand how it is, Osden. You can't see how difficult it is for us to understand. . . . But listen. If it were love, instead of hate and fear. . . . Is it never love?"

"No."

"Why not? Why should it never be? Are human beings all so weak? That is terrible. Never mind, never mind, don't worry. Keep still. At least right now it isn't hate, is it? Sympathy at least, concern, well-wishing. You do feel that, Osden? Is it what you feel?"

"Among . . . other things," he said, almost inaudible.

"Noise from my subconscious, I suppose. And everybody else in the room. . . . Listen, when we found you there in the forest, when I tried to turn you over, you partly wakened, and I felt a horror of you. I was insane with fear for a minute. Was that your fear of me I felt?"

"No."

Her hand was still on his, and he was quite relaxed, sinking towards sleep, like a man in pain who has been given relief from pain. "The forest," he muttered; she could barely understand him. "Afraid."

She pressed him no further, but kept her hand on his and watched him go to sleep. She knew what she felt, and what therefore he must feel. She was confident of it: there is only one emotion, or state of being, that can thus wholly reverse itself, polarize, within one moment. In Great Hainish indeed there is one word, ontá, for love and for hate. She was not in love with Osden, of course, that is another kettle of fish. What she felt for him was ontá, polarized hate. She held his hand and the current flowed between them, the tremendous electricity of touch, which he had always dreaded. As he slept the ring of anatomy-chart muscles around his mouth relaxed, and Tomiko saw on his face what none of them had ever seen, very faint, a smile. It faded. He slept on.

He was tough; next day he was sitting up, and hungry. Harfex wished to interrogate him, but Tomiko put him off. She hung a sheet of polythene over the cubicle door, as Osden himself had often done. "Does it actually cut down your empathic reception?" she asked, and he replied, in the dry, cautious tone they were now using to each other, "No."

"Just a warning, then."

"Partly. More faith-healing. Dr. Hammergeld thought it worked. . . . Maybe it does, a little."

There had been love, once. A terrified child, suffocating in the tidal rush and battering of the huge emotions of adults, a drowning child, saved by one man. Taught to breathe, to live, by one man. Given everything, all protection and love, by one man. Father/mother/God: no other. "Is he still alive?" Tomiko asked, thinking of Osden's incredible loneliness, and the strange cruelty of the great doctors. She was shocked when she heard his forced, tinny laugh. "He died at least two and a half centuries ago." Osden said. "Do you forget where we are, Coordinator? We've all left our little families behind. . . ."

Outside the polythene curtain the eight other human beings on World 4470 moved vaguely. Their voices were low and strained. Eskwana slept; Poswet To was in therapy; Jenny Chong was trying to rig lights in her cubicle so that she wouldn't cast a shadow.

"They're all scared," Tomiko said, scared. "They've all got these ideas about what attacked you. A sort of ape-potato, a giant fanged spinach, I don't know. . . . Even Harfex. You may be right not to force them to see. That would be worse, to lose confidence in one another. But why are we all so shaky, unable to face the fact, going to pieces so easily? Are we really all insane?"

"We'll soon be more so."

"Why?"

"There *is* something."

He closed his mouth, the muscles of his lips stood out rigid.

"Something sentient?"

"A sentience."

"In the forest?"

He nodded.

"What is it, then—?"

"The fear." He began to look strained again, and moved restlessly. "When I fell, there, you know, I didn't lose consciousness at once. Or I kept regaining it. I don't know. It was more like being paralyzed."

"You were."

"I was on the ground. I couldn't get up. My face was in the dirt, in that soft leafmold. It was in my nostrils and eyes. I couldn't move. Couldn't see. As if I was in the ground. Sunk into it, part of it. I knew I was between two trees even though I never saw them. I suppose I could feel the roots. Below me in the ground, down under the ground. My hands were bloody, I could feel that, and the blood made the dirt around my face sticky. I felt the fear. It kept growing. As if they'd finally *known* I was there, lying on them there, under them, among them, the thing they feared, and yet part of their fear itself. I couldn't stop sending the fear back, and it kept growing, and I couldn't move, I couldn't get away. I would pass out, I think, and then the fear would bring me to again, and I still couldn't move. Any more than they can."

Tomiko felt the cold stirring of her hair, the readying of the apparatus of terror. "They: who are they, Osden?"

"They, it—I don't know. The fear."

"What is he talking about?" Harfex demanded when Tomiko reported this conversation. She would not let Harfex question Osden yet, feeling that she must protect Osden from the onslaught of the Hainishman's powerful, overrepressed emotions. Unfortunately this fueled the slow fire of paranoid anxiety that burned in poor Harfex, and he thought she and Osden were in league, hiding some fact of great importance or peril from the rest of the team.

"It's like the blind man trying to describe the elephant. Osden hasn't seen or heard the . . . the sentience, any more than we have."

"But he's felt it, my dear Haito," Harfex said with just-suppressed rage. "Not empathically. On his skull. It came and knocked him down and beat him with a blunt instrument. Did he not catch *one* glimpse of it?"

"What would he have seen, Harfex?" Tomiko asked, but he would not hear her meaningful tone; even he had blocked out that comprehension. What one fears is alien. The murderer is an outsider, a foreigner, not one of us. The evil is not in me!

"The first blow knocked him pretty well out," Tomiko said a little wearily, "he didn't see anything. But when he came to again, alone in the forest, he felt a great fear. Not his own fear, an empathic affect. He is certain of that. And certain it was nothing picked up from any of us. So that evidently the native life-forms are not all insentient."

Harfex looked at her a moment, grim. "You're trying to frighten me, Haito. I do not understand your motives." He got up and went off to his laboratory table, walking slowly and stiffly, like a man of eighty, not of forty.

She looked around at the others. She felt some desperation. Her new, fragile, and profound interdependence with Osden gave her, she was well aware, some added strength. But if even Harfex could not keep his head, who of the others would? Porlock and Eskwana were shut in their cubicles, the others were all working or busy with something. There was something queer about their positions. For a while the Coordinator could not tell what it was, then she saw that they were all sitting facing the nearby forest. Playing chess with Asnanifoil, Olleroo had edged her chair around until it was almost beside his.

She went to Mannon, who was dissecting a tangle of spidery brown roots, and told him to look for the pattern-puzzle. He saw it at once, and said with unusual brevity, "Keeping an eye on the enemy."

"What enemy? What do *you* feel, Mannon?" She had a sudden hope in him as a psychologist, on this obscure ground of hints and empathies where biologists went astray.

"I feel a strong anxiety with a specific spatial orientation.

But I am not an empath. Therefore, the anxiety is explicable in terms of the particular stress-situation, that is, the attack on a team member in the forest, and also in terms of the total stress-situation, that is, my presence in a totally alien environment, for which the archetypical connotations of the word 'forest' provide an inevitable metaphor."

· Hours later Tomiko woke to hear Osden screaming in nightmare; Mannon was calming him, and she sank back into her own dark-branching pathless dreams. In the morning Eskwana did not wake. He could not be roused with stimulant drugs. He clung to his sleep, slipping farther and farther back, mumbling softly now and then until, wholly regressed, he lay curled on his side, thumb at his lips, gone.

"Two days: two down. Ten little Indians, nine little Indians. . . ." That was Porlock.

"And you're the next little Indian," Jenny Chong snapped. "Go analyze your urine, Porlock!"

"He is driving us all insane," Porlock said, getting up and waving his left arm. "Can't you feel it? For God's sake, are you all deaf and blind? Can't you feel what he's doing, the emanations? It all comes from him—from his room there—from his mind. He is driving us all insane with fear!"

"Who is?" said Asnanifoil, looming black, precipitous, and hairy over the little Terran.

"Do I have to say his name? Osden, then. Osden! Osden! Why do you think I tried to kill him? In self-defense! To save all of us! Because you won't see what he's doing to us. He's sabotaged the mission by making us quarrel, and now he's going to drive us all insane by projecting fear at us so that we can't sleep or think, like a huge radio that doesn't make any sound, but it broadcasts all the time, and you can't sleep, and you can't think. Haito and Harfex are already under his control, but the rest of you can be saved. I had to do it!"

"You didn't do it very well," Osden said, standing half-naked, all rib and bandage, at the door of his cubicle. "I could have hit myself harder. Hell, it isn't me that's scaring you blind, Porlock, it's out there—there, in the woods!"

Porlock made an ineffectual attempt to assault Osden; Asnanifoil held him back, and continued to hold him effortlessly while Mannon gave him a sedative shot. He was put away shouting about giant radios. In a minute the sedative took effect, and he joined a peaceful silence to Eskwana's.

"All right," said Harfex. "Now, by my Gods, you'll tell us what you know and all you know."

Osden said, "I don't know anything."

He looked battered and faint. Tomiko made him sit down before he talked.

"After I'd been three days in the forest, I thought I was occasionally receiving some kind of faint affect."

"Why didn't you report it?"

"Thought I was going spla, like the rest of you."

"That, equally, should have been reported."

"You'd have called me back to base. I couldn't take it. You realize that my inclusion in the mission was a bad mistake. I'm not able to coexist with nine other neurotic personalities at close quarters. I was wrong to volunteer for Extreme Survey, and the Authority was wrong to accept me."

No one spoke; but Tomiko saw, with certainty this time, the flinch in Osden's shoulders and the tightening of his facial muscles, as he registered their bitter agreement.

"Anyhow, I didn't want to come back to base because I was curious. Even going psycho, how could I pick up empathic affects when there was no creature to emit them? They weren't bad, then. Very vague. Queer. Like a draft in a closed room, a flicker in the corner of your eye. Nothing really."

For a moment he had been borne up on their listening: they heard, so he spoke. He was wholly at their mercy. If they disliked him, he had to be hateful; if they mocked him, he became grotesque; if they listened to him, he was the storyteller. He was helplessly obedient to the demands of their emotions, reactions, moods. And there were seven of them, too many to cope with, so that he must be constantly knocked about from one to another's whim. He could not find coherence. Even as he spoke and held them, somebody's attention would wander: Olleroo perhaps was thinking that he wasn't unattractive; Harfex was seeking the ulterior motive of his words; Asnanifoil's mind, which could not be long held by the concrete, was roaming off towards the eternal peace of number; and Tomiko was distracted by pity, by fear. Osden's voice faltered. He lost the thread. "I . . . I thought it must be the trees," he said, and stopped.

"It's not the trees," Harfex said. "They have no more nervous system than do plants of the Hainish Descent on Earth. None."

"You're not seeing the forest for the trees, as they say on Earth," Mannon put in, smiling elfinly; Harfex stared at him. "What about those root-nodes we've been puzzling about for twenty days—eh?"

"What about them?"

"They are, indubitably, connections. Connections among the trees. Right? Now let's just suppose, most improbably, that you knew nothing of animal brain structure. And you were given one axon, or one detached glial cell, to examine. Would you be likely to discover what it was? Would you see that the cell was capable of sentience?

"No. Because it isn't. A single cell is capable of mechanical response to stimulus. No more. Are you hypothesizing that individual arboriformes are 'cells' in a kind of brain, Mannon?"

"Not exactly. I'm merely pointing out that they are all interconnected, both by the root-node linkage and by your green epiphytes in the branches. A linkage of incredible complexity and physical extent. Why, even the prairie grass-forms have those root-connectors, don't they? I know that sentience or intelligence isn't a thing, you can't find it in, or analyze it out from, the cell of a brain. It's a function of the connected cells. It is, in a sense, the connection: the connectedness. It doesn't exist. I'm not trying to say it exists. I'm only guessing that Osden might be able to describe it."

And Osden took him up, speaking as if in trance. "Sentience without senses. Blind, deaf, nerveless, moveless. Some irritability, response to touch. Response to sun, to light, to water, and chemicals in the earth around the roots. Nothing comprehensible to an animal mind. Presence without mind. Awareness of being, without object or subject. Nirvana."

"Then why do you receive fear?" Tomiko asked in a low voice.

"I don't know. I can't see how awareness of objects, of others, could arise: an unperceiving response. . . . But there was an uneasiness, for days. And then when I lay between the two trees and my blood was on their roots—" Osden's face glittered with sweat. "It became fear," he said shrilly, "only fear."

"If such a function existed," Harfex said, "it would not be capable of conceiving of a self-moving, material entity, or responding to one. It could no more become aware of us than we can 'become aware' of Infinity."

"The silence of those infinite expanses terrifies me," muttered Tomiko. "Pascal was aware of Infinity. By way of fear."

"To a forest," Mannon said, "we might appear as forest fires. Hurricanes. Dangers. What moves quickly is dangerous, to a plant. The rootless would be alien, terrible. And if it is mind, it seems only too probable that it might become aware of Osden, whose own mind is open to connection with all others so long as he's conscious, and who was lying in pain and afraid within it, actually inside it. No wonder it was afraid—"

"Not 'it,' " Harfex said. "There is no being, no huge creature, no person! There could at most be only a function—"

"There is only a fear," Osden said.

They were all still a while, and heard the stillness outside.

"Is that what I feel all the time coming up behind me?" Jenny Chong asked, subdued.

Osden nodded. "You all feel it, deaf as you are. Eskwana's the worst off, because he actually has some empathic capacity. He could send if he learned how, but he's too weak, never will be anything but a medium."

"Listen, Osden," Tomiko said, "you can send. Then send to it—the forest, the fear out there—tell that we won't hurt it. Since it has, or is, some sort of affect that translates into what we feel as emotion, can't you translate back? Send out a message: We are harmless, we are friendly."

"You must know that nobody can emit a false empathic message, Haito. You can't send something that doesn't exist."

"But we don't intend harm, we are friendly."

"Are we? In the forest, when you picked me up, did you feel friendly?"

"No. Terrified. But that's—it, the forest, the plants, not my own fear, isn't it?"

"What's the difference? It's all you felt. Can't you see," and Osden's voice rose in exasperation, "why I dislike you and you dislike me, all of you? Can't you see that I retransmit every negative or aggressive affect you've felt towards me since we first met? I return your hostility, with thanks. I do it in self-defense. Like Porlock. It is self-defense, though, it's the only technique I developed to replace my original defense of total withdrawal from others. Unfortunately it creates a closed circuit, self-sustaining and self-reinforcing. Your initial reaction to me was the instinctive antipathy to a cripple; by now of course it's hatred. Can you fail to see my point? The forest-mind out there transmits only terror, now, and the only message I can send it is terror, because when exposed to it I can feel nothing except terror!"

"What must we do, then?" said Tomiko, and Mannon replied promptly, "Move camp. To another continent. If there are plant-minds there, they'll be slow to notice us, as this one was; maybe they won't notice us at all."

"It would be a considerable relief," Osden observed stiffly. The others had been watching him with a new curiosity. He had revealed himself, they had seen him as he was, a helpless man in a trap. Perhaps, like Tomiko, they had seen that the trap itself, his crass and cruel egotism, was their own construction, not his. They had built the cage and locked him in it, and like a caged ape he threw filth out through the bars. If, meeting him, they had offered trust, if they had been strong enough to offer him love, how might he have appeared to them?

None of them could have done so, and it was too late now. Given time, given solitude, Tomiko might have built up with him a slow resonance of feeling, a consonance of trust, a harmony: but there was no time, their job must be done. There was not room enough for the cultivation of so great a thing, and they must make do with sympathy, with pity, the small change of love. Even that much had given her strength, but it was nowhere near enough for him. She could see in his flayed face now his savage resentment of their curiosity, even of her pity.

"Go lie down, that gash is bleeding again," she said, and he obeyed her.

Next morning they packed up, melted down the sprayform hangar and living quarters, lifted *Gum* on mechanical drive and took her halfway round World 4470, over the red and green lands, the many warm-green seas. They had picked out a likely spot on Continent G: a prairie, twenty thousand square kilos of windswept graminiformes. No forest was within a hundred kilos of the site, and there were no lone trees or groves on the plain. The plant-forms occurred only in large species-colonies, never intermingled, except for certain tiny ubiquitous saprophytes and spore-bearers. The team sprayed holomeld over structure forms, and by evening of the thirty-two-hour day were settled in the new camp. Eskwana was still asleep and Porlock still sedated, but everyone else was cheerful. "You can breathe here!" they kept saying.

Osden got on his feet and went shakily to the doorway; leaning there he looked through twilight over the dim reaches of the swaying grass that was not grass. There was a faint, sweet odor of pollen on the wind; no sound but the soft, vast sibilance of wind. His bandaged head cocked a little, the empath stood motionless for a long time. Darkness came, and the stars, lights in the windows of the distant house of Man. The wind had ceased, there was no sound. He listened.

In the long night Haito Tomiko listened. She lay still and heard the blood in her arteries, the breathing of sleepers, the wind blowing, the dark veins running, the dreams advancing, the vast static of stars increasing as the universe died slowly, the sound of death walking. She struggled out of her bed, fled the tiny solitude of her cubicle. Eskwana alone slept. Porlock lay straitjacketed, raving softly in his obscure native tongue. Olleroo and Jenny Chong were playing cards, grim-faced. Poswet To was in the therapy niche, plugged in. Asnanifoil was drawing a mandala, the Third Pattern of the

Primes. Mannon and Harfex were sitting up with Osden.

She changed the bandages on Osden's head. His lank, reddish hair, where she had not had to shave it, looked strange. It was salted with white, now. Her hands shook as she worked. Nobody had yet said anything.

"How can the fear be here too?" she said, and her voice rang flat and false in the terrific silence of the vegetable night.

"It's not just the trees; the grasses too . . ."

"But we're twelve thousand kilos from where we were this morning, we left it on the other side of the planet."

"It's all one," Osden said. "One big green thought. How long does it take a thought to get from one side of your brain to the other?"

"It doesn't think. It isn't thinking," Harfex said, lifelessly. "It's merely a network of processes. The branches, the epiphytic growths, the roots with those nodal junctures between individuals: they must all be capable of transmitting electrochemical impulses. There are no individual plants, then, properly speaking. Even the pollen is part of the linkage, no doubt, a sort of windborne sentience, connecting overseas. But it is not conceivable. That all the biosphere of a planet should be one network of communications, sensitive, irrational, immortal, isolated . . ."

"Isolated," said Osden. "That's it! That's the fear. It isn't that we're motile, or destructive. It's just that we are. We are other. There has never been any other."

"You're right," Mannon said, almost whispering. "It has no peers. No enemies. No relationship with anything but itself. One alone forever."

"Then what's its function in species-survival?"

"None, maybe," Osden said. "Why are you getting teleological, Harfex? Aren't you a Hainishman? Isn't the measure of complexity the measure of the eternal joy?"

Harfex did not take the bait. He looked ill. "We should leave this world," he said.

"Now you know why I always want to get out, get away from you," Osden said with a kind of morbid geniality. "It isn't pleasant, is it—the other's fear? . . . If only it were an animal intelligence. I get through to animals. I get along with cobras and tigers; superior intelligence gives one the advantage. I should have been used in a zoo, not on a human team. . . . If I could get through to the damned stupid potato! If it wasn't so overwhelming. . . . I still pick up more than the fear, you know. And before it panicked it had a—there was a serenity. I couldn't take it in, then, I didn't realize how big it was. To know the whole daylight, after all, and the whole night. All the winds and the lulls together. The winter stars and the summer stars at the same time. To have roots, and no enemies. To be entire. Do you see? No invasion. No others. To be whole. . . ."

He had never spoken before, Tomiko thought.

"You are defenseless against it, Osden," she said. "Your personality has changed already. You're vulnerable to it. We may not all go mad, but you will, if we don't leave."

He hesitated, then he looked up at Tomiko, the first time he had ever met her eyes, a long, still look, clear as water.

"What's sanity ever done for me?" he said, mocking. "But you have a point, Haito. You have something there."

"We should get away," Harfex muttered.

"If I gave in to it," Osden mused, "could I communicate?"

"By 'give in,' " Mannon said in a rapid, nervous voice, "I assume that you mean, stop sending back the empathic information which you receive from the plant-entity: stop rejecting the fear, and absorb it. That will either kill you at once, or drive you back into total psychological withdrawal, autism."

"Why?" said Osden. "Its message is *rejection*. But my salvation is rejection. It's not intelligent. But I am."

"The scale is wrong. What can a single human brain achieve against something so vast?"

"A single human brain can perceive pattern on the scale of stars and galaxies," Tomiko said, "and interpret it as Love."

Mannon looked from one to the other of them; Harfex was silent.

"It'd be easier in the forest," Osden said. "Which of you will fly me over?"

"When?"

"Now. Before you all crack up or go violent."

"I will," Tomiko said.

"None of us will," Harfex said.

"I can't," Mannon said. "I . . . I am too frightened. I'd crash the jet."

"Bring Eskwana along. If I can pull this off, he might serve as a medium."

"Are you accepting the Sensor's plan, Coordinator?" Harfex asked formally.

"Yes."

"I disapprove. I will come with you, however."

"I think we're compelled, Harfex," Tomiko said, looking at Osden's face, the ugly white mask transfigured, eager as a lover's face.

Olleroo and Jenny Chong, playing cards to keep their thoughts from their haunted beds, their mounting dread, chattered like scared children. "This thing, it's in the forest, it'll get you—"

"Scared of the dark?" Osden jeered.

"But look at Eskwana, and Porlock, and even Asnanifoil—"

"It can't hurt you. It's an impulse passing through

synapses, a wind passing through branches. It is only a nightmare."

They took off in a helijet, Eskwana curled up still sound asleep in the rear compartment, Tomiko piloting, Harfex and Osden silent, watching ahead for the dark line of forest across the vague gray miles of starlit plain.

They neared the black line, crossed it; now under them was darkness.

She sought a landing place, flying low, though she had to fight her frantic wish to fly high, to get out, get away. The huge vitality of the plant-world was far stronger here in the forest, and its panic beat in immense dark waves. There was a pale patch ahead, a bare knoll-top a little higher than the tallest of the black shapes around it; the not-trees; the rooted; the parts of the whole. She set the helijet down in the glade, a bad landing. Her hands on the stick were slippery as if she had rubbed them with cold soap.

About them now stood the forest, black in darkness.

Tomiko cowered down and shut her eyes. Eskwana moaned in his sleep. Harfex's breath came short and loud, and he sat rigid, even when Osden reached across him and slid the door open.

Osden stood up; his back and bandaged head were just visible in the dim glow of the control panel as he paused stooping in the doorway.

Tomiko was shaking. She could not raise her head. "No, no, no, no, no, no, no," she said in a whisper. "No. No. No."

Osden moved suddenly and quietly, swinging out of the doorway, down into the dark. He was gone.

I am coming! said a great voice that made no sound.

Tomiko screamed. Harfex coughed; he seemed to be trying to stand up, but did not do so.

Tomiko drew in upon herself, all centered in the blind eye in her belly, in the center of her being; and outside that there was nothing but the fear.

It ceased.

She raised her head; slowly unclenched her hands. She sat up straight. The night was dark, and stars shone over the forest. There was nothing else.

"Osden," she said, but her voice would not come. She spoke again, louder, a lone bullfrog croak. There was no reply.

She began to realize that something had gone wrong with Harfex. She was trying to find his head in the darkness, for he had slipped down from the seat, when all at once, in the dead quiet, in the dark rear compartment of the craft, a voice spoke. "Good," it said.

It was Eskwana's voice. She snapped on the interior lights and saw the engineer lying curled up asleep, his hand half over his mouth.

The mouth opened and spoke. "All well," it said.

"Osden—"

"All well," said the soft voice from Eskwana's mouth.

"Where are you?"

Silence.

"Come back."

Wind was rising. "I'll stay here," the soft voice said.

"You can't stay—"

Silence.

"You'd be alone, Osden!"

"Listen." The voice was fainter, slurred, as if lost in the sound of wind. "Listen. I will you well."

She called his name after that, but there was no answer. Eskwana lay still. Harfex lay stiller.

"Osden!" she cried, leaning out the doorway into the dark, wind-shaken silence of the forest of being. "I will come back. I must get Harfex to the base. I will come back, Osden!"

Silence and wind in leaves.

They finished the prescribed survey of World 4470, the eight of them; it took them forty-one days more. Asnanifoil and one or another of the women went into the forest daily at first, searching for Osden in the region around the bare knoll; though Tomiko was not in her heart sure which bare knoll they had landed on that night in the very heart and vortex of terror. They left piles of supplies for Osden, food enough for fifty years, clothing, tents, tools. They did not go on searching; there was no way to find a man alone, hiding, if he wanted to hide, in those unending labyrinths and dim corridors vine-entangled, root-floored. They might have passed within arm's reach of him and never seen him.

But he was there; for there was no fear any more.

Rational, and valuing reason more highly after an intolerable experience of the immortal mindless, Tomiko tried to understand rationally what Osden had done. But the words escaped her control. He had taken the fear into himself, and, accepting, had transcended it. He had given up his self to the alien, an unreserved surrender, that left no place for evil. He had learned the love of the Other, and thereby had been given his whole self. But this is not the vocabulary of reason.

The people of the Survey team walked under the trees, through the vast colonies of life, surrounded by a dreaming silence, a brooding calm that was half aware of them and wholly indifferent to them. There were no hours. Distance was no matter. "Had we but world enough, and time . . ." The planet turned between the sunlight and the great dark; winds of winter and summer blew fine, pale pollen across the quiet seas.

Gum returned after many surveys, years, and light-years, to what had several centuries ago been Smeming Port on Pesm. There were still men there to receive (incredulously) the team's reports and to record its losses: Biologist Harfex, dead of fear, and Sensor Osden, left as a colonist.

WHAT'S IT LIKE OUT THERE?

Edmond Hamilton

Like Murray Leinster, like Clifford D. Simak, Edmond Hamilton is one of the tribal patriarchs of science fiction—a venerable figure who has plied his typewriter for generation upon generation, giving delight to the grandchildren of his original readers. Hamilton's first published story appeared in 1926; within a few years he was one of the most popular science-fiction writers, cherished in particular for his exciting Interstellar Patrol series, collected many years later under the appropriate title of Crashing Suns. *Later, Hamilton was responsible for the* Captain Future *novels and many other tales of adventure in space; the climax of this phase of his career was the splendid epic* The Star Kings *(1947). More recently he has abandoned the swashbuckling style of his youth for a less flamboyant approach—as in this famous short story, written some time before the first astronauts were rocketed into space, which quietly and soberly conveys the nature of the drive that will carry mankind to other worlds.*

I hadn't wanted to wear my uniform when I left the hospital, but I didn't have any other clothes there and I was too glad to get out to argue about it. But as soon as I got on the local plane I was taking to Los Angeles, I was sorry I had it on.

People gawked at me and began to whisper. The stewardess gave me a special big smile. She must have spoken to the pilot, for he came back and shook hands, and said, "Well, I guess a trip like this is sort of a comedown for *you.*"

A little man came in, looked around for a seat, and took the one beside me. He was a fussy, spectacled guy of fifty or sixty, and he took a few minutes to get settled. Then he looked at me, and stared at my uniform and at the little brass button on it that said "TWO."

"Why," he said, "you're one of those Expedition Two men!" And then, as though he'd only just figured it out, "Why, you've been to Mars!"

"Yeah," I said. "I was there."

He beamed at me in a kind of wonder. I didn't like it, but his curiosity was so friendly that I couldn't quite resent it.

"Tell me," he said, "what's it like out there?"

The plane was lifting, and I looked out at the Arizona desert sliding by close underneath.

"Different," I said. "It's different."

The answer seemed to satisfy him completely. "I'll just bet it is," he said. "Are you going home, Mr. . . ."

"Haddon. Sergeant Frank Haddon."

"You going home, Sergeant?"

"My home's back in Ohio," I told him. "I'm going in to L.A. to look up some people before I go home."

"Well, that's fine. I hope you have a good time, Sergeant. You deserve it. You boys did a great job out there. Why, I read in the newspapers that after the U.N. sends out a couple more expeditions, we'll have cities out there, and regular passenger lines, and all that."

"Look," I said, "that stuff is for the birds. You might as well build cities down there in Mojave, and have them a lot closer. There's only one reason for going to Mars now, and that's uranium."

I could see he didn't quite believe me. "Oh, sure," he said, "I know that's important too, the uranium we're all using now for our power stations—but that isn't all, is it?"

"It'll be all, for a long, long time," I said.

"But look, Sergeant, this newspaper article said . . ."

I didn't say anything more. By the time he'd finished telling about the newspaper article, we were coming down into L.A. He pumped my hand when we got out of the plane.

"Have yourself a time, Sergeant! You sure rate it. I hear a lot of chaps on Two didn't come back."

"Yeah," I said. "I heard that."

I was feeling shaky again by the time I got to downtown L.A. I went in a bar and had a double bourbon and it made me feel a little better.

I went out and found a cabby and asked him to drive me out to San Gabriel. He was a fat man with a broad, red face.

"Hop right in, buddy," he said. "Say, you're one of those Mars guys, aren't you?"

I said, "That's right."

"Well, well," he said. "Tell me, how was it out there?"

"It was a pretty dull grind, in a way," I told him.

"I'll bet it was!" he said, as we started through traffic. "Me, I was in the Army in World War Two, twenty years ago. That's just what it was, a dull grind nine tenths of the time. I guess it hasn't changed any."

"This wasn't any Army expedition," I explained. "It was a United Nations one, not an Army one—but we had officers and rules of discipline like the Army."

"Sure, it's the same thing," said the cabby. "You don't need to tell me what it's like, buddy. Why, back there in 'forty-two, or was it 'forty-three?—anyway, back there I remember that . . ."

I leaned back and watched Huntington Boulevard slide past. The sun poured in on me and seemed very hot, and the air seemed very thick and soupy. It hadn't been so bad up on the Arizona plateau, but it was a little hard to breathe down here.

The cabby wanted to know what address in San Gabriel.

I got the little packet of letters out of my pocket and found the one that had "Martin Valinez" and a street address on the back. I told the cabby and put the letters back into my pocket.

I wished now that I'd never answered them.

But how could I keep from answering when Joe Valinez's parents wrote to me at the hospital? And it was the same with Jim's girl, and Walter's family. I'd had to write back, and the first thing I knew I'd promised to come and see them, and now if I went back to Ohio without doing it I'd feel like a heel. Right now, I wished I'd decided to be a heel.

The address was on the south side of San Gabriel, in a section that still had a faintly Mexican tinge to it. There was a little frame grocery store with a small house beside it, and a picket fence around the yard of the house; very neat, but a queerly homely place after all the slick California stucco.

I went into the little grocery, and a tall, dark man with quiet eyes took a look at me and called a woman's name in a low voice and then came around the counter and took my hand.

"You're Sergeant Haddon," he said. "Yes. Of course. We've been hoping you'd come."

His wife came in a hurry from the back. She looked a little too old to be Joe's mother, for Joe had been just a kid; but then she didn't look so old either, but just sort of worn.

She said to Valinez, "Please, a chair. Can't you see he's tired? And just from the hospital."

I sat down and looked between them at a case of canned peppers, and they asked me how I felt, and wouldn't I be glad to get home, and they hoped all my family were well.

They were gentlefolk. They hadn't said a word about Joe, just waited for me to say something. And I felt in a spot, for I hadn't known Joe well, not really. He'd been moved into our squad only a couple of weeks before take-off, and since he'd been our first casualty, I'd never got to know him much.

I finally had to get it over with, and all I could think to say was, "They wrote you in detail about Joe, didn't they?"

Valinez nodded gravely. "Yes—that he died from shock within twenty-four hours after take-off. The letter was very nice."

His wife nodded too. "Very nice," she murmured. She looked at me, and I guess she saw that I didn't know quite what to say, for she said, "You can tell us more about it. Yet you must not if it pains you."

I could tell them more. Oh, yes, I could tell them a lot more, if I wanted to. It was all clear in my mind, like a movie film as you run over and over till you know it by heart.

I could tell them all about the take-off that had killed their son. The long lines of us, uniformed backs going up into Rocket Four and all the other nineteen rockets—the lights flaring up there on the plateau, the grind of machinery and blasts of whistles and the inside of the big rocket as we climbed up the ladder of its center well.

The movie was running again in my mind, clear as crystal, and I was back in Cell Fourteen of Rocket Four, with the minutes ticking away and the walls quivering every time one of the other rockets blasted off, and us ten men in our hammocks, prisoned inside that odd-shaped windowless metal room, waiting. Waiting, till that big giant hand came and smacked us down deep into our recoil springs, crushing the breaths out of us, so that you fought to breathe, and the blood roared into your head, and your stomach heaved in spite of all the pills they'd given you, and you heard the giant laughing, *b-r-room! b-r-r-room! b-r-r-room!*

Smash, smash, again and again, hitting us in the guts and

cutting our breath, and someone being sick, and someone else sobbing, and the *b-r-r-oom! b-r-r-oom!* laughing as it killed us; and then the giant quit laughing, and quit slapping us down, and you could feel your sore and shaky body and wonder if it was still all there.

Walter Mills cursing a blue streak in the hammock underneath me, and Breck Jergen, our sergeant then, clambering painfully out of his straps to look us over and then through the voices a thin, ragged voice saying uncertainly, "Breck, I think I'm hurt . . ."

Sure, that was their boy Joe, and there was blood on his lips, and he'd had it—we knew when we first looked at him that he'd had it. A handsome kid, turned waxy now as he held his hand on his middle and looked up at us. Expedition One had proved that take-off would hit a certain percentage with internal injuries every time, and in our squad, in our little windowless cell, it was Joe that had been hit.

If only he'd died right off. But he couldn't die right off, he had to lie in the hammock all those hours and hours. The medics came and put a straitjacket around his body and doped him up, and that was that, and the hours went by. And we were so shaken and deathly sick ourselves that we didn't have the sympathy for him we should have had—not till he started moaning and begging us to take the jacket off.

Finally Walter Mills wanted to do it, and Breck wouldn't allow it, and they were arguing and we were listening when the moaning stopped, and there was no need to do anything about Joe Valinez any more. Nothing but to call the medics, who came into our little iron prison and took him away.

Sure, I could tell the Valinezes all about how their Joe died, couldn't I?

"Please," whispered Mrs. Valinez, and her husband looked at me and nodded silently.

So I told them.

I said, "You know Joe died in space. He'd been knocked out by the shock of take-off, and he was unconscious, not feeling a thing. And then he woke up, before he died. He didn't seem to be feeling any pain, not a bit. He lay there, looking out the window at the stars. They're beautiful, the stars out there in space, like angels. He looked, and then he whispered something and lay back and was gone."

Mrs. Valinez began to cry softly. "To die out there, looking at stars like angels . . ."

I got up to go, and she didn't look up. I went out the door of the little grocery store, and Valinez came with me.

He shook my hand. "Thank you, Sergeant Haddon. Thank you very much."

"Sure," I said.

I got into the cab. I took out my letters and tore that one into bits. I wished to God I'd never got it. I wished I didn't have any of the other letters I still had.

2

I took the early plane for Omaha. Before we got there I fell asleep in my seat, and then I began to dream, and that wasn't good.

A voice said, "We're coming down."

And we were coming down, Rocket Four was coming down, and there we were in our squad cell, all of us strapped into our hammocks, waiting and scared, wishing there was a window so we could see out, hoping our rocket wouldn't be the one to crack up, hoping none of the rockets cracked up, but if one does, don't let it be *ours.* . . .

"We're coming down. . . ."

Coming down, with the blasts starting to boom again underneath us, hitting us hard, not steady like at take-off, but blast-blast-blast, and then again, blast-blast.

Breck's voice, calling to us from across the cell, but I couldn't hear for the roaring that was in my ears between blasts. No, it was *not* in my ears, that roaring came from the wall beside me; we had hit atmosphere, we were coming in.

The blasts in lightning succession without stopping, crash-crash-crash-crash-crash! Mountains fell on me, and this was it, and don't let it be ours, please, God, don't let it be ours. . . .

Then the bump and the blackness, and finally somebody yelling hoarsely in my ears, and Breck Jergen, his face deathly white, leaning over me.

"Unstrap and get out, Frank! All men out of hammocks—all men out!"

We'd landed, and we hadn't cracked up, but we were half dead and they wanted us to turn out, right this minute, and we couldn't.

Breck yelling to us, "Breathing masks on! Masks on! We've got to go out!"

"My God, we've just landed, we're torn to bits, we can't!"

"We've got to! Some of the other rockets cracked up in landing and we've got to save whoever's still living in them! Masks on! Hurry!"

We couldn't, but we did. They hadn't given us all those months of discipline for nothing. Jim Clymer was already on his feet, Walter was trying to unstrap underneath me, whistles were blowing like mad somewhere and voices shouted hoarsely.

My knees wobbled under me as I hit the floor. Young Lassen, beside me, tried to say something and then crumpled up. Jim bent over him, but Breck was at the door yelling, "Let him go! Come on!"

The whistles screeching at us all the way down the ladders of the well, and the mask clip hurting my nose, and down at the bottom a disheveled officer yelling at us to get out and join Squad Five, and the gangway reeling under us.

Cold. Freezing cold, and a wan sunshine from the shrunken little sun up there in the brassy sky, and a rolling plain of ocherous red sand stretching around us, sand that slid away under our feet as our squads followed Captain Wall toward the distant metal bulk that lay oddly canted and broken in a little shallow valley.

"Come on, men—hurry! Hurry!

Sure, all of it a dream, the dreamlike way we walked with our lead-soled shoes dragging our feet back after each step, and the voices coming through the mask resonators muffled and distant.

Only not a dream, but a nightmare, when we got up to the canted metal bulk and saw what had happened to Rocket Seven—the metal hull ripped like paper, and a few men crawling out of the wreck with blood on them, and a gurgling sound where shattered tanks were emptying, and voices whimpering, "First aid! First aid!"

Only it hadn't happened, it hadn't happened yet at all, for we were still back in Rocket Four coming in, we hadn't landed yet at all but we were going to any minute.

"We're coming down. . . ."

I couldn't go through it all again. I yelled and fought my hammock straps and woke up, and I was in my plane seat and a scared hostess was a foot away from me, saying "This is Omaha, Sergeant. We're coming down."

They were all looking at me, all the other passengers, and I guessed I'd been talking in the dream—I still had the sweat down my back like all those nights in the hospital when I'd keep waking up.

I sat up, and they all looked away from me quick and pretended they hadn't been staring.

We came down to the airport. It was midday, and the hot Nebraska sun felt good on my back when I got out. I was lucky, for when I asked at the bus depot about going to Cuffington, there was a bus all ready to roll.

A farmer sat down beside me, a big young fellow who offered me cigarettes and told me it was only a few hours' ride to Cuffington.

"Your home there?" he asked.

"No, my home's back in Ohio," I said. "A friend of mine came from there. Name of Clymer."

He didn't know him, but he remembered that one of the town boys had gone on that second expedition to Mars.

"Yeah," I said. "That was Jim."

He couldn't keep it in any longer. "What's it like out there, anyway?"

I said, "Dry. Terrible dry."

"I'll bet it is," he said. "To tell the truth, it's too dry here, this year, for good wheat weather. Last year it was fine. Last year . . ."

Cuffington, Nebraska, was a wide street of stores, and other streets with trees and old houses, and yellow wheat fields all around as far as you could see. It was pretty hot, and I was glad to sit down in the bus depot while I went through the thin little phone book.

There were three Graham families in the book, but the first one I called was the right one—Miss Ila Graham. She talked fast and excited, and said she'd come right over, and I said I'd wait in front of the bus depot.

I stood underneath the awning, looking down the quiet street and thinking that it sort of explained why Jim Clymer had always been such a quiet, slow-moving sort of guy. The place was sort of relaxed, like he'd been.

A coupé pulled up, and Miss Graham opened the door. She was a brown-haired girl, not especially good-looking, but the kind you think of as a nice girl, a very nice girl.

She said, "You look so tired that I feel guilty now about asking you to stop."

"I'm all right," I said. "And it's no trouble stopping over a couple of places on my way back to Ohio."

As we drove across the little town, I asked her if Jim hadn't had any family of his own here.

"His parents were killed in a car crash years ago," Miss Graham said. "He lived with an uncle on a farm outside Grandview, but they didn't get along, and Jim came into town and got a job at the power station."

She added, as we turned a corner, "My mother rented him a room. That's how we got to know each other. That's how we—how we got engaged."

"Yeah, sure," I said.

It was a big square house with a deep front porch, and some trees around it. I sat down in a wicker chair, and Miss Graham brought her mother out. Her mother talked a little about Jim, how they missed him, and how she declared he'd been just like a son.

When her mother went back in, Miss Graham showed me a little bunch of blue envelopes. "These were the letters I got from Jim. There weren't very many of them, and they weren't very long."

"We were only allowed to send one thirty-word message every two weeks," I told her. "There were a couple of thousand of us out there, and they couldn't let us jam up the message transmitter all the time."

"It was wonderful how much Jim could put into just a few words," she said, and handed me some of them.

I read a couple. One said, "I have to pinch myself to realize that I'm one of the first Earthmen to stand on an alien world. At night, in the cold, I look up at the green star that's Earth and can't quite realize I've helped an age-old dream come true."

Another one said, "This world's grim and lonely, and mysterious. We don't know much about it yet. So far, nobody's seen anything living but the lichens that Expedition One reported, but there might be anything here."

Miss Graham asked me, "Was that all there was, just lichens?"

"That, and two or three kinds of queer cactus things," I said. "And rock and sand. That's all."

As I read more of those little blue letters, I found that now that Jim was gone I knew him better than I ever had. There was something about him I'd never suspected. He was romantic inside. We hadn't suspected it, he was always so quiet and slow, but now I saw that all the time he was more romantic about the thing we were doing than any of us.

He hadn't let on. We'd have kidded him, if he had. Our name for Mars, after we got sick of it, was the Hole. We always talked about it as the Hole. I could see now that Jim had been too shy of our kidding to ever let us know that he glamorized the thing in his mind.

"This was the last one I got from him before his sickness," Miss Graham said.

That one said, "I'm starting north tomorrow with one of the mapping expeditions. We'll travel over country no human has ever seen before."

I nodded. "I was on that party myself. Jim and I were on the same half-track."

"He was thrilled by it, wasn't he, Sergeant?"

I wondered. I remembered that trip, and it was hell. Our job was simply to run a preliminary topographical survey, checking with Geigers for possible uranium deposits.

It wouldn't have been so bad if the sand hadn't started to blow.

It wasn't sand like Earth sand. It was ground to dust by billions of years of blowing around that dry world. It got inside your breathing mask, and your goggles, and the engines of the half-tracks, in your food and water and clothes. There was nothing for three days but cold, and wind, and sand.

Thrilled? I'd have laughed at that before. But now I didn't know. Maybe Jim had been, at that. He had lots of patience, a lot more than I ever had. Maybe he glamorized that hellish trip into a wonderful adventure on a foreign world.

"Sure, he was thrilled," I said. "We all were. Anybody would be."

Miss Graham took the letters back, and then said, "You had Martian sickness too, didn't you?"

I said, yes, I had, just a touch, and that was why I'd had to spend a stretch in a reconditioning hospital when I got back.

She waited for me to go on, and I knew I had to. "They don't know yet if it's some sort of virus or just the effect of Martian conditions on Earthmen's bodies. It hit forty percent of us. It wasn't really so bad—fever and dopiness, mostly."

"When Jim got it, was he well cared for?" she asked. Her lips were quivering a little.

"Sure, he was well cared for. He got the best care there was," I lied.

The best care there was? That was a laugh. The first cases got decent care, maybe. But they'd never figured on so many coming down. There wasn't any room in our little hospital—they just had to stay in their bunks in the aluminum Quonsets when it hit them. All our doctors but one were down, and two of them died.

We'd been on Mars six months when it hit us, and the loneliness had already got us down. All but four of our rockets had gone back to Earth, and we were alone on a dead world, our little town of Quonsets huddled together under that hateful, brassy sky, and beyond it the sand and rocks that went on forever.

You go up to the North Pole and camp there, and find out how lonely that is. It was worse out there, a lot worse. The first excitement was gone long ago, and we were tired, and homesick in a way nobody was ever homesick before—we wanted to see green grass, and real sunshine, and women's faces, and hear running water; and we wouldn't until Expedition Three came to relieve us. No wonder guys blew their tops out there. And then came Martian sickness, on top of it.

"We did everything for him that we could," I said.

Sure we had. I could still remember Walter and me tramping through the cold night to the hospital to try to get a medic, while Breck stayed with him, and how we couldn't get one.

I remember how Walter had looked up at the blazing sky as we tramped back, and shaken his fist at the big green star of Earth.

"People up there are going to dances tonight, watching shows, sitting around in warm rooms laughing! Why should good men have to die out here to get them uranium for cheap power?"

"Can it," I told him tiredly. "Jim's not going to die. A lot of guys got over it."

The best care there was? That was real funny. All we could do was wash his face, and give him the pills the medic left, and watch him get weaker every day till he died.

"Nobody could have done more for him than was done," I told Miss Graham.

"I'm glad," she said. "I guess—it's just one of those things."

When I got up to go she asked me if I didn't want to see Jim's room. They'd kept it for him just the same, she said.

I didn't want to, but how are you going to say so? I went up with her and looked and said it was nice. She opened a big cupboard. It was full of neat rows of old magazines.

"They're all the old science-fiction magazines he read when he was a boy," she said. "He always saved them."

I took one out. It had a bright cover, with a space ship on it, not like our rockets but a streamlined thing, and the rings of Saturn in the background.

When I laid it down, Miss Graham took it up and put it back carefully into its place in the row, as though somebody were coming back who wouldn't like to find things out of order.

She insisted on driving me back to Omaha, and out to the airport. She seemed sorry to let me go, and I suppose it was because I was the last real tie to Jim, and when I was gone it was all over then for good.

I wondered if she'd get over it in time, and I guessed she would. People do get over things. I supposed she'd marry some other nice guy, and I wondered what they'd do with Jim's things—with all those old magazines nobody was ever coming back to read.

3

I would never have stopped at Chicago at all if I could have got out of it, for the last person I wanted to talk to anybody about was Walter Millis. It would be too easy for me to make a slip and let out stuff nobody was supposed to know.

But Walter's father had called me at the hospital a couple of times. The last time he called he said he was having Breck's parents come down from Wisconsin so they could see me, too, so what could I do then but say, yes, I'd stop. But I didn't like it at all, and I knew I'd have to be careful.

Mr. Millis was waiting at the airport and shook hands with me and said what a big favor I was doing them all, and how he appreciated my stopping when I must be anxious to get back to my own home and parents.

"That's all right," I said. "My dad and mother came out to the hospital to see me when I first got back."

He was a big, fine-looking, important sort of man, with a little bit of the stuffed shirt about him, I thought. He seemed friendly enough, but I got the feeling he was looking at me and wondering why I'd come back and his son Walter hadn't. Well, I couldn't blame him for that.

His car was waiting, a big car with a driver, and we started north through the city. Mr. Millis pointed out a few things to me to make conversation, especially a big atomic-power station we passed.

"It's only one of thousands, strung all over the world," he said. "They're going to transform our whole economy. This Martian uranium will be a big thing, Sergeant."

I said, yes, I guessed it would.

I was sweating blood, waiting for him to start asking about Walter, and I didn't know yet just what I could tell him. I could get myself in Dutch plenty if I opened my big mouth too wide, for that one thing that had happened to Expedition Two was supposed to be strictly secret, and we'd all been briefed on why we had to keep our mouths shut.

But he let it go for the time being, and just talked other stuff. I gathered that his wife wasn't too well, and that Walter had been their only child. I also gathered that he was a very big shot in business, and dough-heavy.

I didn't like him. Walter I'd liked plenty, but his old man seemed a pretty pompous person, with his heavy business talk.

He wanted to know how soon I thought Martian uranium

would come through in quantity, and I said I didn't think it'd be very soon.

"Expedition One only located the deposits," I said, "and Two just did mapping and setting up a preliminary base. Of course, the thing keeps expanding, and I hear Four will have a hundred rockets. But Mars is a tough setup."

Mr. Millis said decisively that I was wrong, that the world was power-hungry, that it would be pushed a lot faster than I expected.

He suddenly quit talking business and looked at me and asked, "Who was Walter's best friend out there?"

He asked it sort of apologetically. He was a stuffed shirt; but all my dislike of him went away then.

"Breck Jergen," I told him. "Breck was our sergeant. He sort of held our squad together, and he and Walter cottoned to each other from the first."

Mr. Millis nodded, but didn't say anything more about it. He pointed out the window at the distant lake and said we were almost to his home.

It wasn't a home, it was a big mansion. We went in and he introduced me to Mrs. Millis. She was a limp, pale-looking woman, who said she was glad to meet one of Walter's friends. Somehow I got the feeling that even though he was a stuffed shirt, he felt it about Walter a lot more than she did.

He took me up to a bedroom and said that Breck's parents would arrive before dinner, and that I could get a little rest before then.

I sat looking around the room. It was the plushiest one I'd ever been in, and, seeing this house and the way these people lived, I began to understand why Walter had blown his top more than the rest of us.

He'd been a good guy, Walter, but high-tempered, and I could see now he'd been a little spoiled. The discipline at training base had been tougher on him than on most of us, and this was why.

I sat and dreaded this dinner that was coming up, and looked out the window at a swimming pool and tennis court, and wondered if anybody ever used them now that Walter was gone. It seemed a queer thing for a fellow with a setup like this to go out to Mars and get himself killed.

I took the satin cover off the bed so my shoes wouldn't dirty it, and lay down and closed my eyes, and wondered what I was going to tell them. The trouble was, I didn't know what story the officials had given them.

"The Commanding Officer regrets to inform you that your son was shot down like a dog . . ."

They'd never got any telegram like that. But just what line *had* been handed them? I wished I'd had a chance to check on that.

Damn it, why didn't all these people let me alone? They started it all going through my mind again, and the psychos had told me I ought to forget it for a while, but how could I?

It might be better just to tell them the truth. After all, Walter wasn't the only one who'd blown his top out there. In that grim last couple of months, plenty of guys had gone around sounding off.

Expedition Three isn't coming!

We're stuck, and they don't care enough about us to send help!

That was the line of talk. You heard it plenty in those days. You couldn't blame the guys for it, either. A fourth of us down with Martian sickness, the little grave markers clotting up the valley beyond the ridge, rations getting thin, medicine running low, everything running low, all of us watching the sky for rockets that never came.

There'd been a little hitch back on Earth, Colonel Nichols explained. (He was our C.O. now that General Rayen had died.) There was a little delay, but the rockets would be on their way soon; we'd get relief, we just had to hold on.

Holding on—that's what we were doing. Nights we'd sit in the Quonset and listen to Lassen coughing in his bunk, and it seemed like wind-giants, cold-giants, were bawling and laughing around our little huddle of shelters.

"Damn it, if they're not coming, why don't we go home?" Walter said. "We've still got the four rockets—they could take us all back."

Breck's serious face got graver. "Look, Walter, there's too much of that stuff being talked around. Lay off."

"Can you blame the men for talking it? We're not story-book heroes. If they've forgotten about us back on Earth, why do we just sit and take it?"

"We have to," Breck said. "Three will come."

I've always thought that it wouldn't have happened, what did happen, if we hadn't had that false alarm. The one that set the whole camp wild that night, with guys shouting, "Three's here! The rockets landed over west of Rock Ridge!"

Only when they charged out there, they found they hadn't seen rockets landing at all, but a little shower of tiny meteors burning themselves up as they fell.

It was the disappointment that did it, I think. I can't say for sure, because that same day was the day I conked out with Martian sickness, and the floor came up and hit me and I woke up in the bunk, with somebody giving me a hypo, and my head big as a balloon. I wasn't clear out, it was only a touch of it, but it was enough to make everything foggy, and I didn't know about the mutiny that was boiling up until I woke up once with Breck leaning over me and saw he wore a gun and an M.P. brassard now.

When I asked him how come, he said there'd been so much wild talk about grabbing the four rockets and going home that the M.P. force had been doubled and Nichols had issued stern warnings.

"Walter?" I said, and Breck nodded. "He's a leader and he'll get hit with a court-martial when this is over. The blasted idiot!"

"I don't get it—he's got plenty of guts, you know that," I said.

"Yes, but he can't take discipline, he never did take it very well, and now that the squeeze is on he's blowing up. Well, see you later, Frank."

I saw him later, but not the way I expected. For that was the day we heard the faint echo of shots, and then the alarm siren screaming, and men running, and half-tracks starting up in a hurry. And when I managed to get out of my bunk and out of the hut, they were all going toward the big rockets, and a corporal yelled to me from a jeep, "That's blown it! The damn fools swiped guns and tried to take over the rockets and make the crews fly 'em home!"

I could still remember the sickening slidings and bouncings of the jeep as it took us out there, the milling little crowd under the looming rockets, milling around and hiding something on the ground, and Major Weiler yelling himself hoarse giving orders.

When I got to see what was on the ground, it was seven or eight men and most of them dead. Walter had been shot right through the heart. They told me later it was because he'd been the leader, out in front, that he got it first of the mutineers.

One M.P. was dead, and one was sitting with red all over the middle of his uniform, and that one was Breck, and they were bringing a stretcher for him now.

The corporal said, "Hey, that's Jergen, your squad leader!"

And I said, "Yes, that's him." Funny how you can't talk when something hits you—how you just say words, like "Yes, that's him."

Breck died that night without ever regaining consciousness, and there I was, still half sick myself, and with Lassen
dying in his bunk, and five of us were all that was left of
Squad Fourteen, and that was that.

How could H.Q. let a thing like that get known? A fine
advertisement it would be for recruiting more Mars expeditions, if they told how guys on Two cracked up and did a
crazy thing like that. I didn't blame them for telling us to
keep it top secret. Anyway, it wasn't something we'd want
to talk about.

But it sure left me in a fine spot now, a sweet spot. I was
going down to talk to Breck's parents and Walter's parents,
and they'd want to know how their sons died, and I could
tell them, "Your sons probably killed each other, out there."

Sure, I could tell them that, couldn't I? But what *was* I
going to tell them? I knew H.Q. had reported those casual-
ties as "accidental deaths," but what kind of accident?

Well, it got late, and I had to go down, and when I did,
Breck's parents were there. Mr. Jergen was a carpenter, a
tall, bony man with level blue eyes like Breck's. He didn't
say much, but his wife was a little woman who talked
enough for both of them.

She told me I looked just like I did in the pictures of us
Breck had sent home from training base. She said she had
three daughters, too—two of them married, and one of the
married ones living in Milwaukee and one out on the Coast.

She said that she'd named Breck after a character in a
book by Robert Louis Stevenson, and I said I'd read the
book in high school.

"It's a nice name," I said.

She looked at me with bright eyes and said, "Yes. It was
a nice name."

That was a fine dinner. They'd got everything they
thought I might like, and all the best, and a maid served it,
and I couldn't taste a thing I ate.

Then afterward, in the big living room, they all just sort of sat and waited, and I knew it was up to me.

I asked them if they'd had any details about the accident, and Mr. Millis said, No, just "accidental death" was all they'd been told.

Well, that made it easier. I sat there, with all four of them watching my face, and dreamed it up.

I said, "It was one of those one-in-a-million things. You see, more little meteorites hit the ground on Mars than here, because the air's so much thinner it doesn't burn them up so fast. And one hit the edge of the fuel dump and a bunch of little tanks started to blow. I was down with the sickness, so I didn't see it, but I heard all about it."

You could hear everybody breathing, it was so quiet as I went on with my yarn.

"A couple of guys were knocked out by the concussion and would have been burned up if a few fellows hadn't got in there fast with foamite extinguishers. They kept it away from the big tanks, but another little tank let go, and Breck and Walter were two of the fellows who'd gone in, and they were killed instantly."

When I'd got it told, it sounded corny to me and I was afraid they'd never believe it. But nobody said anything, until Mr. Millis let out a sigh and said, "So that was it. Well . . . well, if it had to be, it was mercifully quick, wasn't it?"

I said, yes, it was quick.

"Only, I can't see why they couldn't have let us know. It doesn't seem fair."

I had an answer for that. "It's hush-hush because they don't want people to know about the meteor danger. That's why."

Mrs. Millis got up and said she wasn't feeling so well, and would I excuse her and she'd see me in the morning. The rest of us didn't seem to have much to say to each other, and nobody objected when I went up to my bedroom a little later.

I was getting ready to turn in when there was a knock on the door. It was Breck's father, and he came in and looked at me steadily.

"It was just a story, wasn't it?" he said.

I said, "Yes. It was just a story."

His eyes bored into me and he said, "I guess you've got your reasons. Just tell me one thing. Whatever it was, did Breck behave right?"

"He behaved like a man, all the way," I said. "He was the best man of us, first to last."

He looked at me, and I guess something made him believe me. He shook hands and said, "All right, son. We'll let it go."

I'd had enough. I wasn't going to face them again in the morning. I wrote a note, thanking them all and making excuses, and then went down and slipped quietly out of the house.

It was late, but a truck coming along picked me up, and the driver said he was going near the airport. He asked me what it was like on Mars and I told him it was lonesome. I slept in a chair at the airport, and I felt better, for next day I'd be home, and it would be over.

That's what I thought.

4

It was getting toward evening when we reached the village, for my father and mother hadn't known I was coming on an earlier plane, and I'd had to wait for them up at Cleveland Airport. When we drove into Market Street, I saw there was a big painted banner stretching across: HARMONVILLE WELCOMES HOME ITS SPACEMAN!

Spaceman—that was me. The newspapers had started calling us that, I guess, because it was a short word good for headlines. Everybody called us that now. We'd sat cooped up in a prison cell that flew, that was all—but now we were "spacemen."

There were bright uniforms clustered under the banner and I saw that it was the high-school band. I didn't say anything, but my father saw my face.

"Now, Frank, I know you're tired, but these people are your friends and they want to show you a real welcome."

That was fine. Only it was all gone again, the relaxed feeling I'd been beginning to get as we drove down from Cleveland.

This was my home country, this old Ohio country with its neat little white villages and fat, rolling farms. It looked good, in June. It looked very good, and I'd been feeling better all the time. And now I didn't feel so good, for I saw that I was going to have to talk some more about Mars.

Dad stopped the car under the banner, and the high-school band started to play, and Mr. Robinson, who was the Chevrolet dealer and also the mayor of Harmonville, got into the car with us.

He shook hands with me and said, "Welcome home, Frank! What was it like out on Mars?"

I said, "It was cold, Mr. Robinson. Awful cold."

"You should have been here last February!" he said. "Eighteen below—nearly a record."

He leaned out and gave a signal, and Dad started driving again, with the band marching along in front of us and playing. We didn't have far to go, just down Market Street under the big old maples, past the churches and the old white houses to the square white Grange Hall.

There was a little crowd in front of it, and they made a sound like a cheer—not a real loud one, you know how people can be self-conscious about really cheering—when we drove up. I got out and shook hands with people I didn't really see, and then Mr. Robinson took my elbow and took me on inside.

The seats were all filled and people standing up, and over the little stage at the far end they'd fixed up a big floral decoration—there was a globe all of red roses with a sign above it that said "Mars," and beside it a globe all of white roses that said "Earth," and a little rocket ship made out of flowers was hung between them.

"The Garden Club fixed it up," said Mr. Robinson. "Nearly everybody in Harmonville contributed flowers."

"It sure is pretty," I said.

Mr. Robinson took me by the arm, up onto the little stage, and everyone clapped. They were all people I knew—people from the farms near ours, my high-school teachers, and all that.

I sat down in a chair and Mr. Robinson made a little speech, about how Harmonville boys had always gone out when anything big was doing, how they'd gone to the War of 1812 and the Civil War and the two World Wars, and how now one of them had gone to Mars.

He said, "Folks have always wondered what it's like out there on Mars, and now here's one of our own Harmonville boys come back to tell us all about it."

And he motioned me to get up, and I did, and they clapped some more, and I stood wondering what I could tell them.

And all of a sudden, as I stood there wondering, I got the answer to something that had always puzzled us out there. We'd never been able to understand why the fellows who had come back from Expedition One hadn't tipped us off how tough it was going to be. And now I knew why. They hadn't because it would have sounded as if they were whining about all they'd been through. And now I couldn't, for the same reason.

I looked down at the bright, interested faces, the faces I'd known almost all my life, and I knew that what I could tell them was no good anyway. For they'd all read those newspaper stories, about "the exotic red planet" and "heroic spacemen," and if anyone tried to give them a different picture now, it would just upset them.

I said, "It was a long way out there. But flying space is a wonderful thing—flying right off the Earth, into the stars—there's nothing quite like it."

Flying space, I called it. It sounded good, and thrilling. How could they know that flying space meant lying strapped in that blind stokehold listening to Joe Valinez dying, and praying and praying that it wouldn't be our rocket that cracked up?

"And it's a wonderful thrill to come out of a rocket and step on a brand-new world, to look up at a different-looking sun, to look around at a whole new horizon . . ."

Yes, it was wonderful. Especially for the guys in Rockets Seven and Nine who got squashed like flies and lay around there on the sand, moaning "First aid!" Sure, it was a big thrill, for them and for us who had to try to help them.

"There were hardships out there, but we all knew that a big job had to be done . . ."

That's a nice word, too, "hardships." It's not coarse and ugly like fellows coughing their hearts out from too much dust; it's not like having your best friend die of Martian sickness right in the room you sleep in. It's a nice, cheerful word, "hardships."

". . . and the only way we could get the job done, away out there so far from Earth, was by teamwork."

Well, that was true enough in its way, and what was the use of spoiling it by telling them how Walter and Breck had died?

"The job's going on, and Expedition Three is building a bigger base out there right now, and Four will start soon. And it'll mean plenty of uranium, plenty of cheap atomic power, for all Earth."

That's what I said, and I stopped there. But I wanted to

go on and add, "And it wasn't worth it! It wasn't worth all those guys, all the hell we went through, just to get cheap atomic power so you people can run more electric washers and television sets and toasters!"

But how are you going to stand up and say things like that to people you know, people who like you? And who was I to decide? Maybe I was wrong, anyway. Maybe lots of things I'd had and never thought about had been squeezed out of other good guys, back in the past.

I wouldn't know.

Anyway, that was all I could tell them, and I sat down, and there was a big lot of applause, and I realized then that I'd done right, I'd told them just what they wanted to hear, and everyone was all happy about it.

Then things broke up, and people came up to me, and I shook a lot more hands. And finally, when I got outside, it was dark—soft, summery dark, the way I hadn't seen it for a long time. And my father said we ought to be getting on home, so I could rest.

I told him, "You folks drive on ahead, and I'll walk. I'll take the short cut. I'd sort of like to walk through town."

Our farm was only a couple of miles out of the village, and the short cut across Heller's farm I'd always taken when I was a kid was only a mile. Dad didn't think maybe I ought to walk so far, but I guess he saw I wanted to, so they went on ahead.

I walked on down Market Street, and around the little square, and the maples and elms were dark over my head, and the flowers on the lawns smelled the way they used to, but it wasn't the same either—I'd thought it would be, but it wasn't.

When I cut off past the Odd Fellows' Hall, beyond it I met Hobe Evans, the garage hand at the Ford place, who was humming along half tight, the same as always on a Saturday night.

"Hello, Frank, heard you were back," he said. I waited for him to ask the question they all asked, but he didn't. He said, "Boy, you don't look so good! Want a drink?"

He brought out a bottle, and I had one out of it, and he had one, and he said he'd see me around, and went humming on his way. He was feeling too good to care much where I'd been.

I went on, in the dark, across Heller's pasture and then along the creek under the big old willows. I stopped there like I'd always stopped when I was a kid, to hear the frog noises, and there they were, and all the June noises, the night noises, and the night smells.

I did something I hadn't done for a long time. I looked up at the starry sky, and there it was, the same little red dot I'd peered at when I was a kid and read those old stories, the same red dot that Breck and Jim and Walter and I had stared away at on nights at training base, wondering if we'd ever really get there.

Well, they'd got there, and weren't ever going to leave it now, and there'd be others to stay with them, more and more of them as time went by.

But it was the ones I knew that made the difference, as I looked up at the red dot.

I wished I could explain to them somehow why I hadn't told the truth, not the whole truth. I tried, sort of, to explain.

"I didn't want to lie," I said. "But I had to—at least, it seemed like I had to—"

I quit it. It was crazy, talking to guys who were dead and forty million miles away. They were dead, and it was over, and that was that. I quit looking up at the red dot in the sky and started on home again.

But I felt as though something were over for me too. It was being young. I didn't feel old. But I didn't feel young either, and I didn't think I ever would, not ever again.